ALEJANDRO'S LIE

BOB VAN LAERHOVEN

Fin A La Censura

1

For them, our blood is a medal
merited in eternity, Amen
murderers against us all, our men.

A VERSE WAS FROM ONE OF HIS FRIEND VÍCTOR'S LAST songs before he was tortured to death. It tormented Alejandro Juron while he watched the tanked-up demonstration on Wednesday, October 19th, 1983, in Valtiago, the capital of Terreno.

The rally had been announced with much pomp and pageantry as "a powerful expression of the will of the people."

Speakers assured the demonstrators that The People were finally going to defeat the *junta* of General Pelarón.

Their puffed-up rhetoric amused Alejandro:

"Shoulder to shoulder, we will force open the door to democracy promised by General Pelarón!"

"I'll cross my fingers, dimwits," Juron muttered aloud, a habit acquired from years in solitary confinement.

Usually energetic and vibrant with color, today, the large shopping centers on Avenida General Pelarón had the same sullen hue as the Andes Mountains behind the city. Black police buses with armored windows appeared at the end of the street.

Alejandro Juron stepped onto a café terrace. It would normally have been packed with office workers at that time of day, but because of the commotion, it was empty. A police tank blocked the road.

Years back, Juron had been the much-applauded guitar player in a group named *Aconcagua* that was famous across the Latin American continent for its protest songs, but he didn't feel inspired to participate in the protest march.

The demonstrators were out of their minds: the *junta* that governed Terreno for the last ten years wasn't on the brink of collapse like the speakers said. In the last few months, it had made a few compromises to make it look a bit less dictatorial, but Alejandro felt that was all a smoke-screen.

The economic crisis and growing popular protest had recently forced General Pelarón to announce he "would open the door to democracy at the appropriate moment and in the appropriate way."

The opposition, a picturesque collection of splinter groups that were more often than not at each other's throats, took to the streets after the general's speech as if victory were already within reach.

Juron was sure Pelarón made that promise to force his opponents into the open to have them clubbed in the interest of 'national peace.'

He wanted to run, but his eyes held him back—seeing the *fata morgana* that had endlessly tormented him in his prison cell. There she was—shimmering in the mist which rose from puddles of morning rain.

Lucía.

The name of his secret love sounded out of place in these circumstances. While Juron's instincts told him to get the hell out of there, he was unable to peel his eyes away from a woman in the crowd. She had knotted a scarf over her mouth, effectively gagging herself, and was carrying a board around her neck that read *Fin a la Censura* – End Censorship. Her ponytail, the oily sheen on her hair: just like Lucía used to wear it. *Could this be a sign that I can finally shed my penance?*

Alejandro cursed: such were the thoughts of a romantic songster, not of a man who needed to keep a low profile. *Out of there!*

What held him back? He knew bloody well that melancholy was a noxious creation of the ego. After ten years in La Ultima Cena, the prison people called 'The Last Supper' because supper was the only meal they gave you on the day of your execution, Juron's melancholy had decayed like the rotting jellyfish he used to inspect on the beach when he was a boy.

A white Peugeot was parked further down the street, across from the Centro Médico Dental. A man wearing sunglasses and armed with a handgun stepped out and started to shoot at random.

The police used the incident to charge into the crowd. At one moment, the demonstrators were a slowly advancing mass, and at the next, they scuttled in every direction like crazed ants. The man stepped back into his Peugeot and disappeared down the adjoining street.

The police threw tear gas grenades. Alejandro assumed the man in the Peugeot was an agitator, a member of one of the ultra-rightwing factions that enjoyed considerable influence in Terreno. By firing in the direction of the police, he had given the *carabineros* a reason to attack.

Juron wanted to run away, but he noticed that the woman, her mouth still muzzled, *Fin a la censura* still bouncing on her

3

breasts, was running through the clouds of tear gas in the wrong direction. He sprinted towards her. The noise had become deafening in the meantime – shots interspersed with car engines starting.

Juron caught up with the woman and grabbed her by the arm: "Wrong direction, follow me." She looked at him—eyes bloodshot from the gas. Juron pointed to a side street. She realized her mistake, and the two raced into El Paseo de Lyon, a pedestrian street full of shops.

A couple of police jeeps appeared at the end of the road heading in their direction. The buildings disappeared from Alejandro's field of vision. All he could see were the rifles pointing from the jeeps, as if at the end of a tunnel. There was a metro entrance a few meters ahead, so he grabbed the woman and pulled her inside. They had just made it to the stairs when the jeeps passed outside. Alejandro shuddered as bullets punctured the wall above their heads. The woman screamed something incomprehensible. They raced down the stairs and bolted towards the metro tunnels.

Juron looked back. No one had followed them. *You prepare for the worst, and this time, your luck's in,* he thought – not the usual course of events. In the brightly lit corridor leading to the ticket desk, he started to laugh and stopped in his tracks. The woman let go of his hand. She sized him up, pulled the muzzle from her mouth, and stuffed it into her trouser pocket.

"I have to catch a train," she said so quietly that Alejandro barely understood her. She hesitated for a second: "Thank you."

She wasn't Lucía, of course. Lucía was dead, he knew that. He caught his reflection in the window of the ticket desk: the thin pencil mustache he had been cultivating of late and the thick lines either side of his nose. He was small and shabby, not the he-man type with slick, brilliantine hair, not the kind of man a woman like that would look up to.

"I understand," he said, wondering if she'd noticed he'd

been drinking. "You should never miss an appointment with your hairdresser; I get it completely." He knew why he was nasty. Her clothes and hairstyle pointed to money. She was probably one of those left-wing feminists who like to jump into bed with big-talking 'revolutionaries.' It allowed them to flirt with the idea that they were 'in the resistance,' fighting against the *junta* and its old-fashioned views on the status of men and women.

Alejandro smiled in response to the surprise on her face: "Have a good day." He nodded and walked away.

"Hey!" she shouted. "What are you going to do?"

"Get a breath of fresh air."

"Back to the streets?"

"I'm a street brat. Where else should I go?"

"Can't I at least buy you a metro ticket?"

Alejandro stopped. A Terrenean man was supposed to be able to pay for his metro ticket, even if he had only been released from The Last Supper a couple of weeks ago.

"Can't you smell I'm broke?" he asked. He had to quickly ensure the woman despised him; that was the best option.

"That's not what I meant," she said nervously. She glanced at the exit. "I should be up there too, on the streets, with the others."

"Solidarity is a fine quality in a person," Alejandro confirmed. "But not when live ammunition is flying around."

She ran her fingers through her ponytail.

"We should split up," she said as if they'd been in a relationship for years. "What if the police follow us down here?"

Alejandro could see it in her eyes: she had realized that he was pretty well-oiled.

"Where do you want to go? Let me buy you a ticket; I owe you that much at least," she said, her head bowed, rummaging in her bag.

"I'm heading for Canela. I'll pay you back another time."

She smiled for the first time. Alejandro looked away. They

walked to the ticket desk. The woman brought her mouth close to the glass partition to make sure he didn't hear her destination. Alejandro scowled. He had concealed the fact that Canela, the working-class area, wasn't his final destination but the slum just beyond in what they called the *porqueriza*.

"Oink, oink," he muttered. If she was smart – and she looked smart—she would have guessed he lived in the Pigsty by now. The look on her face betrayed that she was feeling less and less comfortable in his company.

They made their way to the platform. A grey metro train arrived. She handed him his ticket. "So, eh... this is my train... Bye." She hesitated. "And thanks again."

"Bye."

The doors glided open. The woman stepped inside.

"What's your name?" said Alejandro through the closed door. "Let me write a song for you." The woman looked at him through the dirty glass and nodded politely. She probably hadn't understood. The train started to move. Alejandro watched it pull out of the station, his arms raised as if he were holding a guitar. He was still standing in the same position when his train arrived.

He got off at the end of Avenida General Pelarón, a journey of several kilometers, and left behind the wealthy districts, his gaze fixed on the Cordillera, now rusty-red like a castellated rampart rising above the city, its peaks covered in snow.

His past was like the mountains: inhospitable.

———

2

Let me tell you a secret,
in the carousel of my pitter-patter heart

I chose a nickname for myself.
A funny rhyme with my little house
of rotting wood and slow decay
where every night I call myself a louse.

Alejandro stood in front of the hovel he called home, disgusted by the cold mud, the stench, and the flaking paint on the Coca-Cola board that served as a door. He pushed it aside. The working-class area, known as Canela, led into what everyone called 'the pigsty,' a slum housing more than one hundred thousand souls. Alejandro was aware that he had to be grateful for the shack his old buddies managed to find for him. Tens of thousands of people in Valtiago were homeless.

For as long as he could remember, ugliness had deeply troubled Alejandro. He once asked his grandfather why things grow ugly. "Grow old, you mean," his grandfather had answered. "Maintenance, that's the key, Alejandro. If you keep things in good repair, they keep their value, and sometimes they even increase in worth."

The ten-year-old Alejandro asked himself if he would keep his value if he kept himself in good repair.

But his worth had not increased, that was clear. Alejandro knew why the *junta* recently released him from prison. The government threw inmates they considered washouts out of prison to lower the exploding prison population.

After the strict regime of The Last Supper, Alejandro found himself in a society that confused him. Ten years behind bars had turned him into a stranger in a strange land. In that same period, the *junta* had succeeded in changing Terreno with the help of the mass media. Nothing was the same, not even the music. The National Government under President Galero Álvarez had seen music as part of the country's cultural heritage; now, it had been replaced by an invasion of American disco.

He quickly realized that resistance against the *junta* had

gone underground and was particularly alive in the poorer parts of the city. Their limited means required them to budget their activities, although their plans were still pretty grand in the scale of things. Many had forgotten the heroes of the past. Álvarez, who shot himself in the head when the army turned its weapons on the presidential residence, was often spoken of in scoffing terms as an 'idiot Marxist' who had steered the country into an economic abyss..

Nevertheless, news of Alejandro's release had quickly done the rounds in the shanty town. People brought him gifts at the start, mostly middle-aged men with children who had no respect for them. Most people over thirty-five still looked up to Víctor Pérez—Alejandro's dead friend and the former popular leader of the band Aconcagua—as something of a hero. For them, Pérez's magnificence as guardian of the country's cultural uniqueness still reflected a little light on Alejandro Juron. But the kids walked past him, indifferent, their jangling radios pressed to their ears: *Whack-a Whock-a.*

Inside his shack, Alejandro watered the plants he was trying to grow in old cardboard boxes, with water from a rusty tin can. He clung to the little things that were meant to make his life bearable. *I live by the grace of people who have little more in life than memories,* he thought to himself, dispirited. *You too, Violeta. More than fifteen years ago, you taught me to play the guitar, and two weeks ago, you found this shack for me. You rested your head on my chest and cried when you met me in front of The Last Supper after my release. I stood there, blinking in the sunlight, a whistling sound in my ear. You may have turned grey, Violeta, but you still believe in the old ideals. I saw you perform a couple of days ago for the people of the campamento. Bitter few had come to hear your husky voice and listen to your songs. You were just as jaunty as in the old days, and your eyes still sparkled under your thinning hair, but your hips were slower than before and your breath shorter. I turned away. I'm pretty sure you saw me leave, and I think you know why.*

Alejandro gritted his teeth, grabbed a tin of Nescafé, and

lit a flame under a pan of water. The light in his *rancho* was filtered red by a sheet of plastic he used as a window. When it was warm, he stored it away, but the wind from the Andes could be cold and blustery in the spring.

He watched the tiny waves of boiling water collide in the pan with the same rhythm as the thoughts in his head. A significant writer once wrote that the sea never stopped moving because if it did, every one of us would suffocate. He felt the steam begin to burn on his face. Some memories were unstoppable, especially memories of the Valtiago football stadium.

Ten years earlier, the army had herded the *junta*'s opponents together in the stadium. Alejandro's memories were repugnant—the rusting bath of boiling water naked prisoners were forced into. The electrically charged batons they used on prisoners' genitals—how they gave off blue sparks in the darkness. The constant screaming that ricocheted off every wall.

Teeth-grinding memories: the self-evidence with which their torturers went about their business, their impunity.

Why did the world look the other way? President Nixon had applauded Pelarón's *junta* when it seized power in 1973 and used words like 'order' and 'calm' and 'economic prosperity' and 'ally.'

Had Nixon given Pelarón *carte blanche* because the general consistently referred to Nixon's opponents as communists and terrorists? Or because the *junta* had borrowed massive amounts of money 'in the people's name' and left the citizens to foot the bill?

Alejandro tried clumsily to remove the pan from the heat, but it fell from his hand, and the water poured down the corrugated iron wall behind the gas cooker.

Morally, he faced an undeniable inner abyss. The woman who bought him the metro ticket was a shadow of flesh and blood, a phantom he had to suppress as quickly as possible.

"I'm an idiot, a complete fucking idiot," said Alejandro as

he picked up the pan. He chuckled and groped under the plank of wood that served as a bed, the safest place to store his guitar. Violeta Tossa had kept it for him when he was in jail. She should never have done it: the guitar made him dwell on the past. Now the instrument seemed insistent that he write songs again in a land that lost its hearing.

All the misery in his life had its roots in the attraction between words and music. It wasn't love at first sight: for much of his youth, the guitar was an unwilling favorite. Violeta Tossa, a cigarette permanently dangling from her lips, taught him with inexhaustible patience how to seduce the instrument. She changed Alejandro's life completely the day she suggested he meet the legendary singer Víctor Pérez.

Alejandro remembered the heat in the air that day, the low horizon induced by the mountains, the mass of clouds reminiscent of Rembrandt's gloomy skies. Violeta and Alejandro were sitting in his parents' garden. Violeta had asked him to write something à la Pérez a couple of days earlier. Alejandro stayed up the entire night working on the verses. He had been drinking, and the words weren't exactly cohesive, but he convinced himself that the world should hear them.

He was nineteen and thought that his brand-new protest song outclassed anything Pérez had ever written. He sang his song and played with passion. But Violeta's eyes narrowed as she listened.

Violeta's reaction to his performance cut into him like a blunt knife: "Spare me the whining, boy!" When she laughed, her motherly breasts would shudder on top of her plump belly. "That's politics you're trying to sing about."

"Of course it is," he answered, pouting at her stupidity. "You wanted something Pérez-style, didn't you? Doesn't he write protest songs? Old-fashioned stuff. My work is the kind of protest song Dylan would write."

"You sound like a bullfrog!" Violeta roared with laughter. "If you shout like that, you'll make people deaf. You have to fill their hearts with passion. You sound like a gringo yelling slogans on TV and driving everyone crazy." She strummed her guitar. "And that guitar, boy, that's not a mangy *burro*. It doesn't deserve the donkey beating you're giving it. It's your very first girlfriend, the one with the hair softer than your cold heart can remember." She plucked a spirited melody that slowly became wistful and sad.

When she looked up, she saw the hurt in Alejandro's eyes. "Chin up, boy, you'll get there one day. You can do it; you can make that guitar sing. It's the voice of the people who lost their tongue." She gestured in the direction of the street.

"Speechless, all of them, struck dumb: all they can do is wait until death comes to get them." Violeta shook her head, and cunning filled her eyes. "Your guitar has to give voice to their silence, coaxing, wheezing, licking, threatening, scream-ing. And you can do it if you weren't so easily satisfied, for Christ's sake. You're no Dylan or Bob Seger. You're Alejandro Juron, and your soul belongs here, in this place. Those miser-able bastards outside deserve *your* voice and not some phony imitation. Go on, play me a Víctor Pérez number!"

Alejandro sighed and strummed a chord. How could he tell Violeta that he was only really interested in fame and often had doubts about those Terrenean protest songs, no matter how popular they were? The only way to become a star in 1970 was with pop music. Víctor Pérez had a decent voice, but the stuff of his songs was folklore. The poor always won. Instead of singing about sex and politics like the American pop stars, his songs were fairy tales. Alejandro felt sure that the love songs he wrote in secret were better than protest songs, certainly if he wanted to make a name for himself. The Terranean poor didn't want to hear about their moral rights. They wanted to dance to the provocative tones of *sizzling love*. Didn't Violeta understand that? But no matter how old-fash-ioned she was, he had to admit that she was and remained an inspiring guitar teacher. His mother—also pathetically corny

— encouraged him to take lessons with her, adding that Violeta didn't accept *just* anyone as her pupil.

Alejandro wondered how long he was going to be able to put up with Violeta. One thing was sure: he was determined to play in a pop band, come what may. He treated her to a Pérez song as she had asked, concentrating on the sound of his voice and guitar. He wanted adoration, even it was only from Violeta, and when he had finished, she said, "Plenty of technique and voice, but a reluctant heart. I'll put you in touch with Víctor Pérez. He's still looking for someone for his new group Aconcagua. Maybe that'll wake you up."

That was 1970, the year in which he found himself, entirely astonished, under the influence of Víctor Pérez and discovering the wealth of Aconcagua's repertoire. Thirteen years later, the radio vomited American pop all day long, and songs by Aconcagua were banned. Alejandro had been right about the future of music, but not in the way he had hoped. Now he was an old man as far as the jittery youth were concerned, and he thought Irene Cara's *Flashdance...What A Feeling* and Cyndi Lauper's *Girls Just Want To Have Fun* were soulless crap.

Alejandro flipped the guitar, sniffed the sound box, and strummed a chord. His fingers glided self-assuredly across the strings. Amazing how they remembered their way through the scales. Alejandro didn't have to search long for a melody: it emerged inside him, languishing with desire. He could fish it up from a timeless reservoir in which every note was as young as the day it was born. But the words resisted. After what he had been through, they seemed infantile. They convulsed like the catch in a fisherman's net. Alejandro took the well-thumbed pages from under his pillow and read what he had written a couple of days earlier:

> *Boots trample grass underfoot,*
> *Mortars leave hearts in ashes.*

But out of their sight,
the passionflower bleeds,
and freedom is weighed up
against an empty death.

Traditionalist and common. He would never be able to imitate Víctor's talent for reconciling tradition with modernity. He remembered how Víctor dismissed his attempts to introduce amusing dance songs into Aconcagua's repertoire. Alejandro reacted by adding insult to injury: here's a piece about a gringo who wants to get laid in Valtiago, Víctor. No? One about Jesus Christ getting lost in the wilderness of Terreno? But while Víctor laughed and shook his head, Alejandro felt envy. He was young, wanted to be like Víctor, only different. Or, better still, take his place.

Alejandro sawed himself into pieces like a magician who jumped too high. Finally, and in spite of himself, the sense of justice innate in Víctor gradually started to affect him, influence him, together with Pérez' seriousness which refused to yield even when the military threatened him and even after he'd spent his first night in jail with intertwined traces of truncheons across his body as a result.

Alejandro was not only enamored and envious of his friend; he was also enchanted by Lucía Altameda, Víctor's wife.

Alejandro ran his fingers over the damp plasterboard that formed the wall next to his bed. The line of Lucía's jaw. He shook his head and started to sing in a falsetto voice, strumming a simple ditty on his guitar:

There was once a country boy
a Terrenean country boy
a man no one could trust.
But he thought he was a hero
A true blue popular hero,

no, no, don't joke with the man.
He had a friend, a genuine friend,
who had a wife, an honest wife,
and when she looked at him,
well now, he just wasn't sure
he was honestly lost for words,
honestly, not a single word.
He was a man you couldn't trust,
he wasn't the faithful type
our popular country boy hero.

Under his breath, as he had often done in The Last Supper, he said: "I might have been worthless, Víctor, but because of you, I slowly came to believe in fraternity, a brotherhood of man. All you lacked was a halo, patron saint of *kiss my ass*." The halo had been sent to heaven ten years earlier after thirty-four bullets had slammed into Víctor Pérez's body. The officer who delivered the final shot as Víctor lay dying in the stadium received the nickname 'Prince of the Night.'

Alejandro made his way outside, stopped, blinded by the sudden sunlight, and mumbled, "I did penance for believing in fairytales! Do you hear me, spirits of the Cordillera?" He collapsed in a fit of laughter. How crazy could he get?

"Out of the way, *borracho*," said a teenager on a rusty bike, sweating his way through the sludge between the *ranchos*.

"So," said Alejandro, staring at the mud at his feet. "If that's your answer, spirits of the Cordillera, snot boys who call me a boozer, then I think it's time I grabbed a drink."

3

That same evening, with a veil of fire-colored clouds in the sky turning the slums orange-red, the paramilitary security police raided the pigsty. The *junta* didn't want the average citizen to know that it could barely maintain control in the *barrio*.

Officially, the reason for the raid was 'to neutralize communist infiltrators.' The police top brass didn't want to—or couldn't—see that some of their men on the ground were taking advantage of a burgeoning trade in poor quality drugs by demanding a share of the profits. Those policemen warned the dealers they did business with that a raid was on its way.

The dealers waited for the police with Russian AK-47s and South Korean Daewoo K1 machine guns on shack roofs. The 'pigs' couldn't use their armored cars in the narrow muddy streets of the *favela*. The inhabitants always carried used plastic supermarket bags with them. They were everywhere. And what was in the bags being carried by the guttersnipes who worked for the drug dealers and called themselves 'soldiers?'

If the 'soldiers' had courage and brains, they got an Israeli Uzi, a great weapon, precise as a poisonous snake. The less talented received Daewoos, awkward, cumbersome, clumsy recoil. But ooh-la-la, what firepower, what tremendous salvo capacity! You didn't just kill your opponents; you ripped them to pieces.

The cops advanced in a tight formation in the alleys. Oops-a-daisy! The plastic bags fell on the ground, out came the weapons. Chaos and destruction to the rhythm of frenetic salvos. The police had bulletproof jackets, helmets, lightweight M16s. They had the advantage of their equipment. The *favela* warriors wore T-shirts over their mouths, knew every nook and cranny of the terrain, and were in the majority.

Gun smoke filled the air. The informants had told the dealers that a particular house in yellow brick would be the target of the attack. The cops knew that it contained a large quantity of cocaine. There weren't many brick houses in the pigsty. The cops advanced towards the location but had to fight for every centimeter of ground.

José Melo, a corporal with the special forces, was sweating profusely under his heavy protective kit. The sun hung low in the sky but was still furiously hot. The red ants of the *favela* had to be eliminated, destroyed, trampled on. That's all they were worth.

The cops arrived at a crossroads and came under fire from above, bullets ricocheting right and left, adrenaline rocketing. The mangy dogs had taken cover on new rooftops! "Cover me!" José shouted to his buddy Rodrigo. Rodrigo fired to his heart's content while José kicked in the door of the nearest slum and ran inside, weapon at the ready. The place was empty. It had only one window, easily smashed by the butt of his M16. José fired at the roofs on the opposite side of the street. Rat-tat-tat, fully automatic. Screaming, not fully automatic, surging and waning.

José peered over the edge of the window sill. Where was Rodrigo? In the corner of his eye: a figure in combat uniform, on the ground, arms and legs spread out. José scowled, glared. Blood dripped from his buddy's mouth. José cursed, wasted a rain of bullets on roofs that were already empty. A rasping sound behind him made him turn. A boy little more than ten years old was pointing a pistol at him. The pistol quivered, shook, juddered. Staring eyes, very dark, shiny as tin.

José stayed where he was, crouched low, and smiled obliquely: "Come on, kid, let's not screw around. If you don't kill me with your first shot, you're a dead boy; I'll shoot you to pieces and feed you to the dogs on the street. I mean it. Are you willing to take that risk? Want to be a man? Then go ahead, shoot!" José thumped his chest in the hope that the boy would fire at his bullet-proof vest. Then he had a chance of surviving the bullet. The boy's mouth trembled. A handsome kid with full lips, an aristocratic nose, intelligent eyes. A doubter: José could feel it.

"There's another option," crooned José, sugar-sweet. "You walk out of here. I wait a couple of minutes and then leg it myself, and no one gets hurt. Let the big boys do the work, kid. Then you might live long enough to know what it's like to fuck a woman." As he spoke, his left hand fumbled unnoticed towards his boot, where he had hidden his throwing knife. José liked to boast to his colleagues that he could earn more money at the circus than with the special forces: *I can skewer a mosquito by the balls from ten meters.*

"Mosquito's balls!" José roared as the blade left his hand. The boy jumped at the sound, took the knife in the belly, doubled over, stumbled sideways, fired a round into the plasterboard wall. Convulsing and bleeding heavily, the young body fell to the ground. José kicked the pistol out of reach. A .38, his professionally trained brain took note. He rested his foot on the driveling child's throat and pursed his lips.

"You should have learned to shoot someone in the back," he said smoothly. "But for you, it's too late." He fired three bullets from his M16 into the body on the floor, which tensed like a spring then collapsed.

The gunfire on the street below appeared to have subsided. José peered outside. He noticed uncontrollable shivers running all over his body as if he had a fever. He'd had enough for one day. No need to push the envelope too far. He planned to stay where he was until his mates retreated and then join them unnoticed. Later a beer, a willing bit of skirt...

Then he saw the plastic supermarket bag beside the table. That wasn't there before. Had to belong to the dead cricket. José inched towards it. It was full to bursting. He opened it.

Moments later, José furrowed his brow, deep in thought.

The plastic bag was bulging with bottles of Polvo de Estrellas, high-quality crack traded by the influential ultra-rightwing secret society, Patria y Sangre. José , like many of his police colleagues, was a member. One of its primary sources of income consisted of importing Polvo de Estrellas by air and sea from Bolivia via Argentina and exporting it from Terreno to the United States.

How did Stardust of such exceptional quality manage to find its way into the pigsty?

————

4

The steel-grey buildings of the National University, a project of the *junta*'s Elemental think-tank, had something Stalinist about them. Not a trace of the architectural finesse of the high mountains or the Italian and French influence evident in the city's older neighborhoods. The buildings concealed a few older constructions built by the National Government before the *junta* threw them out. They were low-built and shaped like a honeycomb.

The woman at the counter of the central administration building was playing it cool. "The law states that you have to pay a registration fee," she said. She slipped a form across the counter and turned back to her Apricot computer. The form stated the fee that prevented country kids and the children of city laborers from registering.

"I already have a degree, thanks," said Alejandro. "I want to talk to the librarian." He took a furtive glance at the computer and felt unsteady.

The woman looked disapprovingly at his clothing. Alejandro tried to smile. "I'm a performer," he explained.

"Señor Vial is in a meeting."

"I can wait," said Alejandro.

The woman ostentatiously flicked a couple of switches on her switchboard. "I suggest you leave. Or would you prefer me to have you removed?"

"If you give Mr. Vial my name, he's sure to receive me," said Alejandro.

"If you don't leave now, I'll call security."

Since the coup d'état, the military ran the universities, and they operated the security services.

Alejandro was about to slink off when the woman he helped during the demonstration walked into the room. She caught sight of him and halted. Alejandro smiled. "Hello, mysterious lady," he said, trying to hide his surprise. "Alejandro Juron, at your service. What a coincidence, meeting you here in this shrine of learning."

"Miss Candalti," said the secretary behind the counter. "This man is…."

"I want to talk to Cristóbal Vial," Alejandro interrupted, without looking away from the woman named Miss Candalti. "It was a great deal easier ten years ago than it is now." Candalti was wearing large earrings and had tied her hair in a bun. She lowered her eyes. She looked bright and competent in her business outfit.

"I'm his secretary," she said. "Does Mr. Vial know you?"

"If he's not suffering from amnesia."

She smiled in precisely the same way as she had after he said he would pay her back for the metro ticket. "I'll take care of it, Luisa," she said to the nervous receptionist. She nodded to Alejandro: "Follow me."

She stood against the wall in the lift, her arms folded over her chest, as far away from him as she could get in the confined space.

"Do you know Cristóbal?" she repeated, this time without a smile.

"From way back, when he used to be an ordinary librarian. He seems to have done pretty well for himself under the *junta*."

"Do you think so?"

"Oh well, maybe not. Cristóbal was running for Vice-Rector under the National Government. Chief Librarian seems like slim pickings by comparison. What happened to Eduardo Corrientes?"

Alejandro noted with satisfaction that Beatriz was surprised he knew the name of the former rector. "Mr. Corrientes is dead."

He nodded as if he didn't need to hear the details. "My father knew him well."

He was a completely different person, Beatriz thought. Yesterday he was a drunk, almost childishly proud; moments ago, he was nervous, a little pompous; now, he was calm, with a bluntness that surprised her.

They headed into the corridor. "Do you know what this building reminds me of?"

"No."

"Bulgaria."

"Were you there?"

"Yes." He smiled. "We gave a concert there, the end of the sixties. Didn't do much for my communist ideals when I realized our Bulgarian comrades were such bad architects."

Cristóbal hurried out of his office. He was short, balding, his scalp brown and shiny, a sturdy fifty-something to whom the years had granted a certain paternal charm. "Cristóbal," said Beatriz. "This man wants to...."

"Alejandro Juron," Alejandro interrupted. "You'll probably remember my father."

"Yes, of course," Cristóbal nodded affably. His defense against uninvited encounters with others was to look like a man in a hurry. It particularly impressed the military he had to deal with. Vial took a couple of steps and then stood still.

"Alejandro Juron?" he said, his eyes pinched. "I read somewhere that you were free again."

"Ten lines on page thirty of the newspaper, I imagine," said Alejandro. "I'm not yet in a position to buy the papers; otherwise, I would've cut out the column and preserved it for my grandchildren."

"Come inside," said Cristóbal without reacting to Alejandro's cynicism. He nodded towards the office door.

"Will you be joining us?" said Alejandro to Beatriz. She turned to Cristóbal.

"Do you know each other?" asked the librarian with an absent-minded smile. Cristóbal was a talented actor who quickly adapted himself to the preconceptions the military had about academics.

"A little," said Beatriz. She had told her boss that morning what had happened the day before during the demonstration. Cristóbal gently chided her for her recklessness.

Cristóbal sighed and turned to Alejandro: "The Last Supper. What was it like? All those years..."

"A picnic," said Juron with a straight face.

Cristóbal's face echoed the expression. "What do you plan to do now?"

"Get out of Terreno as soon as possible. I paid a visit to the Ministry for Foreign Affairs this morning. I noticed that the department dealing with emigration has glass doors. Brought tears to my eyes."

Beatriz frowned.

"I've been dreaming of glass doors for ten years in The Last Supper," Alejandro explained. "But despite that good omen, I was told that even if I got permission, it would take at least a year to leave the country. Not precisely my long-cherished dream of flying through glass doors."

"So what are you going to do in the meantime?" asked Cristóbal.

"That's what I wanted to ask you."

Cristóbal sipped at the cup of tea on his desk. "I can't help you openly. The situation is too delicate for that."

"How many times this week have I heard those words from old friends?" Alejandro smiled. "Not so many, to be honest, but that's because I don't have many old friends left. And precious few of them were willing to talk to me. People have short memories."

"I haven't forgotten you."

"That's still to be determined," said Alejandro bluntly.

"Do you have somewhere to sleep?"

"Violeta Tossa arranged a *rancho* for me in the pigsty."

Beatriz caught herself looking left and then right as if she was following a tennis match. She also noticed that Alejandro's gaze kept drifting in her direction. What was she to think of it? Was he mocking her or just confused? It was hard to tell.

"Let me see if I can find you a decent room. Unfortunately, there's a shortage, so it might take a while." Cristóbal turned to Beatriz: "Did Luisa at the reception see him?"

"Yes."

"Tell her I got rid of him on the spot."

"With a kick in the ass for good measure," said Alejandro.

"Luisa likes to stick to the rules. And she's not the only one at this university." Cristóbal smiled. "I make sure everyone thinks the same about me. Why did you wait so long before coming to see me?"

"Because I wanted to be sure that nobody was tailing me."

"Sensible. Was anyone?"

"I've got a cramp in my neck from looking over my shoulder. But I don't think so."

Cristóbal nodded. "We'll get you some money and do what we can." He stood. "Next time, we can talk about more important matters, things that still have to happen. But not here. What are you going to do?"

Something happened to Alejandro that Beatriz found almost terrifying: first, he looked at her, then his eyes filled with such incredible pain that it cut her to the quick. She noticed that even Cristóbal lost his poise for an instant when Alejandro answered without looking away from Beatriz: "Look for similarities."

The Wind From The Cordillera

1

"RESIDENTS OF THE CANELA-QUARTER, EFFECTIVE TODAY, IT IS forbidden to leave your houses after eleven PM. Violators will be shot on sight."

Beatriz was on her way to meet the Belgian priest René Lafarge, who, according to Cristóbal, could "do something" for Alejandro. As the military jeep passed her, she reacted like all the others in the narrow street. She ambled and looked at her feet. One of the soldiers whistled sharply at her during a lull in the megaphone message. Beatriz didn't look up. The rifles in the jeep tilted upwards. The image reminded her of her ex-husband Manuel Durango when, in bed, he leered at the sight of his erection.

Beatriz didn't have to traverse the *porqueriza* to reach René's home next to Canela's old church. But her curiosity about Alejandro had been growing since he left the university the day before, when Cristóbal told her who the man was. She knew now who the woman was whom she resembled so much. She wasn't flattered but rather painfully shy, to know that she and Lucía, who had been executed in Valtiago's football stadium with her husband Víctor Pérez, resistance hero and singer of the famous folk-group Aconcagua, were outwardly like twin-sisters.

"Similarities, Beatriz," Cristóbal had concluded. "Sometimes, I think life floats on them."

Alejandro walked, tacking between the heaps of rubbish in front of the houses across the street. His head was a beehive of pangs and pains caused by the booze he had bought the day before with Cristóbal's money. His guitar dangled on his back. The years of neglect had dulled her; the snares needed love and attention.

He had two things on his mind: to leave Terreno as quickly as possible and, from now on, to be stubbornly rooted in the mad humor of existence. The first mission was difficult; the second should be a piece of cake. In prison, he survived amongst murderers and rapists. Hadn't they found him irresistibly funny? They had cracked up, the psychopaths, when he played his pranks. How then was it possible that since he was free, no one laughed with him anymore? Alejandro concluded he should stop drinking. You could only be a comedian with a clear head.

He saw Beatriz walking on the other side of the street and stood still. Now that he had decided to take life more lightly, he couldn't just yell *señorita* at her, could he? Too formal. He grabbed his guitar from under his right armpit, cleared his throat, and started singing *Abre la Ventana* as he crossed the street. His strokes, from a hesitant start, grew more precise. His voice, coarse at first, became clear and melodious.

Beatriz stopped, shaking her head, when she saw Alejandro walking over to her. His voice surprised her. She didn't remember it ever sounding so strong and soulful.

A jeep's engine started to whine and subdued Alejandro's voice and guitar. Shots rang; people ran. Beatriz remained motionless. She had to duck, squat down at least; her knees refused. A man ran into the street, chased by a jeep. He charged past Beatriz. Afterward, Beatriz would remember nothing of his face except his half-open mouth, as if he were calling her. The jeep approached Alejandro, who plunged in the mud. The vehicle skimmed past. More rifles fire. The fugitive fell, kicked his legs like a wounded horse, and finally, lay still. The jeep stopped beside the body. Soldiers jumped out. One of them finished the man with a bullet in the neck. They hauled the body in the trunk. The jeep's engine revved up again.

The street was empty now, except for Beatriz and Alejandro. He crawled to his feet and went to her. She gave him a shaky smile and smoothed her hair back. He noticed her earlobes, elf-like and tender.

She suddenly snorted with laughter. "Your pants."

Alejandro stopped and looked downwards. Mud caked his pants, not only at the height of his calves but also on his crotch.

2

"If I were a woman with decent morals, I wouldn't invite you in," Beatriz said with a little laugh, parking in her driveway in Calle Ordoñez, in one of Valtiago's plush quarters. A big patio and a horseshoe-shaped garden surrounded the white-plastered house. "I live here separated from my ex-husband, but our divorce isn't official yet."

The nonchalance with which she said it should've alarmed Alejandro, but he wasn't paying attention. During the ride in Beatriz's Land Rover, with a towel underneath his buttocks, he had been staring at electronics shops and sumptuous Mercedes dealers.

So much had changed during his ten years in prison. Beatriz told him that raids on the shops in the quarter had at least doubled in the last couple of months. Windows with steel shutters, cameras, private militia, and police tanks were needed to protect the city's affluent areas.

"So long ago," he mumbled. "For me, this is 1984."

"That's only next year."

"I mean the novel. Georges Orwell's *1984.*"

Beatriz was surprised. She hadn't seen a reader in him.

"Yesterday, I talked about similarities," Alejandro said. "And look: your house resembles my parents' cottage, only bigger."

"But we're not similar at all," Beatriz said. She had received her house as a present from her father after she married. This fact still irked her every day.

"No," Alejandro answered, misunderstanding her reaction. "I knew early in life what I wanted. I was five and played the piano. I danced in our garden. I told everyone willing to listen that I would become a musician. My father wasn't pleased with my dream. He was a university professor and wanted a Ph.D. title for me."

Candalti got out of the car. Why had he said: *I knew early in life what I wanted?*

"Are you getting out?"

They were walking towards her front door when an absurd thought struck her: *I would like, just once, to see him dancing in my garden.*

In her living room, she noticed that he looked more at her than at her furniture.

"Drink?"

"Would be nice."

"Meanwhile, you'd better take off your pants before you sit down."

He lowered his eyes. "Don't need to. I'll stand."

"Don't be silly, Alejandro."

Sheepishly, he pulled off his pants. He wore neat but thread-bare boxer shorts.

"I'll take a look in my man's closet. You can change in his bedroom."

He was skinny and sinewy. And shy. Very shy.

She went up to the first bedroom. Her ex-husband had honored his judgment that twin beds also had to be in separate rooms in the American style. It gave him the further advantage of being able to sneak up on her unexpectedly at night, something he found mightily arousing. Beatriz felt a wave of nauseous memories.

She felt a surge of resistance washing over her, reminding herself that she was thirty-two, past it by Terreno's macho-standards, and shouldn't want to spoil the contact with the man in her living room, whom she found interesting despite everything.

There was little subtle about the yearning glances he cast on her when he thought she didn't notice. But the compatibility between them, as her father liked to put it, how about that? After a few months of being secretly involved in the resistance, shouldn't she be cautious when choosing a man? Alejandro would be the worst possible choice for a partner.

She tried to suppress the rising turmoil inside her. Her father had chosen her husband. Now she would use her own values to pick a new partner.

She went back to the living room with a forced smile.

"Here are some new clothes. You can change in the bedroom."

He threw one of his shy glances that were already beginning to feel familiar. Despite his big mouth, he had eyes that made her feel strong and wanted.

A few minutes later, he came back. Manuel's pants were baggy on his frame, but for her, that added to his physical appeal.

"Here, take this." She touched his fingers when she gave him his *cup maté*.

He accepted the calabash, rapidly withdrew his fingers,

and spilled the hot tea over his new pants and the living room rug. He tottered to and fro, his face contorted, his hands over his crotch. "Haven't had *maté* for ten years…Made me forget how hot it is," he snorted.

Beatriz warned herself that such a clumsy man was not a match for her. She realized at the same time that he aroused her sense of humor.

Alejandro noticed her amused eyes and grinned. "No worries, I'm only practicing some old dance moves," he said, strutting like a peacock. "I used to be an irresistible salsa dancer, but, at my age, I need a cup of super-hot *maté* on my loins before I find my juice again, you savvy? And…"

"Take them off. The pants, I mean. No problem. Manuel has left dozens of them. He's convinced that someday he'll regain his place as 'master of the house.'"

Beatriz went back up to Manuel's bedroom and opened his closet again. Which color would suit him even more? Light khaki? When she went back, she heard the front door opening. The door to the livingroom bounced hard against the wall. Manuel stood in the doorway, cheeks red, eyes trying to focus, swaying slightly on his feet. *Borracho*, as so often.

"*Puta*," Manuel lisped when he saw Beatriz with his pants in her hands and Alejandro in his boxer shorts in the middle of the room. He spread his arms dramatically, threw his head back, and roared, "Whore!"

Beatriz reacted instinctively, as she had done on previous occasions that spelled marital violence. She turned and ran to the patio to escape via the garden. Durango bolted after her but collided with Alejandro who, with his arms spread peacefully outward, wanted to soothe the situation.

"*Mierda!*" Manuel grunted. He tried a left hook to floor Alejandro. Alejandro ducked the blow, jumped aside, grabbed his guitar, and held it in front of his body as a truncheon.

"Come and get me, anteater." He hunched down and swayed to and fro with his guitar.

Manuel straightened his back and looked scornfully at Beatriz, who watched the scene from the back door.

"Oh, I see, the whore is in heat for stray dogs who don't fight like real men," he said. "My *carabinero* friends will be very pleased to hear that, my little dove."

He turned with the flair of a toreador, left the room, and banged the front door shut with a resounding blow. Alejandro sighed and looked at his guitar. "If this had been a massive Fender, he'd have been a headless chicken by now," he mumbled. Despite her shaking knees, Beatriz grinned.

"Go now, quickly, Alejandro," she said. Her eyes betrayed the opposite of the light-hearted tone she tried to use. "You have to go now. He'll come back with the cops. When they catch you here in the house, I'll legally be a prostitute, even though Manuel and I live apart."

"I've heard about that stupid law." He shook his head. "Will I see you again, Beatriz?"

She noticed the sudden emotion in his voice when he said her name and lowered her eyes. "Yes, of course. Cristóbal has asked me to take ca…help you."

Through the window, she watched him leave the house, fiddling with Manuel's oversized trousers. He looked so droll. Her first impression of him had been that he was a typical Terranean macho. She started to suspect now that he was a proud, sensitive man who was broken and sloppily put back together.

She had lied to him. She knew that Manuel wouldn't return with the police. He was way too vain for that. Her ex would find another way of punishing her. She knew the kind of violence he liked. How had he managed to get a key to her front door when she had the lock replaced months ago? She knew she had better not kid herself. The way the *junta* governed this country gave Manuel every opportunity to see her as prey. The police wouldn't stop him.

She hadn't sent Alejandro away because of Manuel but for

herself. She turned and looked in the mirror and fumbled with her hair. Her thoughts walked beside him as if she were at his side: what did all of this mean?

———

3

Even in his hospital bed, Ernesto Candalti managed to project narcissism. Bone-scrawny, skin with the texture of putty, his head swollen (in his opinion a result of the 'voodoo' of 'those medical quacks'), cork-dry lips: nothing seemed able to break that self-assured look in his eyes. His pepper-and-salt mustache didn't move a millimeter when Beatriz leaned forward to kiss his cheek.

"Hello, papa."

"You're late. Your mother was never late."

Beatriz sat down on the chair next to the bed, crossed her legs, looked at her shoes.

"Who has come to visit you today?"

Ernesto gave her a detailed record of the business partners who had come to his sickbed that day.

"Humberto Laínez comes every day. And he's an employee, admittedly my right hand, but still an employee. He visits me more often than my only daughter."

"Humberto doesn't have a job that keeps him busy for many hours a day."

"If you had listened to me, you wouldn't have to be working. And the university closes the day after tomorrow. You'll have a vacation for two weeks."

Beatriz looked at the window. "The house has to be maintained and cleaned."

"I don't understand why you can't get a cleaning woman with what you earn and what you get from me."

When Beatriz was little, her father had always punished

her in the same way: he pressed her head between his knees and methodically slapped her buttocks. He never noticed the fierce look in her eyes, and the tightness in her lips, afterward. Years later, he took her with him for a trip in his Cessna Skymaster 337. During the flight, she asked to try steering the plane. The sight of his unruly, fifteen-year-old daughter at the controlling filled Ernesto with so much pride he taught her how to fly afterward.

"The daughter of Ernesto Candalti is working as a secretary in a trashy university. No wonder I'm sick."

Why did she keep on visiting him? Eight years ago, she had won—or lost, what did it matter?—the battle of wills between them when she'd cut her wrists in the bathroom of her parents' house. She had been found just in time, precisely by him.

"What are you sitting there laughing for?"

"You look better, papa."

"That's because of my faith in God. You don't want to admit where your profanity has brought you. Why did I bother to pay for your expensive education? You're still young and beautiful but so stupid and stubborn. It hurts for a father to have to say that. It was good that Manuel wanted to discipline you. You never knew your place."

"That's not -"

"You can't deny it."

Twelve years earlier, when the socialist government of President Alvarez made it hard for her father 'to do business as real men should,' he had been as self-assured as now: that *compañero presidente* would quickly learn who wielded real power in this country!

Beatriz's mother told her daughter every day how brave her husband was in his battle with the 'Government of the People'. She didn't suspect that her sermons automatically turned Beatriz pro-Alvarez, even though she wasn't interested in politics. Her parents had gone to extremes to inculcate obedience. She was twenty-one and the product of a strict Catholic boarding school. All kinds of obligations that went with her social class ruled her life, but she kept refusing to make the necessary adjustments that all genteel Terrenean girls accepted for the sake of a profitable marriage.

In the *poblaciónes*, she had seen young women who defended themselves fiercely against seduction by young men. At first, she had been impressed, until she discovered the rules of the game: despite these girls' combative attitude, they wanted nothing more than to melt, cooing, into the arms of a worshipper who promised them the world.

Terrenean girls believed their husbands would free them from the suffocating moral and economic yoke of their parents and dress them in silk frocks and jewelry. Treating a worshipper with condescension was a move in the game that led to the final surrender, after which they wanted to marry and have children as early as possible. As honorable, married women, they became peripheral to their husbands' world, focused on the hunt for money, hours of drunken conversations with their friends, and making wild plans for the future. Before long, the wives were trying to perfect the image they had of themselves as young girls: a tight skirt, a lush décolleté, and parading on the edge of adultery. They covered themselves with make-up and dazzling smiles and anxiously tried to avoid more children.

"Manuel was a good husband for you," her father went on.

The rolled-up paper with which Manuel slapped her, the raw pain. A tug at her blouse, buttons ripped off. Ducking, her hands protecting her face, moaning softly while his hands lashed her body.

Sometimes, she had screamed at Manuel. That only made it worse. One sunny day, against the howling backdrop of the military jets that attacked President Alvarez's residence, Beatriz had resolved to use whatever it took to survive her own battlefield. During the following weeks and months, she was barely startled by the racket from Valtiago's football stadium where opponents of the new junta had been rounded up. The main thing it meant to her was that Manuel wouldn't be home for days. Her husband was an important member of the extreme right militia that had played a decisive part in the rise of the *junta*. That was all she knew and more than she wanted to know.

Years went by, and her marriage became a cat-and-mouse game. She evaded Manuel as much as possible; he found it thrilling to hunt her down. Her only consolation in that period was alcohol. She quickly understood that alcohol was dangerous for her. It made her fitful, and when Manuel was at home when she was drunk, she often reacted so crankily that he hit her until he drew blood. In the church of the *barrio alto*, the Belgian priest René Lafarge preached soulfully about the ravages of alcohol and drugs. René wasn't kind to the *junta* either. Still, people kept coming to hear his sermons, thinking that the *junta* wouldn't dare to muzzle a priest of the influential Catholic church.

Beatriz went to church not for God but for Lafarge's harsh and critical words. After the third time she went, she spoke to him. He was lanky, barrel-chested, with a thick, grey mane, prominent forehead, deep-set eyes, and full lips. Her visits to René became a habit.

Lafarge, a stubborn, often contradictory, and mettlesome man, had been able, after a string of long and fruitless efforts, to help her to escape her hellish marriage. He found a judge who, in exchange for a large sum, ruled that Beatriz could get her divorce on account of her husband's physical assaults. The separation gave her a degree of independence but didn't free her completely: although he had to leave the house, Manuel Durango acted as if this new situation was only temporary because, for the first two years, Terrenean law forbade a divorced wife from living under one roof with another man.

Those two years were a 'reconciliation period' in which man and wife were urged to renew their marital vows.

"I know why you don't answer me," her father said. "You can't deny that Manuel was a good husband for you." He lifted his eyes to the ceiling as if he were pleading with God to show his daughter the evil of her ways.

Her smile was tight. "Manuel is a proud and dangerous man, and you know it, papa."

"You exhausted Manuel's patience. Do that, and you can expect anything! Your decision to divorce him was foolish and bad—you didn't need to make it worse. No decent Terrenean girl lives by herself. Out of pure parental love, I suggested you come home, never mind the shame you had heaped on our name. Back home, you would have retained your status, regardless of your stupidity. But no, you had to become a secretary. It won't be long before Manuel catches you in bed with another man. He'll have the right then to have the police chase you out of the house—the house that I paid for! What should I do with you *then*? The chaplain visits me every day. I talk about you all the time. He shares my point of view on the whole affair and congratulates me on my patience. You can't expect as much patience from a young man like Manuel as you get from your father."

Ernesto gasped and coughed in his handkerchief. He tried to hide his bloody spittle from his daughter.

Beatriz kept her silence.

"I pray every day for you," her father went on laboriously. "Your communist friends have turned you into a daughter I don't recognize. Manuel has confessed that he still loves you. You should've seen the tears in his eyes, the poor boy. He was so ashamed that he whispered when he told me that you're a woman who can't leave other men alone." Ernesto Candalti turned his head away dolefully.

"Manuel only loves himself and the lies he's spreading around."

"Damn it, girl, won't you ever learn? Why are you such a mule? Tell me honestly, can you live on your money?"

"You know all too well what's happened with inflation in Terreno, father. And how inadequate wages are, especially those of academics."

"You're short of money? And you don't even have to pay rent to live in my house? Manuel has…."

"Manuel is an executioner of the junta." She could have cut her tongue out for saying it, but the way he had said '*my house*' had broken her self-control.

As a secretary, she earned 14,000 pesos per month. In the event of the slightest setback, she would have to get rid of her car, rent out the house, and be forced to look for an apartment in one of the less-favorable neighborhoods. But nowadays, exorbitant prices were asked even there. The city, pasted like an ulcer against the Andes, was struggling with a growing housing shortage.

"What did you say?" Her father almost whispered. To her surprise, Beatriz saw terror in his eyes.

"He may not be an official executioner," she said, "but I'm sure he has something to do with it." Her resentment turned against herself because she backed down so easily.

Ernesto Candalti lowered his head into the cushions. "Who told you that?"

"What?"

"That Manuel is an executioner for the junta."

"No one."

It seemed as if he hadn't heard her. "How can you believe such lies?"

"Which lies?"

"That this regime has executioners. Under that ridiculous People's President, anarchy and economic chaos prevailed. Everywhere, you had political hotheads; splinter groups were arming themselves, and..."

"Daddy, I didn't come to get history lessons."

"Sometimes I think you're out of your mind," Ernesto said. "Why are you like this? I've asked God this question countless times. I was a righteous father. And now that I am sick and powerless, you try to hurt me. You keep claiming this government is monstrous because you know that I hold General Pelarón in high esteem. That's how you try to make me into a monster, even though, in spite of everything, I keep throwing money at you. Why?"

"I don't know, daddy."

"Is that your answer? You've made nothing of your life; you've given me no reason to be proud of you. You come to insult me, and at the same time, you beg me for money. What am I going to do with you, child?"

Why do I always have to lose? Beatriz wondered.

"I don't know, daddy."

Ernesto broke the meaningful silence. "Are you short of money?"

"Yes."

He is just a dairy cow, she reminded herself. It doesn't affect me that I have to humiliate myself to get him to the point where he gives me money.

"How much?"

She mentioned the amount. Her father sighed, shook his head, grabbed his glasses and checkbook from the bedside box, and decisively wrote out a check. He handed it over carelessly. She put it away and kissed her father on the cheek.

"Thank you, daddy."

"When are you going to talk to Manuel sensibly and politely?"

"I don't know yet, daddy. When I am ready for it."

"I'll be here in Observation for at least another fortnight," he said, invigorated by the ritual they just had performed. "You'll come and visit me every day, won't you? A man of my age needs the love of his child."

"Yes, daddy." She took a deep breath. "There is something else."

He shook his head. "Yes, girl, what?"

"After all this time, I would love to make another flight," she said with a heart-warming smile. Her father's Cessna had been standing unused for a long time at the private airport of the flying club to which he belonged. Years ago, he had told anyone who would listen that his daughter could fly. A Terrenean girl who could do something other than dress up and cook!

"It's been such a long time," she continued with downcast eyes. "I always feel better when I can fly." When she was married to Manuel, she had borrowed the plane regularly. When the Cessna sheared past the mountain peaks like a firefly, she had felt herself another person, calm and self-confident.

"Hmmm," he said. He stroked his balding skull. "Do you promise to be careful?"

"Yes, daddy."

"Well then," he said with a sigh as if his benevolence were an almost unbearable burden. "Fine-tune the details with Humberto Laínez. I'll tell him that it's okay."

When she kissed his cheek, she was struck by his gaze, which suddenly seemed shy. For a moment, his hand went in her direction. It changed course; he took off his glasses.

"Bye, daddy."

"Bye, child. Till tomorrow."

When she was at the door, he said: "And don't wear such tight skirts, Beatriz!"

———

4

That evening, Beatriz Candalti went to sleep around eight o'clock. Her father was like a dose of benzodiazepine, sucking away all her strength.

Two and a half hours later, she woke up covered in sweat, struggling in the sheets. Her nightmare disappeared, but the sadness of it remained. It was a depressing feeling, the realization of the uselessness of her life.

Just before her teenage years, her friend Pietro – she called him her boyfriend - had asked her in the summer house if she would ever want to marry him.

"Yes," she had answered enthusiastically. "And then you have to make a lot of money, and I have to make a lot of children."

She hadn't 'made' children, and that had been Manuel's first disappointment. It had been for her too. The tight feeling in her uterus that haunted her after learning she was infertile had long since faded. After all, it was a blessing to not have children in this desolate country.

She got out of bed and walked under the spell of her memory to the bathroom. Even then—so young still—she was under the influence of her parents' standards, which meant breeding many children for a rich husband.

She found herself fretting over her past self a lot recently: the Beatriz of ten years ago in no way resembled the Beatriz of today.

How was it possible she remembered nothing of the last year of the *Gobierno Popular* government, except her resentment that the economic downturn made the latest Paris fashion unavailable?

For herself, for her rights, she rebelled against her family. Still, she had almost imperceptibly adopted the world view of her social class.

She never really noticed the solidarity of the People's

Government, the local initiatives, the citizens' committees. She missed all that, living squeezed into her straitjacket of 'appropriate' friends. Why hadn't she realized that even they tried to streamline her for the ideal husband?

In the shower, she let hot water flow over her body and cried, hunched over. Manuel had always urged her to walk upright: otherwise, her breasts would droop. Well, they were drooping now, and she couldn't care less. She felt ugly in the mirror, the reflection of powerless resentment.

She separated her anger from sorrow and stood straight. Men had dominated her all her life. Getting rid of Manuel and tricking her father for money was no longer sufficient as revenge.

She thought about the cargo that, as soon as Cristóbal Vial got the all-clear, she would pick up with the Cessna in the desert of the north where the Andes train crossed the Cordillera. She was afraid of this mission even though she had volunteered when Cristóbal had told her what goal the resistance was after.

She acted out of pride because she had an airplane at her disposal and out of shame of her origins. Since joining Cristóbal's circles, she read very different literature: the lifestory of Marianela Garcia Villas, for example—the lawyer for tortured and missing political prisoners in El Salvador until she found herself kidnapped, stripped naked, and tortured by soldiers.

Beatriz read about the brave mothers of the Plaza de Mayo in Argentina, demanding to know what had happened to their missing children.

About Maria Lionza, who stood up, for free and for nothing, for the poor in Venezuela.

Reading about these heroines led her to conclude that she no longer wanted to be mediocre. She was going to do something about that now. By her mission, soon.

But also by finally dominating a man.

Beatriz knew who she could succeed with in doing that, even before the curfew call at midnight emptied the streets.

———

5

Look how they slithered closer, the memories. Alejandro, lying on his back in his cot, admonished himself that he should leave his shack and take a breath of fresh pigsty air. Too late. The memories had already numbed the impulses necessary to get up and go. With eyes closed, Alejandro Juron kept lying on his back, sinking back in time.

Every time the soldiers had entered his cell in The Last Supper and put the blindfold on him, the hair on his arms had stood up. They had led him through the corridors, through the now familiar maelstrom of agonized sounds in every register. His heart was beating faster; his throat went dry. He felt the infernal circles of Dante surrounding him. The poet was wrong: not in some hollow in the underworld dwelled the demons; they lived among us.

They led him into a room. The voice, always the same voice, was mild and talked somewhat ponderously as if the speaker were reflecting between the words.

The words 'state interest' and 'conscientious' often resurfaced, as did 'patriotism' and 'necessity.' In the long run, Juron lost his understanding of the voice's reasoning. Then came the threats. Cozy enough, the voice told him what they were going to do to him if he did not give up the secret address of 'public enemy number one,' Víctor Pérez and his family. Pérez, the voice went on, was the symbol of anarchy, chaos, and destruction in Terreno, a demagogue who wanted to get rich off the backs of the poor who worshipped him.

Again, Juron couldn't make much of what the man said. However, the threats his interrogator uttered were specific, detailed, cold. Juron listened to them like the last prayer at the deathbed of a believer. He admitted that he had weak nerves. He was a sensitive artist. That was true, according to the voice. It told Juron that it wanted to spare him a mountain of moaning and groaning. That fanfare was too humiliating for an artist with so much talent, wasn't it?

"I do like your guitar work," the interrogator concluded sweetly. It was that word: guitar work. Making it seem honest and hard-earned, not just frivolously picking on strings.

How many days did this continue? The blindfold, the sounds, the voice? Difficult to say. Then, unforeseen came the change. The voice monotonously told him what they were going to do with him, which electrodes they would attach to which places, the duration, the pain level, the inevitable result. The voice now sounded like a salesman summing up a catalog.

Alejandro was unable to stand on his legs when they took him away after that session. The world span 360 degrees. Midway back, they turned and brought him back into the room. The voice spoke again, recited one of the verses from a resistance song by Víctor Pérez that Juron had played so often.

> *Brother, they will cage you,*
> *and tear your skin to patches.*
> *Brother, they'll grub you up*
> *and later you'll be horribly sorry,*
> *because of my name, my dugout, my last*
>   *little bit*
> *You gave them everything they asked you for.*
> *For you are weak, and they are rabid.*

On hearing that strophe, Alejandro Juron burst into tears and soaked his blindfold. Pérez was a prophet: he was weak, and the voice was rabid.

Ten years later, Juron opened his eyes and looked at the

corrugated sheets of his roof. One word remained, grinding in his brain, stinging like a wasp.

Dissociation.

———

6

Beatriz stepped out of the bus and looked around before glancing at her watch. The Canela district was built in a low-lying area on the outskirts of Valtiago.

The actual pigsty, as the slum area of Canela was often called, stretched across the foothills of the mountains next to the highly polluted River Mayu and close to the derelict old freight station. When Beatriz asked to get out at the nearest stop, the bus driver had looked at her with the corners of his mouth pulled down disapprovingly.

"Surely, you are not going to the *porqueriza*?" he said. "You are playing with your life, *señorita*: they're all perverts and addicts."

"I'm aware of that," she replied evenly, telling half the truth: with the Belgian priest René, she had often walked through the neighboring district of Canela. During the daytime, she knew her way around. But now, she stood in doubt in front of the entrance to the pigsty. The spring days were still short; it was already twilight.

She orientated herself on the church, the only significant building that stood close to the slum. Her boots became dirty because of the mud from the heavy rainfall of the last few days. Further on, the mud reached her ankles, and the path became slippery.

Alejandro had told her about the church on the left, to walk across the wasteland, and then take the second street on the right. A strong wind came down from the Cordillera. The weather was harsh and unstable for the time of year. There was hardly any electric light in the slum. The few electricity poles were skewed; most of the lines were cut long ago, and nobody was able to pay their energy bills, so illegal tapping was the commonest activity. In the 1970s, the People's Government had erected solid wooden barracks to replace the hovels. Under Pelarón, who liked to call himself 'The general of the poor,' the huts had returned faster and more numerous than ever. The pigsty was now more than ten kilometers long.

The second street. A little further, Beatriz heard a man's voice shouting something unintelligible. A new gust of wind. Beatriz realized that a spring storm, feared for its unpredictable character, could arise at any moment. She also became aware that she had not taken into account that Alejandro might not be at home. A thumping sound behind her. She turned halfway around. A man came running in her direction, followed by two others. Beatriz squatted behind a pile of old wheel rims in front of a barrack that had been somewhat recalibrated to serve as a local shop. The pursued man swung with his arms and ran with his head thrown back. He was gasping for air. The other two slowly gained ground on him.

They ran past her. Beatriz waited a while, heard a scream. And another. She quickly got up and ran further into the street. Nobody seemed to be bothered by the groaning up ahead.

She stopped in front of a barrack that had previously accommodated several families but now stood at an angle, halved by a collapse, sloppily closed at the back with a corrugated sheet of metal, a few car tires, and more barely recognizable debris. It was closed off with a rotting wooden fence topped with faded curlicues.

As she stood in front of the shack, she heard guitar music. A man's voice started a song, a jumpy dance tune. It was not Alejandro's voice. The man was singing an English song she didn't recognize. The song stopped. A few seconds later, crackling and noisy, she heard it again with more instruments and a different voice. Alejandro started to sing along with the tape recording. Loud voices came closer from the direction where the men had been. They sounded elated.

Beatriz knocked on the wooden Coca-Cola board. "Alejandro!" she called out. Two shapes emerged behind her.

"Good evening," said the first one, pulling his hat deeper over his eyes. "We have a party down the road. You could become the star of the evening."

The fence was pushed aside. Alejandro stood in the opening, in his left hand a guitar, in his other a knife.

"Go and party with yourselves," he said. "You have precisely the right mug for that. Make fun until the morning comes, so you don't have to see the day. Snuff some more rubbish in your nostrils; they're not big enough yet."

The men looked at each other. "We'll do that," said the first man. "And then we'll come back, street-musician." They sank backward, slowly, without turning their gaze away from him. "You're just a scrawny jailbird who has nothing more to say," said the second.

Alejandro balanced on the balls of his feet: "Shall I show you what I had to say in The Last Supper?"

The men turned around and disappeared, mumbling among themselves.

"I missed my bus," said Beatriz. "It was the last one. That's why I've come."

Was this her way of dominating a man?

Alejandro looked at her, surprised. "It's not safe to miss your bus," he said gallantly. In The Last Supper, he had learned almost everything about using a big mouth when afraid and had forgotten nearly everything about gallantry.

7

Beatriz watched Alejandro uncorking the bottle of wine she brought before he poured two glasses.

"Those two men didn't like you."

He shrugged his shoulders. "Young wolves. We don't stay young for long in Terreno, but we all have wolf blood."

She did not ask what he meant by that. "Don't you think it's stupid what I did?"

"What? Missing your bus?" He chuckled. For a moment, he looked like a man who wanted to slap his thighs from pure pleasure but forgot how.

"Searching for you." She took a sip from the wine, a big one.

They fell silent. Alejandro seemed suddenly inaccessible. Beatriz looked around. What did she do in this shack full of shadows?

"Sometimes, I feel like a silly woman. Suddenly, I'm standing in front of your door, and you don't even know me that well. I've caused you problems."

He lifted his glass at her: "Don't say that, Beatriz, it makes me sad." He smiled at her questioning gaze. It was a miracle she was sitting in front of him. He would never have dared to dream of her showing up at his door. Those dark, insecure eyes could study him so haughtily, that shiny black hair, the way she held her head: he thought it was all marvelous. Like a photograph, the image of Lucía slid in front of his eyes, playing in the surf during a holiday twelve years ago on the coast; how he had watched Lucía, how he imprinted every line of her body into his memory. Under that tailored jacket of hers, Beatriz would be precisely like Lucía: girlish suppleness matured poignantly by small imperfections here and there. A healthy body filled with unconscious grace.

"You weren't afraid a moment ago," she said. "I was."

Answering that remark with a lie was easy for him. "I used

to be far too scared about everything, but that was a while ago."

"You sing well."

"It's just an imitation."

She lifted her head a little, and there it was: as he sat opposite her at the Formica folding table, he felt like he was looking at himself. He often felt the same sensation in his cell: he saw himself sitting before his mind's eye, usually surrounded by a grey light, his face squeezed into a rigid expression.

"Why are you laughing?" she said.

"I'm laughing at myself."

"I've spoken to René Lafarge."

"That Belgian? A parish priest, right? I'm not a priest lover. I'm not even a believer."

"René supports the poor. He will help us try to find you an apartment as soon as possible."

"Who is *we*?"

"Lafarge and friends at the university."

"Friends of the Resistance?" He asked bluntly. "*Indignados*?"

She shrugged her shoulders. "If you want to see it like that. Cristóbal tries to help as many people as possible. Because of the cultural institutes connected to the university, he can do more than you would suspect, so...."

"Come on, Beatriz," he interrupted. "You can trust me. Tell me the truth."

"I know very little about the resistance. Cristóbal is quite discreet." It was a white lie. She drank from her wine.

He nodded, but his eyes looked at her with amusement. "Okay, you know almost nothing, message understood. I will refrain from asking for any further information." Abruptly, he changed the topic. "Did your ex-husband come back after I left your house?"

"No. But that only means he's waiting for a better opportunity."

"Does he like music?"

What weird question was that? "He loved Frank Sinatra."

"Frank Sinatra. And who do you love?"

"What do you mean?"

"Which music?"

"From Víctor Pérez."

"From Víctor Pérez. Everyone loves Víctor Pérez." Alejandro poured another generous amount of wine. "Why have you come? I know that you've nothing to find here, and you know that too."

He looked at her so cunningly that she laughed. "I felt alone."

"You can choose better friends than me. Reliable."

"I felt like listening to some music."

"Then go to the discotheque."

"I wanted to hear you playing the guitar."

"A song by Pérez, maybe?"

"Why not?" she said airily. "You were the lead guitarist in his band." The situation was more difficult than she had imagined. Today, he seemed different, as if he'd forgotten his hungry glances at her the day before.

Alejandro shrugged, grabbed his guitar, struck a chord, picked a low, sonorous sound. He looked at her from beneath his eyebrows; pityingly, it seemed.

"Cristóbal must have told you a few things," he said. "I was a teacher at the Instituto de Extenstión Musical. I also was Aconcagua's guitarist. And I was Víctor Pérez's friend, at least, everyone said that." He began guitar picking an erratic dance tune. "But now I'm not any of those things anymore. Now, I am an ex-con. Ten years in The Last Supper turned me into a jailbird. I've also become a whore runner. Women with delicate skin like yours are better off going around a few blocks when they see me coming. I stink like a billygoat." He pulled a funny face and shook his head like a horse on a meadow.

"What should I believe of this inventory?"

"The worst." He switched to a vibrant rhythm and flawlessly sang the first strophe of *Requiem for Carmencita*, the famous song Pérez wrote for his little daughter.

Thirteen years earlier, Beatriz's father had forced her to participate in a conspiracy of women who wanted to give a boo-concert during a performance of Víctor Pérez's group Aconcagua. The concert was put on for the benefit of the People's Government, which was already reeling. Two days before the concert, Beatriz wisely became ill. The national radio and television station broadcasted the performance. Her parents didn't allow her to watch it. She heard fragments of nostalgic songs on the radio during moments when the masses of drummed-up women from the better circles were gasping for breath, tired of booing. The tight drum rolls and the thin, eerie sound of the *quena* fascinated her. It was the first time she had heard Terreno folk music and became impressed by the whimpering of the mountain flute. At home, they listened to Bach and Händel; sometimes, it was Julio Iglesias' turn. She was addicted to John Travolta's songs and would've liked to see his movie *Grease*. After that mutilated radio concert, she had slowly become acquainted with the poetry of Pérez.

> *The street, Carmencita, is your dance hall.*
> *The street that never sleeps,*
> *and confuses love with money.*
> *Your feet are swollen, Carmencita,*
> *you're wrapped up, your arms on strings.*
> *That is the street where each bed*
> *is set to the edge of the slit.*

"Requiem for Carmencita," she said.

He nodded. "That song is old now. I didn't think you would be familiar with it."

He was a sad man, no matter how much he tried to hide it under his mannerisms. She smiled and shook her hair. She knew how lush it was. She grabbed his hand, small and robust with well-formed fingers and dirty nails. His skin was rough. "You sing it beautifully. Almost as beautifully as Pérez himself."

His hand in hers tightened. For a moment, Beatriz had the impression that he was going to withdraw it. But he shrugged again and poured out the last remaining wine with his free hand.

"Was it so bad in prison?"

"Nothing that I can't forget."

"And how are you going to forget?"

"By leaving Terreno," he replied. "I must have money to leave this unpleasant piece of land, stuck between the mountains and the sea." He laughed, full of self-mockery. "The Last Supper left me thinking of this country as a prison. I had to keep them all at bay, the rapists, the sadists, the lunatics. I pretended I was even crazier than they were. I sang songs about street whores in the chow room. The guards laughed their heads off. If the tensions ran high because yet another prisoner had run amuck and was beaten to a pulp, I played the clown. And at night, in my dreams, I gave the most beautiful concert Aconcagua has ever performed in London. When I awoke, I could smell the aroma of fish and chips in Hyde Park in my cell."

He lifted his glass: "*Salud!*" He emptied it in one gulp and took from under his bed the *charango*, a small guitar made out of the shield of an armadillo. He struck a few chords. Beatriz leaned over to him: "Now I remember. On the radio. When Aconcagua performed, the sound of the *charango* sounded so painful and yet mesmerizing. That was you."

"Aconcagua," he said, averting his head. "The Stone

49

Sentinel, the highest mountain in the western hemisphere, up there in the high and mighty Andes. We thought we were giants, but the giants had feet of clay. The government tortured Víctor to death. I've been in prison for ten years. Andres and Mauricio, the other group members, have been reported as 'missing,' which means they've been thrown on a stack of anonymous corpses."

"Will you never perform again in public?"

"No," he said. He laughed, "Or yes. Yesterday when that jeep almost knocked me down, I gave you a serenade then, didn't I?"

"A beautiful..."

"Do you know why I did that?"

"No," she said, knowing all too well why.

"Because you resemble Víctor's wife, Lucía, with whom I was hopelessly and sneakily in love."

In the silence that occurred between them, she realized that she hadn't expected this kind of unease between them.

"You can always write new songs." She kept her eyes on his guitar.

"Oh, about what, then? "

"About the missing persons and their mothers who keep watch in front of General Pelarón's palace until the police chase them away. The next morning, they return."

"If I do that, they'll silence me for good this time."

"You think so? Major changes are on the way. The future amendment of the constitution is just one of them. The people are on the move, Alejandro." Didn't this sound too pamphleteer? She added quickly, "I was at a protest demonstration with René in the government square less than a week ago. The protesters were singing Aconcagua songs."

Why did she bother so much? Did she paint the future so rosy to give him courage? The demonstration had become a nightmare, no matter how poetic the beginning might have been. "Forward, mothers, into the lizard's beak!" an old

Indian woman from the Andes had shouted, the kind of woman with old-fashioned flowery language who still seemed misplaced in the streets of Valtiago. Shoulder to shoulder, she and René had walked with the protestors to the government palace.

At last, the people had become combative. And she played a role in it, just as she had dreamed she would. She had laughed at René, and he had put his arm around her shoulder for a moment, drummed together as they were by the advancing crowd. Then, unforeseen, the water cannons came into action. The thumping of the water hoses was drowned out by screaming. A water cannon had appeared in front of her, a giant iron iguana, hissing and spitting. The world had faded in tornadoes of water. A stinging ray of water shaved past her. She had fallen, her breath cut off by a tingling, wet cold. Lafarge had picked her up from the street. He pulled her away while she was staring at a middle-aged woman who was hit in the chest by the water lance. The force of the water had smacked her against a lamppost. Instead of the name of her missing son, blood came out of her mouth. René saved Beatriz from the chaos of the fleeing mass.

His old Citroën was packed with people when they fled. All that Beatriz remembered from that ride was that René revved up the engine way too much.

"They were singing, boy, oh, boy." Alejandro shook his head as if she had told a good joke.

"The junta is less locked in the saddle than it was a year ago."

"The junta has become lazy because it's so firmly saddled," he replied sarcastically. "It takes more to wobble the generals than a few mothers jumping out of their skin in front of the government palace."

"You talk like my father," she said, poised between bewilderment and anger. "You're smirking at me because you think I'm a woman for whom you need to simplify everything."

His astonishment seemed sincere to her: "What do you mean: 'simplify'?"

"The junta has become lazy because it is so firmly saddled," she rehashed ironically. "This is not true, and you know it well enough: the junta is under pressure from abroad, and from America in particular, to give Terreno at least a democratic tinge. We can benefit from this. It's a beginning."

"I ask you again: who are *we*?"

She started laughing. "You probably see me as a spoiled woman who flirts with the romantic, virile image of the *guerrillero*."

René Lafarge had told her that in the middle-class neighborhoods, which were now in upheaval because of high inflation and the unfortunate economic situation, certain women had these compulsive urges.

Alejandro looked insulted. "How do you simplify me now? As the guitarist of an engaged group who has been in prison as a martyr for the people?"

She knotted her jacket with numb fingers. "It would've been better if I hadn't come," she said stiffly.

"What brought you here? Your romantic dreams? Or did you come because I'm so funny?" He rose angrily. "Do you have any idea what you're doing to me? Because of you, I talk about the past after I locked it out for ten years to survive. Why should I go back into that emotional hell? I wasn't your beautiful singer. That was Víctor; I didn't sing the songs that captivated your heart so much!"

Beatriz suddenly felt calm and purposeful. Through this mixture of misunderstood intentions on both sides, he had shown her a distressed part of himself that affected her.

She stood up and bent to his right ear. "You have a beautiful voice. It's better to sing from now on instead of complaining."

A blast of mountain wind rushed through the *porqueriza* when she kissed him. The flimsy walls shook; a thunderous blow followed. The noise got worse and worse, a cracking and thumping that effortlessly drowned out the wind. The ground was shaking. The rickety walls around them wobbled.

"An earthquake." He gave her a push. "Outside."

She stumbled. Alejandro pulled her along. The earth shook again, this time more violently. The whining wind threaded the giant blows together. Outside, Beatriz involuntarily froze. A dozen barracks, built on poles because the mud pools in the alleys were so large, fell with a grotesque squatting motion in her direction. She saw people tumble out of the dilapidated boxes, distorted as if the wind were crushing them. Dust covered the devastation with a yellow-brown veil. The ground became a rolling carpet under her feet that made it impossible to stay upright. She fell. A piece of torn lime-stone plate hit her hard in the back. Once again, the wind struck the neighborhood and laid hovels flat as if they were reeds. Alejandro yelled something. She couldn't understand him, didn't see him through the dust and debris. She remained on the ground, her fingers pressed into the mud beneath her.

It started to rain.

———

8

An old, sodden mattress stuck like a giant discolored tongue in the fragments of a house. Beatriz tugged at it. If she could get it into some shelter, there would be one less injured person in the mud. The thing was too heavy. She called Alejandro. He grabbed her by the arm and gestured silently.

Behind the mattress lay the crushed corpse of a child. Beatriz wiped wet strands of hair out of her eyes and turned around. The disaster had erased more than a third of the *porqueriza* as far as she could see. "Go and get help," she said.

She stooped, grabbed the dead child, a boy of perhaps

ten, and hauled him out of the rubble. A small woman pushed her aside, pulled the corpse out of her hands, and began to sob, holding the dead boy tight in her arms.

Hours later, she felt exhausted. Only now were the emergency services becoming more or less organized.

While she had been helping recover the bodies of strangers from the rubble, she lost sight of Alejandro. Now she turned away from the carnage. She could no longer endure all that mutilation and death.

She stood there, staring at the mountains in the distance. Then, she saw Alejandro approaching in the uneven light of the railway lamps near the Canela district, which, after much squabbling, had been ignited at full power. He walked a bit insecurely and swung a bottle of *pisco* in her direction.

Closer to her, he threw her a cunning gaze, his chin slightly raised, his lips folded with a bizarre sort of pride. "How brave of you," was all he said. He gave her the bottle; she took a sip.

"The great Stone Sentinel has a heap of hors-d'oeuvres behind his teeth." The way he said that was malicious.

"Is that your way of describing this?"

"How would I describe it otherwise, *mamita*? That's what we are, right? Hors-d'oeuvres for the eternal Andes." He handed Beatriz the bottle again. Juron shook his head. His gaze swept over the devastated slum. "The poor bastards. Aconcagua performed songs about the beggars of this country, but I never dreamed I'd become one of them. Now I've got nothing left, and yet I still can't feel like one of them. My shack is a shambles. Where should I go? Will I be able to feel like a true beggar now? Like a lost rat, just like them?"

She made a decision. "Your house is gone, Alejandro, but mine is still standing."

———

9

He stood naked next to her bed and covered his penis with his hands when she came out of the bathroom and quickly laid down underneath the sheets. That bathroom next to the bedroom had been Manuel's refuge. After sex, he'd always rushed in there while she remained in bed, staring at the ceiling. Once, she had caught him in the en-suite, looking in the mirror and admiring his shoulder muscles. At that time, it hadn't been funny, but now that she saw Alejandro's sinuous body, standing beside the bed, entirely different from Manuel's fat-wrapped muscles, that image of her ex-husband returned to her, and she had to laugh.

"Why are you laughing?"

"Nothing. Come, Alejandro, don't just stand there."

He obeyed. His toes were cold. He put his face in the cavity between her shoulder and neck and sniffed the scent of her skin. "Maybe I won't meet your expectations," he whispered.

"Why not?"

"How do you think I satisfied the beast in myself in prison? In all loneliness, of course. That is at the expense of technique and stamina."

"Square ass!" She pulled his hair playfully. "Do you think it's wrong that we are lying here?"

"Yes," he said. "After all, you're still a married woman."

"No, I mean, after what happened a little while ago. The dead, the wounded..."

"Is this priest, this René, teaching you to think like that?"

"What do you mean?"

"In prison, a chaplain occasionally visited me. I had to renounce my sins, show repentance. Then everything would be in all right again. The man was old and half deaf. I told him hundreds of times that Jesuits had raised me until I was seventeen, but he kept asking me whether I was a communist.

That would have been a mortal sin for such a nice man as he saw in my inner self. I'm sure he was quite myopic."

"René is not like that."

"Then you don't have to feel bad. I'm not a huge fan of guilt; others are too quick to take advantage of it."

He brushed his lips along her neck. She felt the sensation in her toes. He chuckled. "Maybe we should agree on a symbolic price. I'll feel at home then. It will work wonders for my libido." He clamped her with his arms and legs in such a tender way that she could only laugh.

"Hmm. I don't get the impression that you're particularly uncomfortable now, even without a fee."

"What you feel is only an illusion," he mumbled. His mouth slid over her right nipple, but his voice was grave.

She grabbed his head and forced him to look at her. "Do you think this is good?"

"Yes," he said. "We're holding each other tight, Beatriz. What else can we do?"

René Lafarge could have said a similar thing, she thought. Juron's body already seemed familiar, but she didn't get a grip on his mind. She remembered Manuel's dominance, pushed Alejandro onto the pillows, and straddled him. "My husband thought he was quite a macho."

"And was he?"

She laughed. A sudden feeling of victory increased her excitement.

"He believed he was." She bent forward to Juron's almost hairless chest and sucked on a nipple. He tried to push her away clumsily.

"Oh no, Beatriz, I can't stand that! It tickles!"

"Come, Alejandro. A Terreno stud of your caliber can handle a few volts."

He giggled almost girlishly and pushed her mouth away from his nipples. "My mother did that too when I was little.

The Mapuche Indians think men will better understand a woman's soul if their nipples are sucked when they're children. That's how the mother blows the female soul into the male so that, as an adult, he'll have a twin soul. Only then will he be able to see what real beauty is. And the mother has to start sucking when the baby boy is still very young, otherwise..."

"I want to know everything about you, Alejandro Juron, including your sensitive nipples. But not now. Come closer to me."

He was silent for a moment. "That's not easy," he whispered. "Every inch of my belly is covered by your belly."

"We still have a way."

———

10

He appeared naughty and cute in the early morning light with his small nose above his trimmed mustache. Beatriz had noticed that his head rarely stood still when he was awake. His lower lip puffed out a little, which gave him the air of an innocent ten-year-old boy. His little teeth were a bit ambiguous, making him look like he would cry or become angry. But then again, his round chin and delicate facial features made him attractive. Beatriz lay close to him and stroked his thighs. She felt that his skin was surprisingly soft. His crotch was the most delicate of all, a warm, varied spot that reminded her of the downy softness of Bulo, the Labrador her father had bought for her when she was little.

In his half-sleep, his penis started to grow. Beatriz tightened her grip a bit. The phone rang just as he slung an arm over her shoulder. She pressed her breasts against him and pushed her body even closer. His legs opened up for her gently caressing fingers. She had touched Bulo like that when he was lying on his back, wagging his tail, helpless when her hand slid over his belly.

The ringing didn't stop. Could it be Manuel had found out that she was in the house with a man?

"I have to answer this."

He mumbled something incomprehensible. Beatriz got out of the bed, looked back, half hoping that the ringing would stop. She saw him looking at her. She automatically pulled her back straight, went down to the living room, and lifted the receiver

"Beatriz?"

She took a deep breath. "Yes, René."

"Beatriz," the Belgian priest said, "I need your help. The people are bringing the wounded from the pigsty to the church. The emergency services have simply ignored them. I know you helped a lot last night, but we need everyone willing to help. Can you come?"

"I'm coming," Beatriz said. "I'll call the university and ask if any others will come along too. And I'll bring Alejandro with me."

René was silent for a moment. "Good. Thank you, Beatriz."

The way he said her name made her think that he suspected that Alejandro was lying in her bed.

And that he was jealous.

The Doubt Of A Priest

1

RENÉ STOOD IN FRONT OF THE ALTAR. BEHIND IT WAS THE massive cross on which a brown-skinned Christ turned his heavily accentuated eyes to heaven. Underneath the cross stood the black-haired Virgin Mother on her canopy. She wore a crown and a white lace cloak decorated with gold brocade. The Virgin had downcast eyes, which gave her a bitter expression. Morning light entered through the stained glass windows depicting the twelve disciples. Their colors were pale.

René addressed the crucifix: "Thank you for proving once again that misfortune is a must for the poor, undoubtedly to promote their spiritual development," he said in a muted voice. The damp chill in the church was far from optimal for the wounded behind the altar. A few hours after the emergency services had left Canela, the procession of poor lice from the pigsty, neglected by the rescue services, started filing into the church. René offered them shelter. He had called friends and asked them if they could collect medicines and food. Until they showed up, he couldn't do much.

People with Indian blood populated twenty percent of the slum. For centuries, René's predecessors had tried to defeat the faith of the Native Andeans. They had at last succeeded through a combination of violence, indoctrination, and rituals which they had adopted - and adapted - from the Indians. The priests were smart enough to lure the Indians away from their mountain slopes. They sensed that their crucified god and a virgin could not compete with the centuries that looked down upon them. But even after intensive massacres and deportations, the mountains remained Indian territory. In the mid-seventies, the brand new junta had forced them to work in the mines. In barely four years, the miners drained the mountains close to Valtiago.

American advisors located new mining sites higher up the Andes. The indigenous tribes who had worked in the depleted mines were dismissed and forced into slums, cut off from their cultural roots, and dependent on alcohol and drugs.

No longer did they turn their eyes to the mountainsides where the spirits of their ancestors lived and on whose ground their parents had buried their umbilical cords, according to the old custom. They only saw the rot in front of their feet now, forgetting the mysterious majesty above their heads— needing to instead focus on surviving to the next day.

In his sermons, René spoke little about God, preferring to remind them of their ancestors and culture. He had a voice for it: melodic, heavy, emotional. The priest provided food and clothes through all kinds of institutions from Europe. He convinced the elderly to go back to the mountains to live off the yields of their bean fields again. However, the young people, who were ideal targets of the growing drug trade, stayed.

Two loud popping sounds echoed from the front porch of the church. On the floor around René, the wounded hardly moved.

Three young men stood in the semi-darkness of the church portal. The first one pointed a gun, with which he had shot in the air, at the priest. They had scarves wrapped over their faces.

"We want money, padre," said the first one. "We are dangerous. We want the money you have raised."

René threw his head back. In a few steps, he stood in front of them, the palms of his hands turned outward. "Do you want money? Go and ask for money on the plaza in front of the government building. Do you want food? You can get that. Do you want drugs or liquor? You don't get that for the simple reason that I don't have those things." He clamped his lips together. "Do you want to shoot? So shoot."

The first boy held the gun sluggishly at him. René pushed the weapon away. "Go away," he said without a trace of contempt. "I can't give you anything at the moment. Go away and come back like real men. Then you can help me to relieve the suffering of these poor people."

The youngsters were members of one of the many street-gangs in the pigsty. They glanced at each other, turned around, and walked out, glancing over their shoulders at him.

Looking at their backs, René felt an unexpected and painful memory: sixteen years earlier, as a young and restless priest in the Belgian city of Charleroi, he had one evening visited a divorced woman with two children, a regular church-goer who was having a hard time. She was small, had big, sad eyes, and lively gestures, betraying her Spanish origin.

They talked for hours. Finally, René admitted to her that he could no longer cope with the Church. He no longer knew how to deal with himself, his priesthood, and with God. She listened to him as he tried to unravel his life.

Stay with me tonight, the young woman had said when he didn't know what to say anymore. *You can stay for the night.*

She was sitting next to him; he could feel her warmth

while he was looking at his shoes with his head in his hands. She would be good for him; it was as simple as that. But all this confusion, this inability, this desire. He sat frozen on the sofa until he whispered that he had to leave; it was already so late, too late.

The priest turned to the altar and looked at the statue of Christ. It had taken Lafarge quite some time to get used to the sugary romanticism it radiated. *I don't remember who I am anymore*, he thought. *I am displaced, just like those young wretches, just like you.*

From his love for God, only a feeling of incapacity had stayed; from his human love, just pain and confusion had remained. Of all the people he had called for help that morning, Beatriz had been the last.

"*Los huevos!*" screamed a shrill voice behind him. René turned around. A parrot had flown into the church, pale, lean, and nervous, crowing *Los huevos!* The beast landed on the altar and looked at René with its head tilted, suspicious and begging at the same time.

René sighed, "If this is your messenger, God, you could at least have taught him proper Spanish. If the subject has to be 'balls,' *cojónes* sounds a lot more civil than *los huevos*, doesn't it?"

2

René shook hands with Alejandro. "Alejandro Juron," said the priest. "I am an admirer of Aconcagua's music. Your friend Víctor was a great man. Together with Terrenean priests, I tried to mediate after they locked him up with his family in the stadium..."

The Belgian shook his head. He fell silent when he noticed that his words had fallen into the wrong soil. He could see it from the way the man in front of him lowered his eyes. Juron turned around and looked at the silent wounded in the church. Beatriz glanced at Alejandro. René noticed it and felt irritation. On which long toes had he stepped?

The other man in Beatriz's small group had the build of a wrestler. He was at least one meter ninety. His shoulders and neck were particularly impressive. His broad head showed africoid features, but his eyes were surprisingly light-colored.

"I brought João Pereira from the Instituto de Extensión Musical," Beatriz said. "I also called Cristóbal Vial. He will try to round up some more people, but you know that the university will be closed for another two weeks." João extended a massive hand to René.

"I've heard a lot about you," said René. The muralist João Pereira was known throughout Terreno for the joy of life that his colorful paintings radiated. He kept his distance from politics, and the junta considered him harmless. It had authorized João to run an art village in the Andes, financed by an American organization.

The village got the idyllic name La Paloma and lay close to the observatory that the Americans had built in the mountains to take advantage of the clear Terrenean nights. La Paloma had quickly become a stopover for tourists who wanted to photograph the observatory.

René turned to Beatriz. Alejandro still seemed to be inspecting the church. His back radiated rejection. "It's a pity that Cristóbal was unable to do more. He's otherwise so helpful."

Beatriz pursed her lips. She was not used to the Belgian priest's sarcasm. For many years, René had been friends with Cristóbal. He bombarded the librarian regularly with daring cultural projects criticizing the situation in the country, ranging from subtle to overt. Cristóbal usually managed to be diplomatic when he torpedoed René's malapert proposals.

"I think Cristóbal has become more careful," João chuckled.

"If Cristóbal heard that, he would have had a coughing fit," René replied, trying to clear the atmosphere with a joke. Cristóbal was known for his angry coughing when he disagreed with something but couldn't say it openly. The priest noticed Beatriz and Alejandro had moved away. They stood a little further in the main nave. Alejandro said something to her, a few words that Lafarge couldn't catch.

"Shall we start?" René asked a little louder than necessary. As they approached, he had the unpleasant feeling that Alejandro was looking sourly at him. "I've been able to cadge food parcels from the diocese," he continued. "Could you transport them to the church with your Land Rover, Beatriz? The parcels are waiting at the Diocese Head Office in Calle Valdivieso."

A little later, Beatriz had left, and João and Alejandro were busy with the children. Some of them were seriously injured. Lafarge had done what he could, but medical equipment and drugs were urgently needed. He called the emergency services several times, but no one had turned up.

The children who could still walk were roaming the church or sitting quietly in a corner. René saw Alejandro kneeling in front of a girl who had crawled into a confessional. He said something to her. A little later, the girl lifted her distraught face. The priest saw how Alejandro took the child in his arms and cradled her.

Abruptly, a group of soldiers entered the church with their weapons, ready to fire. The soldiers spread out. The captain went to René.

Out of the corner of his eye, René saw Alejandro put the girl down roughly before retreating to the altar, kneeling and pretending to be absorbed in prayer. The abandoned girl started crying again.

"René Lafarge?" said the officer, positioning himself in front of the priest.

"Present," said René without flinching a muscle in his face.

The captain raised an eyebrow. "We have been informed delinquent inhabitants of the *población* have sought refuge in the church. Among them are a few notorious drug traffickers who we've been tracking down for a long time."

"That's nonsense," René said. "What we have here, *mi lugarteniente*, are people whom the emergency services didn't care enough to rescue—people who dared speak out against your government."

The small man pushed René's chest with his right palm. It was a vicious gesture, fueled by René's deliberate misinterpretation of his rank. The heavily-built priest barely took a step backward. René, in his heart a fierce and proud man, almost raised his fist. The officer was waiting for this, as was clear in his eyes.

"I've been warned that you are a priest who 'interprets' the teachings of our Holy Mother the Church rather nonchalantly. You have been faulted for inflammatory activities before. You're a European and a priest; therefore, you believe you're above our laws. You need to start believing differently, René Lafarge." He signaled to his soldiers, "Take them all with you."

"You can't do that," René said. "Some of these people are seriously injured."

"I'll spell it out one last time, Lafarge: we're following orders from a high level." The captain smiled; his eyes under the *kepi* were provocative.

The soldiers dragged the wounded away. The children were herded together and driven out of the church. João Pereira continued to dab a woman's feverish temples until a soldier tried to pull him to his feet. João shrugged his large shoulders, and the soldier almost fell over. The painter looked back, his pale eyes completely innocent. He stood up. The soldier took a step backward and gestured with his weapon that the half-blood had to retreat. Alejandro had also risen. He breathed heavily as if he could faint at any moment.

"No," he said when one of the soldiers came up to him. "Not me. I do not belong to them. I'm not a resident of ..."

"Those two are part of my crew," said René, frowning at Alejandro. "They are lay brothers of my parish."

The captain nodded to the soldier, who turned around and walked away. The parrot stuck his head out of the confessional and screamed with his shrill echoing voice: "*Las güevas!*" Startled, a young soldier turned around and fired. The shots boomed through the church. The bird flew up and described agitated, quacking circles. The captain stared at it.

"Shots in my church," said René Lafarge, who saw an opportunity. "That will surely ..."

"Silence!" snarled the captain. He glared furiously at the soldier who had fired the shot.

"You should leave my church," René resolutely continued. "My bishop will not take shots fired in the house of God lightly." He knew how heavily this argument would weigh in staunchly Catholic Terreno.

"I will..." started the captain.

"You are leaving my church," René interrupted. "Now."

The captain moved his right shoulder as if he were going to hit Lafarge. The priest took a step forward and made an impertinent gesture that, in this country of high masculinity, no one would tolerate. The captain stared amazed at the Belgian, pulled his gun, and pointed it at the priest. René saw his eyes narrow. His abdominal muscles tightened. The man in front of him swallowed visibly and struggled to keep himself in check. "Of course, padre," he said, barely audibly. "In the house of God, you're in charge. But you aren't here all the time." He turned to his soldiers: "The Reverend Father asks if we would kindly evacuate God's temple faster, so do your best!"

The soldiers lugged up the wounded a lot more roughly than before and carried them out on the run. "*Salaud*," said the priest in his Walloon mother tongue. "*Sale salaud.*"

The captain smiled; his eyes did not change expression: *my time will come, son of a whore…* He turned around and walked away. A little later, the church was empty.

René looked around him. The parrot landed again on the altar and strutted up and down with his head shaking to and fro. The priest saw that Alejandro was sitting on a bench with his hands in front of his face. João kneaded the skin around his eyes with a tired gesture. René walked to the altar, took a bottle of wine from a chest underneath it, and took a big sip of it. "Here," he said, extending the bottle to Alejandro. The guitarist avoided his gaze and made an averting gesture, thought twice, and drank. At just that moment, Beatriz entered the church.

"What happened?"

Alejandro did not answer. He looked at the priest. Looking back, René tried to guess whether he had made a friend or an enemy.

———

3

In the coolness of the night, Alejandro was woken up by something pressed against his throat. Asleep, Beatriz had laid her left arm over his neck. Carefully, he turned towards her and stroked her belly. If he stayed with her, the dissociation in his mind and the ten-year stay in jail would slowly fade until they seemed unreal.

And, eventually, he would be able to forget what he had done.

He profoundly regretted accompanying her that morning to the church where he had shown his cowardice when the soldiers wanted to take him. Beatriz had been away at that moment, picking up food parcels, but René had seen it; João had seen it. Sooner or later, Beatriz would hear about it. Alejandro wondered when René would tell her and how she would react.

Before being imprisoned, he had been a somewhat hypocritical musician who paid lip service to the socially engaged status of the group in which he played. In his true essence, he was a dreamer longing for fame and money. He felt hurt and humiliated when he noticed that he could compose music and provide ideas for songs, but that writing lyrics with real emotional content eluded him. Víctor twirled those songs in his fingers, the singer, the idol, the soothsayer.

In darkness came the memory of a night when he was thirteen. His mother had taken him into the mountains, to the feast of the *abuelos*, an Indian ritual in Tierra Amarilla that she wanted to investigate. She had asked Alejandro if he would dare to participate and afterward tell her how it felt. That caressed his vanity. Him? Scared of silly Indian hocus pocus? How was it possible that his mother could think so?

The fire, clear blue against the red ground, carried a cloak of grey smoke that lingered despite the wind. The smoke caused the faces of the Indian boys to fade around the fire. Juron stood between them. An *abuelo* jumped out of the bushes, his coat undulating in the heat of the fire, the hood over his head tightly closed, the mask for his face representing a mythical animal. A wide strap with bells hung crosswise over his chest. The bells signaled the rhythm of his wild jumps; the bang of the whip swung at its own pace through the rhythmic ringing. The whole scene was eerily threatening.

The "grandfather" shouted his admonitions in Quechua with a hoarse voice. Although Alejandro didn't understand most of the words, the throaty sounds made him flee with the others from this old incarnation. It was a game; of course, it was just a game. But Alejandro had felt movement in his soul:

something in him had awakened when for the first time he had seen the symbol the old man personified.

Although still young, Alejandro had seen a glimpse of himself in the fire, a young boy with a hump of darkness weighing on his back. He'd felt sadness in his core, without knowing why.

Squinting in the dark, he lay next to Beatriz with his hand on her belly. Images appeared in his mind: the old, toothless Aymara women hanging a condor upside down on a pole during the feast of the Immaculate Virgin; the long-haired *huaso* who stormed towards the bird on his horse and punched it with his fist in the hope of killing the wildly fluttering beast, thus claiming the honor of the most audacious horseman in the village; the reflection of an Aymara boy squatting in a mud pool, his arms wrapped around his head.

And then the contours of a face behind a bright lamp when his blindfold was taken away in one of the stadium's torture chambers: "I'm Captain Astíz, and I'm going to make sure you get to know yourself better."

A man who had got to know himself better knew he didn't belong in this soft bed with this well-meaning woman.

Alejandro got up and dressed. At the door, he glanced at her: in the vague light of the bedroom, she was only a shape. He blew her a kiss and went down to the living room, where light entered from the patio. A minute later, he stood in the garden. He wanted to orbit the house but remained motionless. The image of the Indian fire that he had circled came back before his mind's eye and turned into the flame of the lighter with which Captain Astíz had lit his cigarette in the semi-darkness of the cell. Alejandro pushed the memory away and looked up to the starry sky. It was foolishness to look for words for something he had no words for.

Chirpy, chirpy, cheep,
I am a fearful parrot,

my colors in the sun
shine like a lemon.
My beak is big,
wide as the world,
but all I can do,
cracking like an old shoe,
is chirpy, chirpy, choo.

Alejandro kept on staring at the rushing clouds and the moon crescent. He had just left someone who might have dispelled the bitterness in him with her sweetness. What more could he do to write at last a heart-gripping song without his constant acidic mockery?

Chirpy, chirpy, choo.

"Alejandro." Beatriz stood on the patio in her underwear, pushing her hair out of her face. "Did you do the same with your hookers? Steal away in the middle of the night?"

"You don't understand."

"I'm afraid I don't."

"Look at Aconcagua." He pointed to the Andes. The moonlight brushed down the slope of the two peaks that towered just above the *barrio alto* so that the light seemed to drip from them like milk. "Only the Stone Sentinel was high enough to meet my ambition. And what's become of it?"

She did not react. The light from the patio fell over her shoulder, turning her skin golden.

"You should've seen me in your friend's church, trembling like a leaf for the soldiers, screaming like a girl that I didn't belong to the slum gang."

"That's normal after what you've experienced."

"I knew you'd say that," he said. "For me, it's not normal. I have to face myself finally: I am a coward."

"Cristóbal told me a few things about your prison days. You've lived in hell for ten years. It's time you realized that you don't have to be a fairytale hero."

Her logic made him angry. He showed his palms and took a step backward. "That's not what it's all about. When I played with Aconcagua, I sang the second voice. Our songs were all about poverty and oppression, but I only wanted admiration, money, and fame. Víctor was the soul of the group. I tried to compose songs too, but they weren't good enough. I lacked the talent to be a real songwriter, but I could find the right melody for every word Víctor wrote. Víctor said that we were blood brothers, but he was the great darling of the masses, not me. I got even more envious when we became internationally known. And still, everything revolved around Víctor Pérez, the dedicated, singing poet with unprecedented talent." He paused and shook his head.

Beatriz folded her arms over her chest. He coveted her all of a sudden, but even more, he wanted to hurt her, leaving her behind like a broken doll. But when he was close to her, he put his arms around her and buried his face between her breasts. Her fingers grabbed his neck forcefully, and suddenly he knew. While he had thought that the years behind him had made him vigilant, they had instead distorted him. He was a vague shape in a thick fog, nothing more.

This insight made him more afraid than the soldiers who had invaded the church. Maybe that's why he pushed her so suddenly when the phone rang in the living room.

"Who can that be?"

She rubbed her upper body where he had hurt her like a skittish horse. "How can I know?"

"At this hour? Who…."

His confusion and fear dispelled her anger. "Shall I pick up?"

"It is already after midnight."

"Maybe it is important."

"It'll certainly be that priest again."

"Why do you say that?"

He turned his head away. She no longer waited for an

answer and felt his gaze on her back when she went into the living room. She lifted the receiver.

"Beatriz? Is it you, Beatriz?"

She took a deep breath: "Yes, father."

A long silence followed. "Daughter, I feel as if the world is collapsing around me," said Ernesto.

The Dove In The Mountains

1

Dear Gui,

I'm afraid you may be worried about me as it's been a long time since I wrote to you, and you've always fretted about me like a father. But I just had a dream about you which reversed these roles. You were no longer my older brother but a little boy abandoned in an underground maze, deep inside a mountain. I wandered through the corridors, and the sounds of your terror made my skin crawl. I could hear your crying and its inconsolable sorrow made me desperate for it to stop. Now and then, I glimpsed a tiny silhouette through cracks in the rock, and without knowing why, I was sure it was you. But when I finally reached you, you had vanished. Someone else had taken your place: an adult who looked like you but had a mournful manner and asked me a question as he stood there under dripping rocks. I woke up in the deepest darkness, not so much around me but within myself. The dream-man had asked me: Who are you, and what are you doing here?

Nightmarish fears usually give way to relief when one wakes, but not this time. The question is correct: how did I end up in Terreno, and what is left of all my ideals?

Who am I? A miner's son from Charleroi with a taciturn father, who coughed up blood and died at just the age I am now. And you, Gui, my big brother – at the time our father died, you were a young man recently widowed, when your wife and baby died in childbirth, just seven months after your marriage. The bigots of the neighborhoods thought it was God's punishment for your "disgraceful premarital sex."
All through our youth, our parents banged into us that God governed everything. By the time your wife died, I was old enough to realize that, in fact, God's special talent was the spreading of disasters. To appease Him, I decided to become a priest. And because Mom always said that poverty was a disgrace one had to put right, I ended up in Terreno, the land of the chronic poor.

With a character like mine, I already had problems with the authority of the Holy Mother at the beginning of my vocation. These problems with hierarchy have increased year by year. A priest who cannot keep his mouth shut about injustice will sooner or later end up in trouble in a country like this.

Can character be traced back to critical moments in one's youth? I don't know, but I do know that all my life, there has been too much confusion between me and my 'true self.' Too many compromises, too many disappointments, and too much guilt.

Tonight, I have admitted to myself what I have known for a long time: I have lost my faith. These days a priest who loses his faith is a banal cliché. But the seed has long been taking root and I didn't dare to admit it. I preferred to go on sacrificing my hypocrisy to God - not the sensitive God I felt in my mystical and naive young rapture, but a sullen, incomprehensible tormentor who demanded lip service.

I would give everything I have to relive the moments of ardor and ecstasy I knew at the seminary. Those moments turned me into a popular left-wing priest in the slum area of a fractured South American country. Once I was here and felt how the poor people looked up at me, there was no way back: I had to efface myself and give them my best. I saw that as the divine verdict over the crime I committed years ago.

The Andes handed down a verdict two days ago. As usual, it is hard for the have-nots. An earthquake destroyed three-quarters of my parish. The working-class district nearby suffered less; nevertheless, many people died. We do not know how many: the homeless in the slums are innumerable, just like the blessed souls in heaven.

I notice that I automatically translate the human suffering around me into the political context and thus into numbers. That's because there is no alternative in Terreno. In my constituency, the People's Government was engaged in building projects, but they stopped ten years ago when the junta seized power. Since then, the living conditions here have dramatically worsened. Now, I fear that real uprisings are about to occur. If that happens, the riots will give General Pelarón the excuse to attack the pigsty.

Last night, the military emptied my church of wounded people. They claimed activists were hiding amongst them. The wounded were mainly Indians whom the emergency services had abandoned on the streets. It is true that the Indians have discovered their rights over the past year and are starting to assert them - but calling them activists is an overstatement.

This country is on the verge of chaos. The wealthy are dancing the rumba in luxurious nightclubs; the poor grab leftovers in the garbage dumps. In recent months, the junta has been trying to show a veneer of democracy. Still, I fear that the growing resistance will lead it to revert to its usual brutality. Terreno is a country full of contradictions and teeming with underground parties and resistance groups. I have heard that rebel groups are smuggling in arms from Cuba. The middle class hesitates; the oligarchy has resolutely sided with the junta. Right now, the left-wing *opposition is still fragmented, but the signs are that a broad front is gradually becoming possible.*

What will be the role of the Catholic Church when it comes to a revolt? My boss, Cardinal Subercaseaux, is a man who equates God with authority. Yesterday, he summoned me to his office for a slap on my wrist. When I entered the pastoral office, Monsignor was reading a book. He let me wait without inviting me to sit. When he considered the humiliation sufficient, he turned his gaze to me.

"We have heard bad news about you from the government," he said.

"I meticulously reported to your secretary what has happened in my church and asked if the Church would make a complaint," I replied. "One of her priests was threatened."

The monsignor sighed. Four years ago, when he was just an obscure Terrenean Bishop, he visited the junta's extermination camps. He praised the military's 'commitment to the homeland' and their determined resistance to 'forces of evil that weaken the sacred values of God, family, and patriotism.'

He had a motive for this behavior. General Pelarón devoutly visits the City Cathedral every Sunday, but his government was roundly reproaching Rome for being too critical. Rome relented and put Subercaseaux forward as the new face of the Terrenean church. He is now Terreno's only Cardinal and best buddies with the junta.

"I don't understand where you're coming from, Lafarge," said the prelate. "Further resistance on your part would have been a political act. Our Holy Mother does not interfere in politics. Surely, you don't suppose that the military came to pick up suspects in your church without good reason? You talk too much about this world, René, and too little about God."

He is so eloquent, Cardinal Subercaseaux, and so different from my former bishop, the old Monsignor Tibeira, who, at the time of the coup,

when the stadium in Valtiago was bursting with prisoners, worked tire-
lessly to save as many people as he could. Subercaseaux has his mouth full
of God, and he licks his lips as if talking about a delicious dish.

After his sermon, I took stock of my life, Gui. I am not staying here
because the people of Canela need me, but because I feel as if I am stuck
in a pithead and cannot escape.

RENÉ LAID DOWN HIS PEN, COVERED HIS EYES WITH HIS hands, and sat in his chair for a long time. Then, he took a new sheet of paper and wrote on it hastily:

My dear Cristóbal,

I called Beatriz a moment ago. She suggested that we organize a benefit
concert for the reconstruction of Canela and the slums. What do you
think? Will the junta allow such a peña? Beatriz has told me that she
wants to persuade Alejandro Juron to perform. With Aconcagua's ongoing
reputation, which could prompt harassment by the authorities, it seems to
be better that we reject this proposal. Can't you come up with an excuse to
keep Alejandro away from the event? I also suspect that the man is unreli-
able. I had heard that he had come to live in the porqueriza, but I had not
met him until last night. I felt sorry for him over his experience in jail.
Now that I have encountered him, however, I believe that he has a
cowardly character. I think he is clinging to Beatriz for opportunistic
reasons.

I intend to discourage Beatriz from seeing him any further, but perhaps
she has already wrestled herself from my influence. I apologize,
Cristóbal, but Terrenean women are incomprehensible to Europeans.
Beatriz may be beautiful, but why is she so stupid as to be taken in by
a man who wears the halo of a folk hero without deserving it?

Alejandro whined like a scared kitten when the soldiers arrived in my church.

Admittedly, if I'd had his years imprisoned in The Last Supper, then perhaps I would also be afraid - I've heard the horror stories that go around. All the same, I do not like him; I cannot look him in the eye; I do not understand why Beatriz chose him instead of...

René laid down his pen again and stroked his forehead. He ripped the letter apart, got up, and walked to the window of his office. His house next to the church was the first built under the People's Government in the workers' district. René looked over the monotonous rows of Canela houses, all dark at this hour, and he shook his head.

At this very moment, he knew that, while he was pondering his faith and his infatuation, others in Terreno were plotting murder and manslaughter, whether for drunken or envious reasons or in the service of guerrilla attacks and subsequent reprisals. He needed a drink. Hadn't he read somewhere that sobriety was a deplorable state of affairs? "I'm drinking to you, Beatriz," he mumbled as he poured a glass of wine.

Despite her good intentions, she was a spoiled woman. Her laughter and ambiguous glances under her beautiful eyebrows made him uneasy. Could she ever have considered the possibility of taking a priest to her bed?

René grinned sourly and downed the wine in one gulp. All women in Terreno were raised to please and to be dependent. They were defenseless without parents or husbands. They could turn their hips voluptuously during the salsa. But they were prudish and spoiled cozy creatures who were only interested in American movie stars and tight dresses.

What an embarrassment it was to be a man-priest, imagining Beatriz in a close-fitting white dress, dancing the salsa during a gala ball at the university.

He poured himself a new glass.

Her voice on the phone this morning when she asked if he knew more about the homeless whom the soldiers had taken with them: she was Mary Magdalene, converted by the sweat of charity, her voice full of longing.

"I should give up," said the priest under his breath. "Drop the 'Holy Mother' like a brick." He grimaced, momentarily seeing himself as a graying knight, redeemed from his vow of chastity, galloping on a white stallion to conquer Beatriz. Undoubtedly, he would come a cropper along the way. "I lack coolness, that's it," he said out loud again.

Then a feeling of love overwhelmed him, making his heart skip a beat. Annoyance, doubt, and resentment fell away, and he was rapt in a spiritual embrace that enveloped the world, a feeling so profound that tears came into his eyes. But just as abruptly as He had come, God disappeared again. Worse still, the place where He had been seemed emptier than ever.

Perhaps he should have prayed now, but René had not done so for years: his God had become too personal for that, a part of himself that he spoke to like a silent father. Lafarge walked to his desk and grabbed a new sheet of paper. Pressing hard on his ballpoint pen, he wrote:

Gui,

I have to get away from here, or I'll go crazy. On the one hand, the Terreneans are bozos, but on the other, I love them dearly. I have heard today that a guerrilla group is preparing an assault on Valtiago. How did I hear this? It sounds incredible, but I'll tell you: the rebels call themselves communists, but one of them came to me in the confessional this morning. He said he had no choice. His faith compelled him. He began begging my blessings for the terrorist plans of his group. A 'communist' in the confes-

sional, where else than in Terreno is this possible? I allowed him to leave with my absolution and a promise of secrecy...

With a final gesture, the Belgian priest grabbed the two unfinished letters to his brother and opened a desk drawer. He placed them on top of the stack of other messages he had never sent.

———

2

Beatriz Candalti stood by the bed Ernesto now invariably called his death bed. She asked why her father called to say his death warrant had been signed.

"The doctors have a diagnosis," he said, looking her in the eye this time. "I don't have long to live anymore." Beatriz thought she could hear in his words: *I fell seriously ill because you are such a bad daughter, and I will die from sorrow now.*

"What kind of diagnosis?" She noticed that her voice was unsteady.

"Pancreatic cancer."

"Are they sure?"

"Yes."

Beatriz stood next to the bed and told herself to take her father's hand.

She couldn't.

For a long time, silence cloaked the hospital room.

"Beatriz?"

"Yes."

"Before I die, I want to be certain that you're happy. And that you will go back to...".

"You shouldn't be so gloomy, daddy. You always have to ask for a second opinion."

Saying these words, Beatriz felt an unexpected pain. She realized that there was only one way that her father could make her happy.

———

3

Beatriz had gone to the hospital, and Alejandro was alone with himself. He couldn't escape the memory of the officer who had called himself Captain Astíz. That permanently glowering face haunted him even when he was hiding on the patio in the morning sun with a bottle of wine.

Why should he go on trying to write songs? Even from the tomb, Víctor remained in command. In one of his final lyrics, Víctor predicted everything that Alejandro wanted to express.

> *Brother, you exchanged life for death*
> *You were paid with interest for this trade.*
> *But, brother, your soul is in great need.*
> *You have tightened the screws*
> *to stop hearing the screams*
> *but listen, brother, what's that sound?*

Alejandro emptied his glass, grabbed the bottle, and looked at the sun through the flask. The sunlight was the color of blood diluted in water.

"Artists are sensitive people," Astíz had said from behind the powerful lamp that shone in Alejandro's eyes. "But is that the case? I wonder. You know: one of Víctor's last songs has inspired me to do a small experiment. I would've liked to experiment with Víctor himself, but one of my colleagues has unfortunately been too conscientious. He has sprayed poor Victor and his wife with an unnecessarily high number of bullets. You, Alejandro, are my second choice, but let's not be sad about that. I suggest the following to you. You learn to interrogate prisoners. It's tiring and dirty work, and we don't enjoy it, so if you take the work off our hands, we have to repay you somehow. For every prisoner who loses his life by your hand, I will release one of his children. An innocent party in exchange for a guilty party. Surely, that cannot pose too horrible a moral dilemma?"

Juron listened in disbelief. He could hardly take it in: this lunatic told him that Víctor and Lucía had been shot.

But Astíz's sugary voice went on: if Alejandro's tender soul could not bear this proposal, there was another option.

He would "question" Alejandro himself.

―――

4

After visiting her father, Beatriz sat in the hospital garden in the sun. She looked at the tall waving cypress trees bordering the terrain. Her thoughts circled the commitment she'd made some time ago to Cristóbal and João. The approaching death of her father made the engagement she entered much more meaningful.

"It will be the first public act of rebellion, Beatriz," Cristóbal had said.

"We want to make clear to the *junta* that there'll be a massive popular uprising if it doesn't step down," João had continued.

Beatriz was proud to be a pivotal figure in making this act of resistance possible. But at the same time, she was ashamed because she was afraid.

She was not self-confident like the five heroines who, years ago, on hunger strike in Bolivia, woke up the people until they took to the streets *en masse* and overthrew the dictatorship.

Nor was she a member of a Sandinista group who dared risk their life in Nicaragua with a Kalashnikov in hand.

She was Beatriz Candalti, a bling-bling child, high society daughter, nervous wreck, and insecure marionette. She lived in Terreno, where most people looked away from the injustice mumbling: *there will be a reason for this, do not interfere, please, do not interfere.*

Soon, she would fly her father's Cessna to Arini in the north of the country, where she would collect a consignment of smuggled explosives. This pack would be thrown out of the Andes train near the Salitreras, the northern salt mines of Terreno, and picked up by *guerrilleros.*

In Beatriz's eyes, the target Cristóbal and João selected for a homemade bomb was ambitious and dangerous. She also wondered whether now was the right time to act when the junta seemed prepared to make concessions. However, in the underground resistance groups, the leadership contradicted her: they were sure that the military was merely spinning things out and would use force regardless. An assault at this juncture could show the world how desperate the situation was in the country. Beatriz knew that if the plan leaked out, even her background would be no protection. But in her eyes, coincidence, inevitability, fate—that Holy Trinity which Alejandro always called on so ironically—had brought her to this point in her life. She was scared, but she wouldn't turn back. That had to do with Manuel Durango and with a maze of feelings that she didn't want to disentangle.

Beatriz had another few days off, and Cristóbal, who had a network of informants in all sorts of groups and agencies, had told her that Manuel was running a construction project in the south of the country. He would be away for a few weeks.

On hearing this good news, Beatriz had told herself that

she could enjoy Alejandro's company until she left for Arini. Her belly felt warm, and the sun shone on her shoulders: that was what she wanted to focus on now. Coincidence, inevitability, and fate caused her father to become ill at the right moment. The Holy Trinity was now making arrangements for his death, after which she would be free. It had also put Alejandro on her path.

Beatriz felt the excitement tingling like spring water in her belly. Lust for life crashed over her like a wave, making her gasp for breath. Every day, the Terreneans sank more into disorder. Barely a day passed in Valtiago without demonstrations or marches. The people demanded the abolition of curfews, freedom of press, better wages, and social conditions – and even elections.

Cristóbal Vial claimed that Pelarón was having increasing difficulties with the Americans. The Yanks felt that he gave the left-wing resistance too much space and wanted "corrections."

What was unthinkable a few months ago had now happened: people expressed their opinions; newspapers such as *Pronto* and *Hiel* published increasingly barbed opinion pieces.

The government banned them, but after a few days, they released new editions. The situation in Canela, and in particular in the *porqueriza*, was ultra-tense. No action had yet been taken to alleviate the homelessness caused by the earthquake, and the inhabitants of the *población* were becoming noisier by the day. The police had placed a cordon around the neighborhood, but for the time being, they did not enter it.

As if to temper her sudden optimism, Beatriz heard a police siren wailing. *The days of madness are not over. They have yet to begin.*

———

5

"And?" asked Beatriz. "Are you going to play at the *peña*?"

Alejandro, opposite her on her patio table, laid down his newspaper. "*Mamita*, do you truly think they want to hear Alejandro Juron at your benefit concert? Nowadays they want disco. Aconcagua's popularity is long gone. The folk festival as we knew it is a thing of the past."

"That's what you think."

"Your brave René will surely succeed without me, Beatriz."

"You don't have to sing the old songs," she said, ignoring his veiled allusion. "Write a few new songs; that'll do you good." He shook his head. "Well, if you don't do it, you don't do it. But then at least write a love song for me."

She noticed his relief and wondered what lay behind it.

"That's simple," he said. "But I want to do something special for you... Wait, I feel a flash coming: the rhythms of the *altiplano* mixed with rock. Beware if you like it because then I'll become a graying rocker, and the young girls will be lying at my feet by the dozen."

He pulled his guitar against his belly, hit a fiery rhythm, and sang a silly song with lots of 'yeah' and 'rock you all night.' His English was not bad at all. He got up while playing, and swayed his hips suggestively to the rhythm.

He became increasingly rapacious until he collided with one of the garden chairs. He tried to maintain his balance, stumbled over a chair leg, and fell. She burst out laughing, got out of her chair, and bent over him. He grabbed her by the arms and pulled her on top of her.

"You see?" he laughed. "They'll break down the tent when I play your love song; we'll be filthy rich before you know it!" He kissed her and rolled with her over the grass, away from his guitar that had ended up next to him. His warm body on hers, the smell of grass in her nose, the pressure of his lips on hers, his tongue in her mouth, how could she still doubt him?

"We have to leave, Alejandro," she said teasingly when his hands began to stroke her legs. "João expects us."

"João doesn't run away, but you will if I don't sprinkle salt on your tail," he whispered.

From across the street, Manuel saw through his binoculars how they kissed each other and felt a satisfaction that he liked to call 'icy,' a word he was fond of.

The *coligüilla*, the slut, had `found someone else.

Manuel made a wise choice when he rented this apartment for the militia Patria y Sangre as a meeting room a few months before. The condo offered a beautiful view of Beatriz's house and garden. He often used the flat to spy on her in the garden behind the house.

As small as a doll she'd seemed, a graceful puppet. In his mind, she was naked when she bent over her flowers. He loved looking at her dresses, imagining how he would tear them away from her body.

Now it was another man who untied these dresses. Her father should know that it was a jailbird with a guitar. Look, the waster offered her a serenade. Manuel knew everything about him now.

This Alejandro Juron would be as easy to squash as a banana. The coward already proved that over and over. But the leader of Patria y Sangre had ordered Manuel to leave the turtle-doves alone for the time being.

Alejandro could still be useful: sooner or later, he would lead them to people who were worth far more. Manuel consented, but it was merely a postponement.

Beatriz thought she could have her own life, but he would show her how wrong she was when she least expected it. She had betrayed her family and husband, who, through the holy sacraments of marriage, remained her master, despite the legal tricks she used.

Manuel knew her: when the hour of revenge had struck, she would beg for mercy.

And do anything to receive it.

————

6

The paved mountain road was not wide but in reasonably good condition. A truck loaded with sewer pipes drove in front of them. The diesel engine boomed when they reached the steep stretches.

"You drive well." Alejandro looked outside. Just a few meters to the left of their car, there was an abyss covered with bushes. "But suppose the engine of that truck breaks down. His brakes may be bad, or the driver panics. The truck would roll back towards us."

"What an unpleasant imagination you have."

"That's because I listen to sounds," he said, apparently light-heartedly.

That afternoon, they had heard on the radio that political parties might be an option again in the future. Pelarón had declared on the radio that "perhaps the time is ripe for a gradual return to a democratic form of government, provided that the Terrenean people show good sense."

Afterward, they made love, and Alejandro had sweated like never before, while Beatriz raged like a cat on heat. Afterward, pressed against his body, she wondered if her mission was still necessary—the situation seemed to be evolving so rapidly.

While Alejandro stood in the shower, she called Cristóbal.

Cristóbal told her that she had to pick up the explosives in any case. However, whether and when the attack would take place would be decided by a 'revolutionary council.'

"How long have you known Cristóbal?" asked Alejandro

while she slowed down to put more distance between their car and the truck.

"I worked with him setting up the administration for La Paloma."

"Why did Cristóbal choose him to lead the village?"

"Why are you so curious about João?"

He shrugged. "Because João was in the church and heard me whine when that soldier wanted to take me with him."

"His mother was a Brazilian," Beatriz said. "He was in Brazil when the *junta* seized power. He returned only later to his father's country. I've always found that strange: why did he come back when he knew about the situation here? João pretends not to care about politics. When Cristóbal nominated him as the CEO of the artists' village, the *junta* readily gave permission."

Alejandro skewed his mouth. "I have known Cristóbal since he studied law. We called him 'the smooth egg.'"

A little further on, the road made a bend to the right. Near the abyss stood some crosses.

"Those crosses tell a story," said Alejandro. "It was trumpeted in The Last Supper many times over. All inmates loved bloody stories from 'outside.' Two years ago, a Ford Falcon stopped here. The bodies of three Indian leaders were taken out and tipped over the edge. The Indians claim that since then, three black condors regularly circle above this place." He smiled. "When I was little, I thought that the condor was the king of the mountains. I was a lonely kid, so I flapped my arms and declared myself the biggest condor of all. That lasted until I heard that the condor was a carrion eater, a huge vulture."

"There it is," said Beatriz, wondering about the meaning of Juron's continuous self-mockery. The road descended abruptly; the lorry sped down, the sound of its engine reduced to a distant staccato. The valley lay open in front of them, beige, with green patches of bean fields, and behind it rose the stone grey of the lower mountain peaks. The artists' village comprised about eighty clay-colored houses with blood-red roofs from anti-corrosion paint. And behind the tops, controlling the field of vision like the head of a mythical creature, sea blue, ending in an unattainable, bright white, lay Aconcagua.

Upon seeing the mountain, Alejandro felt a knot in his heart: every thread of it appeared to lead to even more confusion. Beatriz saw the tension in his shoulders. "Hey," she said. "Relax. João and his artists are having a party. We're not going to a funeral."

He laughed, hugging her with his left arm over her shoulder. "Terreno, the country where even a funeral is a party," he pealed. "Or is it the other way around?"

———

7

The attractions of the potter's workshop and the cabin where young artists painted everyday scenes from Indian life could not keep Alejandro's eyes from wandering toward Aconcagua. In reality, it was far away, but the snow effect made it seem close.

The mountain top radiated a magical white sheen over the village. The houses were simple but clean and accommodated about three hundred people.

"La Paloma, where people live from the sale of tapestries, paintings, and pots. The idea alone gives me wings," Juron said to Beatriz after they visited several studios with João. He pointed to Aconcagua. "If it goes on like this, I'll soon be flapping upwards for a quick visit to the mountain top."

The mountain was surrounded by a wavy fog that performed a dance around the summit.

"What's that mist?" Beatriz asked.

"Snow blowing south at more than 120 kilometers per hour," said Alejandro.

"A mighty sight," said João. "Before I came to Terreno, the highest summit I had ever seen was what you'd call a *hill*."

"Why did you accept this appointment, João?" Alejandro's voice remained light-hearted.

"Because the university asked me to," João answered amicably. "The Americans rob Terreno's mineral resources, but in return, those cute Yanks support our, ahem, culture. Our folk art is popular in the United States, so non-stop production is inevitable until the Americans are tired of their new toy. Yep: our powerful northern neighbors are such genuine advocates of values and norms."

"We were able to test our values and norms against reality in Lafarge's church," said Alejandro. "Did you notice, João, how bravely I defended the poor?"

"You were about as afraid as I was. But when I start trembling, they think I'm tightening my muscles."

"Maybe you're an even better actor than a painter," Alejandro said nonchalantly.

"And maybe you're better as a guitarist than as a folk hero," answered João without hesitation.

Alejandro laughed, a little exaggerated. "I didn't want to offend you."

"Here," said João, pointing to his eyes, "lives the painter in me. You'll have to make do with that."

Juron noticed that Pereira's eyes turned to Beatriz after he had said that.

The almond tree in the village square was large and idyllic. Juron sat on the bench underneath it and drank a glass of cold mountain wine. Life was so beautiful, *que vida tan sabrosa*. With friends, drinks, and the pure mountain air that made one forget the gasoline smell of Valtiago, he could start to understand his parents' passion for the mountains.

João and Beatriz discussed Pelarón's speech that morning

on the radio, in which the general had promised, among other things, a revision of the constitution.

"A revision of the constitution," Juron said. "What kind of twerps believe that will ever happen?"

Pereira shrugged his shoulders. "I create naive art, so I think I stand a good chance as a twerp." He raised his glass to Juron.

"Forget it," said Alejandro. "They'll shift some points and commas, that's all. And after that, when people are flocking to the streets, up in arms, Pelarón will be rubbing his hands."

"Why?" said Beatriz.

"What better than riots to give your police the order to shoot? Pelarón wants to get the resistance on the streets. Then, he'll have an excuse to restore tranquility with a strong arm. He'll only resign if he's forced to."

A silence fell. Again, it struck Alejandro that João and Beatriz exchanged a look full of a meaning he could only guess at.

"I want to dance," Beatriz said. She jumped up. "Alejandro, grab a guitar. João, call your friends. You wanted to party, didn't you?"

———

8

Another dance song, why not? The guitar, although not his own, had a clear sound. Women in white dresses performed traditional dances. After all, this was a village that had to represent South American folk art: tourists wanted it that way.

In the romantic light of the lamps dangling from the tree, the panorama was enchanting. The full moon colored the mountains pale purple. The heat rose from the ground and kept the cold of the night at bay. Beatriz, in jeans, held her hands along her hips as if she were wearing the same white skirts as the village women. She was so lithe and self-aware. And they served the best homemade *pisco* here. Alejandro spontaneously played the folk dance songs from the early days with Víctor: the *cueca* and *cumbia* and *sirillas* and *sambas*. Two men accompanied him on the *zampoña*, and it worked well, although drums wouldn't have been out of place.

But everything sounded beautiful and striking, playful and inviting, completely different from the electronic thump that excited the young people in Valtiago.

What did they do here in this village, the young people? While they munched *sopaipillas*, homemade pumpkin rolls, they stomped with their feet and heels to the beat of the music.

Alejandro especially watched one girl; she was maybe just five. She looked like Carmencita, the daughter of Víctor and Lucía. In this blessed moment, the image did not provoke self-reproach in him; instead, it evoked a series of memories: the scents of spicy olives, garlic, lemon, herbs, and red peppers, which Lucía prepared in the kitchen for the *arrollados*. Carmencita, then four, always wanted to taste before the food was on the table.

Carmencita, who called him *tío*, uncle. The sound in her voice when she said she loved him a lot, almost as much as she loved her parents. *Tío, tío, I dance for you, look at me, do you think I'm beautiful?*

Alejandro stopped playing, passed on his guitar to a man with a felt slit hat, and moved among the dancers to Beatriz. He bent down to her neck. Her smell had become so familiar to him.

She kissed him. "You're so beautiful when you play the guitar. You should perform again, Alejandro; I would love to see you play at the *peña*."

He stopped dancing, immediately short-tempered. "As a curiosity for rich parasites? That's why your priest friend wants to lure me to his benefit, right? *Look, there you have Juron, who sat in the tank for years; you can see it by the lines in his face.*"

"I didn't mean that." She looked at him, offended.

In prison, he had become so accustomed to ambiguous remarks full of venom that he didn't expect anything else anymore. Juron realized that it was the memory of Carmencita that had suddenly made him sour. He looked at João dancing nearby, his smiling face raised to the skies. He avoided Beatriz's gaze, knew she was waiting for a reaction. What was he supposed to say to her? *Do I have a short fuse?*

A boy pulled Alejandro's sleeve. "This is for you from La Paloma," he said. He handed Alejandro a painting. It was a mountain scene, very colorful, with primitive but carefully painted figures, one of the successful pictures of the village, sold by the hundreds.

"What do you think of our present, Alejandro?" João shouted, laughing. "We hope you won't sell it to a tourist for a lot of money!"

"So much joy," said Alejandro. "It tires me out."

"Come Alejandro," said Beatriz. "Let's have one more drink."

Alejandro made a wide gesture, suddenly realizing how much he'd already put away. "Yes, let's have another drink— to forget our worries and especially ourselves."

Behind Pereira, who looked at him a bit mockingly, he saw Mount Aconcagua. That stupid mountain was even more ghostly in the bright moonlight. Dizzy, he closed his eyes.

Around them, the dancers spinned wildly. The elderly watched and clapped their hands. The mothers had baked tortillas, and the smell made everyone happy. *Did you have to feel self-hatred at such a moment?*

João grabbed Alejandro by the arm and took him to the stall where they served drinks. They all cared about him; he felt that. He didn't understand why this annoyed him.

"I'm just a drunk old jailbird, plinking the guitar,"
Alejandro snapped, more sharply than necessary.

"Ah, Alejandro, you're in a bad mood again," Beatriz
said sympathetically; it cut him up that she was right. A bad
mood. A sullen child who couldn't stand himself. He associ-
ated this thought with her hands passing over his belly, so
feather-light, so attentive. It turned his sourness to excitement, but the force of it only threw him further out of
kilter.

He grabbed her by the arm, pinching it. He didn't mean
all this; surely she knew that he sometimes lost his cool? A
villager approached João, pointing in the direction of the large
studio. The painter said something to Beatriz and went with
the man. Alejandro noticed that he didn't understand what
Pereira had said. There was only one remedy for that buzzing
in his ears. He poured himself a stiff one. That tasted, yes...
Ooh la la, a song bubbled up in him, made him swoon, even
more, the tune of the great puppeteer:

> *General Pelarón-rón-rón,*
> *Oh so old and dumb,*
> *You have hangmen as biceps,*
> *a mouth that preaches lies,*
> *eyes like brass buttons,*
> *sweat like molten copper.*

"I have sweat like molten copper," Alejandro said. The
veins in his forehead were throbbing.

"What did you say?" Beatriz asked.

A man with a gaucho hat and the weathered face of a
mountain *mestizo* started a new song. Alejandro was pissed: the
songs, always the same songs... *Vamos, friends, learn to read and
write and make Terreno a better homeland. Come, friends, grab the white
paper and write down your dreams; they will make this land fertile.*
When was it that Víctor Pérez had written this nonsense?

Mid-seventies? How often had he played the notes of that song?

João returned and mingled with the dancers, towering above them, clapping his hands. Alejandro tried to get a grip on himself. A little irony would work wonders. Come on, that panic in him, soaring in all directions: it couldn't be so bad, could it? Alcohol and memories were to blame.

For now, he needed a bold statement that illustrated that he was still quite clear-headed: "This country makes you weak. The mountains limit our brain. We are an island."

"Who do you mean?" said Beatriz with something disconsolate in her voice. "The two of us? Are we an island?"

"Yes," he said. Beatriz had deliberately misunderstood him. "Especially the two of us." He took the jar from the table between them and brought it to his lips. The wine dripped down his neck and ended up on his shirt. When nothing dripped into his mouth anymore, he looked into the jar and became dizzy.

"What do you mean by that?" she asked.

"I need to think about that very carefully."

"Just tell me what's wrong with you, Alejandro." She stood close to him. He only had to make a small movement to touch her, but there was fog between them—the dense mountain fog suffocating him.

"You know what's wrong with me," he said.

She seemed to be nodding. Her face looked thoughtful and indifferent, both at once. Or was he seeing wrong? Maybe he saw everything wrong. He put his fingers in her glass of *pisco* and rubbed his eyes with the caustic drink. That stung; that was delicious.

"What are you doing now?" said Beatriz.

"I wash my eyes out," Alejandro said. "I think I see things wrong."

"Alejandro." She held out her hand to him. "What do you see wrong? That you and Víctor used to sing about love?"

How venomous that name made him.

"I'll tell you who Víctor Pérez was," he snarled at her. "Víctor was a great artist: hurrah, boom boom, good for him! He loved poor people, but he also loved Mercedes sedans. Want to know more? He loved Lucía, but he loved many women. Lucía knew it, but she chose to see only the gifted artist, not the man, just like all of you."

He looked at her wryly. "Sometimes, I was satisfied with his leftovers, if you understand what I mean," he continued. "And then I imagined that this woman was Lucía."

Her hand shot up to slap him. The blow was well-targeted, but she pulled back just before she made contact. She shook her head, turned around, and walked away. She seemed to melt away in the crowd. He knew he should follow her and stop her before she turned out to be a dream. But he remained there, with the empty jar in his hands, paralyzed.

The numbness in his body was the same as he felt when Lucía was close to him. Deep inside, he twisted and writhed, but he couldn't follow Beatriz. The feeling of loss took his breath away: their fragile togetherness, their sheer self-deception, it had been so brief. His knees knocked as he abruptly turned away.

Quickly, he left the partying crowd behind him. In a detached way, as if it were about someone else, he knew what he was going to do: earlier on, she had left the keys in the Land Rover's ignition. He would leave this dove in the mountains.

———

9

Alejandro drove through the night. It came to his mind what he had just recognized in Beatriz's eyes: she'd looked as if she had expected this break-up.

What else could you expect?
I read our destiny in your eyes.
You knew me better than I dared to hope.
How could you, otherwise, feel compassion?

Did he have to drown himself in a flood of alcohol before this third-rate poetry would dissipate in him? He raised his speed, the light of his headlights floating in the bright moonlight. Instead of taking the road for Valtiago, he turned left at the crossroads, heading for the grayish-white teeth of the Payachatas mountain, veiled in mist and moonlight. The valley was stained orange by the waste from copper ore. The mountain road meandered through like a beige ribbon towards the buildings of a deserted mine.

Alejandro stopped at the beginning of the valley. His stomach started to heave. The two lakes close to the old copper mine looked like solidified mercury, saturated as they were with deposits of hot liquid minerals. He accelerated again, drove into the valley, and towards the half-collapsed buildings. He opened the window completely; he needed air.

Juron reached the mine, parked the Land Rover behind one of the filthy hangars, and got out. His stomach churned, and acid burned in his throat. He threw up violently and sat down against an old cabin. After some time, he noticed a glow of light to his right. He got up but crouched again when he saw that the glow came from the headlights of trucks, coming down the same road he had traveled. The moonlight touched their olive-green flanks. His nausea gave way to tightness in his chest.

If he drove away, they would see him. The trucks stopped with squawking brakes at the lake, about twenty meters away. Alejandro peered round the corner of the cabin. For the time being, he and the Land Rover remained invisible behind the building. Soldiers jumped out of the lorries and began unloading sealed brown bags. Alejandro saw how the mercury-silver water hardly rippled as the bags were tossed into the lake.

One of the last ones broke open during the unloading. The body of a child dropped out, a girl. In the bright Andes night, Alejandro recognized the black hair and the broad face. The recognition was so overwhelming that he felt he could distinguish her scent. He'd smelled her when he'd held her in his arms in Lafarge's church before the soldiers had arrived, the little girl who had lost her parents during the storm. The soldier hastily stuffed the body back into the bag. The calm water swallowed it all.

One of the soldiers ran towards the abandoned mine buildings. Alejandro got up halfway, almost overwhelmed by the reflex to run.

Ten more strides, and the soldier would see him.

Alejandro pressed his fist against his mouth to suppress a wild giggle when the soldier stopped in front of the cabin, dropped his pants, and squatted down. *He didn't care about hygiene: look how quickly he pulled up his trousers and ran back.* They were in a hurry, these young soldiers. A little later, Alejandro saw the convoy driving away. When the trucks disappeared behind the ridge, he looked at the water of the lake.

A bleaker coffin was inconceivable.

10

João Pereira was amazingly flexible for such a big man. Spectators had formed a circle in which Pereira performed martial dance movements of the *capoeira*. His moves were in time with the drum rhythm played by a toothless old man grinning beneath oversized glasses.

Beatriz clapped her hands just like the others. *See? A man could be himself, not a nervous troublemaker like Alejandro, who didn't know how to handle his feelings.*

Beatriz had told João that Alejandro had run away. João had taken her by the shoulders and spoken encouraging words. "You can count on me," he had said.

Beatriz recognized that attitude. João had wooed her before and had made no big deal about her cautious rejection. This time, however, his piercing gaze at her breasts excited her – before shame intruded, like a reflex. Beatriz reprimanded herself. Why should she feel ashamed? When she was young and inexperienced, a husband who had beaten and humiliated her had been forced upon her. A priest had looked at her sideways with the same expression as João did now, but his desire was like a father's and therefore forbidden. And a mentally ill man confused her by the way he treated both himself and her.

Men were so often pathetic. They begged to be used. At heart, they were clumsily romantic but self-absorbed. From now on, she would make use of their weakness. After all, it was true perhaps, as her father used to say, that she was a 'depraved girl.' She no longer cared. She had enough years of barbed wire behind her.

Beatriz suspected that João was performing the *capoeira*, especially for her. Alejandro's desertion had stimulated him. That assumption kindled anger in her.

That, and the realization that Alejandro had been honest in his way: he had told her that he had forgotten how to love someone. She reacted shocked as if she'd forgotten that she had recently been looking for a man she could dominate. Nothing ever turned out as she expected. She clung to her resentment to stop anger giving way to sorrow: she had to avoid that. So she moved with the rhythm of the drum and kept her eyes on João.

João's movements were hypnotizingly slow and then again dazzlingly fast. He had told her that the *capoeira* originated from the martial art of Brazilian *mestizo* culture. That was what she wanted to do herself: fight. Did men want her? Then they would have to...

Two arms wrapped around her, and a kiss burned into her neck.

"I'll tell you about Lucía and Captain Astíz," Alejandro whispered in her ear. "Afterwards, you'll understand better the man I've become. Shall I tell you about fire and water, *querida?*"

It was that last, husky whisper that made Beatriz turn around: "*Dear one.*" Alejandro's eyes shone when she put her arms around his neck. What round, beautiful arms she had, created for embracing men.

"Alejandro," said João apparently cheerfully as he knocked Alejandro off balance with a light kick on his shin, then bumped him smoothly on his hip so that he tumbled backward. At the last moment, just before he smacked the ground, the giant's left arm caught him. "I've heard that you've become a car thief these days. You're going to end badly, Alejandro, truly badly." João slowly lowered Alejandro to the ground.

Alejandro looked up at the stars and the two faces that hovered above him. João's face, in particular, was a mystery.

"I think I'll sing a new song on the *peña* of your clerical friend, Beatriz," he said. "I already have some initial sentences, tick-tock, like a silver clockwork:

> *Bury me in the womb of the mountain,*
> *in a bag, mercury like silver, heavy as pain.*

My poetic brain still has to figure out the rest. But it sounds already a bit as if Víctor has written it, don't you think so?"

João looked at the smiling Beatriz. "The liquor," said the half-blood shaking his head. "It's robbed him of the last vestiges of his sanity, poor wretch. The booze, or you, Beatriz, what's the difference?"

———

11

They reached a pact, the nervous bard and the insecure woman. It was not very logical, but Alejandro thought he saw secret courage in Beatriz, and she saw in him a man who was tormented by a talent he misunderstood. The university was still closed for a few days. Beatriz wanted to devote that time to care for the inner scars that made Alejandro so capricious. She tried to learn how to reduce his self-reproach and recrimination. For his part, Juron listened to her stories about her father: how Ernesto Candalti had cried covertly at his wife's death, how he had kissed the picture of Beatriz's mother in the living room every time he entertained guests but the rest of the time ignored it.

Did they get to know each other better in those few days? They tried to believe they did, but their togetherness remained only skin deep, though characterized by exaggerated promises and grand expressions of love. Several times, Alejandro came close to telling the truth about his past, but each time he retreated into lies that he wanted to believe.

It was as if the world were holding its breath out of solidarity with the delicate ribbon around this young love affair, for not a single time did Beatriz's phone ring in those days. Every day, she visited her father who was trying a 'revolutionary treatment' from the United States. Beatriz was her former self during those visits and shamelessly molded her father, who once again hoped to be healed, to her will.

Back home, she kicked off her shoes; the rest followed quickly. Alejandro and Beatriz, what an Olympic endurance they demonstrated, and what inventiveness for people whose sexuality had been starved for so long. Even Manuel didn't disturb them, although Beatriz continually violated the Terrenean law that determined that a divorced woman, caught with a suitor, lost all the possessions acquired during the marriage.

They lived like that for three days. At the end of the third day, in bed, Alejandro said, "I still have to make you a confession, *querida*, the last one."

Beatriz smiled. How many times had he said something along these lines in recent days?

"It's about my music. Over the years, I have made myself believe that it wasn't a problem that I didn't have enough writing talent. The truth is more subtle than that: I have the subjects, I have the images; it's just that I can't express them properly."

She said nothing; her silence encouraged him. "At the beginning of Aconcagua, Víctor was looking for beautiful words to use in simple love songs. He did indeed have some pretty words, even though he was an uneducated farmer's son. They were like gold nuggets in the furrows that he plowed. The way he put them together, the rhythm, the sound: pure magic. But when the military coup took shape on the horizon, I offered him socially engaged themes. It soon became clear: I was the thinker. He was the poet." Alejandro grinned sheepishly. "Criticizing the gap between rich and poor, and the attention to injustice in our music, turned Víctor into a popular hero. That's how Aconcagua's grand period began. I had resigned myself to the way fate had chosen: Víctor was the shining star, and I was the guitarist who stood behind him. We went to Cuba, Germany, we performed in France, Peru, England, Bulgaria. Víctor not only wrote the songs about the subjects I gave him, but he added a special glory to them by the way he sang on stage, his commitment, his surrender."

"But you've always said that you'd rather have been a rock star," Beatriz said.

A crooked smile. "Self-deception – theatrical but also

meant. In my youth, I liked to flirt with the idea, but later I understood that imitation would never make me an authentic artist." Juron spread his hands, dropped them on the sheet. "The thing is that I've always felt two men in me: I was the cynical intellectual, but I was also the musician who wanted to see faces shimmering with hope, with joy, with surrender... Always that same word!"

As if he had made a decision, Juron looked Beatriz Candalti in the eyes. "The other man in me was my salvation in The Last Supper. And now I have the feeling that, in those years, he killed the musician."

She put a hand on his arm.

"When they released me, I noticed that I could still play my guitar, but I could no longer make it *speak.* Since I lost Víctor, the songs don't want to come anymore. And only now, I understand that I was born in the depths of my heart for *Canto a lo humano,* Beatriz. No matter how much I play someone else, I'll never be anyone but a musician who wants to touch the heart." Juron took a deep breath. "That's why I will play at Lafarge's *peña.* I will sing the Aconcagua songs written by Víctor and no other."

She nodded, and the love he saw in every pore of her face grabbed him by the throat. That love reminded him he was still a liar, something he had gradually forgotten in the fire of his argument.

"There's one more thing you should know," he continued in an attempt to dilute his lies with a little truth. "Víctor and his family went into hiding just before they arrested me. Captain Astíz and his team tortured me to know where Víctor was hiding. I pretended not to know, but one morning they came and said they had picked up Víctor, Lucía, and Carmencita. The night before, I had decided to give up. I would've given them all away if fate hadn't been ahead of me." Beatriz wanted to say something, but he raised his hand. "Did you hear what I said?" he asked. "I would have told them where they were. For years I've lived with that knowledge without being able to talk to anyone about it." He bowed his head; his right hand was clutching the sheet.

Her heart filled the whole room. Her hands went over Alejandro's belly, her mouth followed.

Did she want to show him what his words could be worth?

However badly he wanted to deny it, he knew what they were worth.

The Paths Of Power

1

"THANK YOU FOR GETTING HERE SO QUICKLY, RENÉ," SAID Cristóbal. "I have something important to tell you."

"Does it have anything to do with the pigsty?"

René looked tired. That morning, the military reported on the national radio that the situation in the shantytown had become 'unacceptably' dangerous. The police had cordoned off the *porqueriza*, and strict controls were now in place. The *carabineros* wanted to evacuate some of the slums, but they were obstructed by the barricades of debris the earthquake constructed.

Foreign journalists indignantly reported that police were shooting unarmed people. The national radio called the *población* a "hotbed of left-wing terror" and threatened radical measures.

There was no mention of a return to democracy.

"For weeks, the government has done nothing about the situation in the neighborhood," continued the Belgian priest. "They let people rot in their own filth. Where are they supposed to go? If the *junta* wants to chase them away, they'll fight. And there are more than a hundred thousand of them."

"I called a few people in the know," said Cristóbal. "They told me that the generals can't agree amongst themselves. Some of them think that the situation is being mishandled, but the hawks in the government are vehemently opposing them. I don't know what will happen to your neighborhood. Perhaps the international attention will force the junta to decide on a real aid program. Let's hope so."

"These are going to be difficult days," replied Lafarge.

"I didn't just ask you to come because of Canela and the pigsty," said Cristóbal, with a worried expression.

"How do you mean?"

"Someone is preparing to assassinate Pelarón," Cristóbal replied bluntly.

René Lafarge kept his face neutral, remembering the confession of some time ago. The fact that Cristóbal could see into his confessional, so to speak, didn't surprise him too much.

"Now?" he said. "Just when there's a slight chance that Pelarón will take a more democratic course?"

The priest watched how the chief librarian looked at him: layers of hesitation and calculation hidden in his gaze.

"Is that all you have to say on the matter?" Cristóbal pressed.

Lafarge didn't answer.

Cristóbal frowned, then continued: "The resistance thinks Pelarón's new approach is just paving the way for him to become a legally elected president. That nothing will change, except that the government will have a democratic mask. Pelarónism will go on and with it the disastrous liberal economy and the growing gap between rich and poor."

"Why are you telling me this?" asked René.

"Yes, why should I do that?" Cristóbal asked, his voice tainted with hidden meanings.

The two men averted their gaze at the same time.

"What do you want to say?" Lafarge finally said.

Cristóbal tilted his head. "You know what happened to this university during the coup: the arrests, the massacres. The military still considers us subversive. You also know what happened to my predecessor and how careful I have to be."

"Get to the point, Cristóbal," said René Lafarge.

Cristóbal put his palms against each other and twisted his lips. "I'll allow your *peña* for Canela and the *porqueriza* to take place on our grounds. But after that, you should break all ties with the university for a while. And, René, think carefully. I tell you this as a friend: Pelarón's death won't change anything in this country. On the contrary, the chaos would only get worse."

René Lafarge stared at the small Terrenean. Cristóbal was a typical inhabitant of this country: he rarely showed his hand.

The priest understood that Cristóbal warned him in his veiled way. The thought that the librarian believed he could be involved in an assault on Pelarón was so grotesque that Lafarge could only shake his head.

———

2

"Lots of people, but not enough of them paid for tickets," said Cristóbal.

"Did you expect anything else?" asked René, pretending that he was in a good mood.

The priest seemed to be looking around the large auditorium but was secretly keeping an eye on Cristóbal.

Since their conversation a few days ago, the librarian had treated him as cordially as before, but Lafarge knew that after the *peña*, Cristóbal would cut off all contact with him.

His first reaction after their meeting had been anger. These people! Their predilection for complicated social exchanges drove him wild sometimes.

Afterwards, however, he realized Cristóbal had tried to do him a favor by politely warning him. Did the man seriously believe that he would support or aid an *assassination* attempt? René hadn't asked Cristóbal where or from whom he had picked up this rumor. In this country, you didn't even ask your best friends things like that. But who had spread this dangerous lie? And above all: why?

"I certainly didn't," the priest stiffly replied.

"What?"

"Hope there would be more paying fans."

"It was our cultural duty to help the inhabitants of the poor district." René noticed the librarian's formal tone and understood why when he glanced over Cristóbal's shoulder.

Kurt Fitzroy was joining them - a Terrenean who held a vague government office that had something to do with the American Embassy.

Kurt was fifty-something, tall, with wavy grey hair, thick horn-rimmed spectacles with tinted lenses, a beard, and a gentle expression. Next to him stood a slim girl of about fourteen. She was shy, but there was something proud in her posture.

René smiled at her. When their eyes met, the priest felt as if his bones were turning to water. The girl smiled hesitantly, and the dimples on her cheeks swung him back ten years in time.

"Hello, Father, I have heard a lot about you. Nice to meet you," Kurt said. "I am coming to make my contribution to your neighborhood. I hope the government will resolve all difficulties soon." He nodded to the girl. "This is my daughter, Amanda. It's her first *peña*." He smiled at the teenager and stroked her cheek. "I warned her about the extravagant characters she would see here, Cristóbal. That made her a little shy." Kurt winked at his daughter, and she blushed.

"Excuse me," René said. His voice sounded stifled. He nodded at the company and walked to the bar. What he had seen made his heart beat faster. The priest looked back at Amanda.

Should he believe his heart or his mind? Could it be true? He remembered the officer's voice ten years ago: "I can't let you take the daughter of Víctor Pérez. Look at her: she's too sensitive, too fragile, to be raised by simple peasants up in the barren north. What she needs, and what she'll get from me, is an education that fits such a rosebud. Take the other children, priest. This one I'll keep."

René recalled the eyes that mocked him in the stadium when the chief officer of the secret service said those words. He thought that he would never forget them.

A blond man without a beard or glasses, about forty-five years old, civilized, and handsome. He was utterly different from the peasant soldiers in the stadium who had casually let René through when he showed them the official documents allowing him to save as muich children as he could from the stadium.

The blond man was in civilian clothes, but René realized he was a ranking officer. At first, the priest had thought the man's eyes were mocking him, but they also had a gleam that reminded him of fanaticism.

The man claimed Víctor Pérez's daughter as his own as the stadium's execution squad led her parents away. Lafarge knew he was facing a man who laughed in the face of moral decency.

His gaze wandered back to Kurt. Was it possible that Kurt was that man? What made that blonde hair so gray? And why did those eyes, partly hidden behind beer-colored glasses, seem so meek, so different from ten years ago?

The priest concentrated on the girl. Why was it that this

teenager had suddenly reminded him of Victor's four-year-old daughter? He had seen Carmencita a few times in the stadium, that was all.

The eyes. It was the eyes. The toddler had her father's black, penetrating eyes with the longest lashes he had ever seen. The way she had looked at René ten years ago when he held her in his arms in that terrible place: he had been frightened but also determined to rescue her. This girl had precisely the same eyes, the same expression.

Fitzroy seemed to feel Lafarge's gaze and looked in his direction. René turned his head away and pretended to scan the audience. He saw a striking number of young people with long hair. The Tereneans liked to wear their hair long, but when the fragile economy faltered, and the *junta* was irritated, patrols came out on the streets and shaved off their hair on the spot.

The girl was tall for her age. Did she seem happy? Or at least no more unhappy than any other teenager in this country, restricted by rigid regulations?

Why did he feel Amanda was Carmencita Pérez? For years, he suppressed the episode in the stadium. The memory of that place, where thousands of opponents of the regime were tortured and killed just after the coup, made him simultaneously despondent and restless. Why did he stay in a country where such things were possible? Monsignor Subercaseaux would be over the moon if he left Terreno.

He squeezed through the busy queue in front of the bar until he stood next to Beatriz Candalti.

"Among all those people, I saw the circle of your hair as a jet-black pearl."

Beatriz looked at him, surprised. She had put her thick hair in a knot and was wearing a white blouse, jeans, and sneakers. She looked fresh and young.

"Where's Alejandro?" the priest continued. He saw how

Beatriz looked at him and wondered if she noticed something going on.

"He's preparing himself. He's nervous."

"That's understandable after all these years. Are you going to dance?"

She smiled faintly. "Yes, of course."

"Cristóbal has put together a clever program," René hastily continued. "At the beginning of the evening, some American pop to attract the youngsters. After that, the better work – including your friend. They've got him coming on as a 'surprise gig' so he didn't have to appear on the guest list Cristóbal submitted to the government. By the time he sings, the rich, noisy boys will be bored of all this charity and will have left for their nightclubs. So the cocktails go into the closet, we'll drink real *pisco*, we dance the rumba, and we'll all forget our worries." He grimaced. "Until tomorrow." *Why was he nervously rambling on like this?*

"We?" said Beatriz, raising her eyebrows. "Do you dance too?"

"Yes," he said. "With you, if you like." He didn't understand where he got the courage to say that.

Again, that surprised look from her. René remembered everything she told him when he'd helped with her divorce. Beatriz felt so close to him then, a painful contrast to this forced atmosphere now. She would more than likely be thinking it wasn't right for a Terrenean woman in a relationship to be intimate with another man, especially if that man was a priest. Moreover, the dark-headed guitarist with his tormented eyes disliked him. As a true Terrenean macho, Alejandro would surely have forbidden Beatriz to socialize with him. René Lafarge was shocked by the anger he felt at this thought.

"Excuse me," he said, turning around. He made his way through the people without looking back.

With his empty glass in his hand, he looked at the dancers.

The auditorium, a large concrete cone, was almost packed full. They had placed a wooden dance floor in the middle, with olive green metal tables and folding chairs around it. Garlands were hanging from the ceiling and trestle tables at the edge. Behind them, volunteers filled glasses. The music system blared.

Behind one of the trestles stood a young man in a white shirt and a bow tie, clearly from a wealthy family.

He juggled a shaker with a broad smile on his face. In front of his improvised bar stood well-dressed young men who cheered him on while casting their eyes towards the heavily made-up girls at the tables who, in turn, were sneaking glances back. A bit further on stood an Indian woman who had overcome her shyness. Her bowler hat, large build, and strong arms aroused the ridicule of the rich *pitucos*. She pretended not to notice.

Mestizos clapped cheerfully to the beat of the music and danced. Foreign guests, mostly Americans and some Europeans, sat at tables and talked with their heads close together. In the past, René had been at folk festivals where people listened to the music, commenting loudly on the lyrics. This custom had almost disappeared in the past ten years. This *peña* was hardly distinguishable from any party anywhere in the world.

"What do you think of the party, René?" asked a friendly voice. He looked sideways. Kurt grabbed René's glass and filled it with a bottle he carried. "Cheers," he said.

"*Gesundheit,*" said René. Kurt Fitzroy's eyes above the glass did not change.

"Perhaps your reputation as a militant priest stops you from enjoying a bit of fun," said the man with a smile.

René ignored the hidden barb. "I'm less militant than you think."

Kurt grinned as if René had told a good joke. "I can imagine that," he said with his civilized accent. "We Terreneans like to exaggerate. Honor, blood vengeance, inevitability, fate. These concepts are familiar to us. The dramatic expression, sensuality, cruelty, exuberant love, the man as a flamboyant conqueror; we find these aspects of life worthwhile. You as—"

"What an exalted analysis," René interrupted. "You're not afraid of using clichés to describe your countrymen."

Kurt laughed and stroked his beard. "Do you think that the people here tonight are dancing and drinking for the sake of the *porqueriza*? Of course not: they have a reason to let themselves go. Tonight they get drunk, and then they say: who cares about tomorrow?"

"I think you underrate these people. Maybe they dance because they hope that tomorrow the constitution will be amended and elections will be possible again."

"What a funny comment. Your irony is quite special. You reserve it for atheists like me, I assume, because, to believe in a god, we need *le plongée dans le néant*, don't we?"

"That sounds like profound French, but I still don't know what you think of the recent political momentum." René kept his voice airy, his body language nonchalant, though inside, he tremored from head to toe.

Kurt poured again. "A while back, a military dictatorship was virtually the only form of government in all of South America," he said. "A few years ago, democracy began to reappear. It's not always a wind that delivers prosperity and happiness. Stroessner in Paraguay is a classic dictator, but I would rather call Pelarón an enlightened *despot*. I wonder if the time is ripe for democracy in Terreno."

"Do you think that there'll be constitutional reform?" At the same time, the priest thought: *Why can't I keep my mouth shut?*

"You don't seem to have much faith in Pelarón's democratic intentions, René," said Kurt, addressing the priest by his first name for the first time. "Or are you so discouraged because the situation in your neighborhood is deteriorating so quickly?"

During the last two days, the riots in the *porqueriza* had spread to the entire district of Canela. The police responded with a show of force that was reminiscent of the *junta*'s first months.

"Who knows?" said Lafarge as he turned his eyes to the dancers. The smell of *arrollade* hung appetizingly in the room. The University hadn't gotten permission to hold the *peña* in the faculty gardens. The authorities claimed a benefit gig for Canela in the open air would attract disorder.

"Democracy is a label like any other," said Kurt. "I've just spoken to a young man here who swore black and blue that he was a communist. I asked him if he knew what that meant."

"And?" asked René.

"I got a Terrenean version of Robin Hood," chuckled Kurt. "Taking everything from the rich to give to the poor, nationalizing industry, trade with Cuba, the works. I had to use all my tact to shake off that silly youth. His theories were as long-winded as Das Kapital."

René laughed cordially but was more than ever on his guard. The conversation stalled.

"What are you looking at, dear René?" Kurt asked amiably, a little later. "I may assume that you're not leering at the dancing girls, right?"

"Pour me another glass, dear Kurt," answered René light-heartedly. "Where's your daughter?"

Kurt looked at the priest. In the light of the auditorium, his eyes behind his tinted glasses seemed very dark. There was suddenly something between them, an invisible field of energy that jumped between the two men: *deep in our hearts, we are enemies*.

"She was tired," Kurt said. "She's only fourteen, and it's late already. A friend of mine took her home." He smiled. "A high-ranking officer who was here too. So you see, René, the military caste also wants to support your charity. You ought to be optimistic."

"You're right," replied René. "This isn't an evening to become gloomy. Maybe, as a man of God, I'll even risk a few dance-steps." He wondered why Fitzroy had sent his daughter home.

Kurt laughed jovially. "Are you going to do that to the music of your protégé?"

"Hmm?" said René, as if he was distracted.

"Alejandro Juron," said Kurt with a mischievous flicker in his eyes. "Ex-member of the famous Aconcagua. Cristóbal's just told me that you unexpectedly picked him up in the *población*. Juron doesn't appear on the list of artists submitted to the authorities, but it's only a sour-puss who grumbles about that, eh René? Cristóbal assures me that Alejandro won't sing inflammatory songs from Aconcagua's old repertoire; he'll stick to classical love songs from the *altiplano*. A pity, really: Aconcagua's repertoire was full of true gems. You do have a talent for surprises, René."

Lafarge's hand holding his glass froze just in front of his mouth. Kurt elegantly tapped his glass against René's and downed it in one draft.

———

3

Alejandro clamped his guitar in his hands. He felt melancholic but at the same time excited. He thought of Aconcagua's first gig, almost fifteen years ago now, and of Víctor getting drunk afterward. Juron never forgot Víctor's words at that time: "If only you could see me now, father! There was blood on the walls of our hut in Tampu each time you hit mother. I secretly poured away the leftovers of the *pisco* to stop you pouring it all in your stomach. You were a good-for-nothing, and I was destined to follow in your footsteps. But look, father, I defy you. I'm becoming someone."

"I'm ashamed, Víctor," Alejandro muttered under his breath. "I am humiliated."

Two men entered the dance studio that served as an artists' dressing room. "Is it my turn?" asked Alejandro.

Without a word, one snatched the guitar out of his hands and shattered it on a table.

The years in the cauldron of The Last Supper were now Alejandro's salvation. He saw the glint of a boxing brace on the fist that swung in his direction, and he ducked. Alejandro threw a chair in front of the second attacker's feet and ran out of the room.

In the corridor stood two men; they were surprised when they saw him; he knew one of them.

"Damn it!" snarled Manuel Durango. "Get him."

Alejandro slipped past them. He felt a hand on his shoulder, kicked backward. He ran on, knocked open the double door at the end of the corridor, and ended up on the auditorium balcony. Downstairs, Beatriz was talking to Lafarge. The music had been turned off; everyone was waiting for Alejandro to come on.

He called, "Beatriz!" as the doors flew open behind him. He jumped from the gallery and landed with a shock on the lower floor, hurting his left knee. Manuel Durango followed on his heels, along with the three members of the fascist group Patria y Sangre.

The audience instinctively parted for Alejandro, then closed ranks against his pursuers. A blast sounded: to force a passage through the crowd, one of Manuel's thugs fired into the air. Panic ensued. People rammed each other in their flight to the exit. René and Beatriz tried to reach Alejandro, who was wrestling against the current of people. As his pursuers drew near, Alejandro reached Beatriz and the priest.

René went to stand in front of them.

"This is..." he started.

The first fascist swung the barrel of his gun against Lafarge's head. He staggered and fell. Then, the man pointed his weapon at Alejandro. In turn, Beatriz stepped in front of him. Manuel shouted something but was drowned out by the noise of the fleeing crowd.

"Stop at once," a voice echoed through the sound system. "We have called the police."

Manuel pushed the man with the gun aside and snapped something inaudible at him. Cristóbal stood on stage and spoke into the microphone, "Consider the consequences of this illegal aggression."

Manuel looked at Beatriz, who trembled but held his gaze. He turned around, walked with big steps to the stage, jumped on it, and snatched the microphone from Cristóbal's hand.

"Go home!" he bellowed. "I can inform you on behalf of General Pelarón that the government will rebuild the *población* with stone houses at a small rent. The general represents the future and prosperity of this country. Anyone who claims the contrary is a scabby asshole and deserves to be executed."

Manuel turned to Cristóbal and continued calmly: "I can also inform you that the name of the *población* will be changed to the Residential District Antonio Pelarón. This university has gone far beyond its mandate with this festival. A bunch of communists abusing drugs and bootleg liquor...."

Manuel dropped the microphone with a bang on the floor, beckoned his men with a nod, and left the hall. It remained silent behind them. Everyone stood still. Cristóbal bent down and picked up the microphone. "The *peña* has ended. You should leave the university grounds immediately. Thank you for your understanding."

"Go get some water," Beatriz said to Alejandro as she tried to help René to his feet. Blood dripped into his eyes from a head wound.

"Not so bad," the priest muttered. Beatriz had to repeat

117

her request twice: Alejandro was staring at the stage where, a few minutes ago, he had wanted to give his first performance in years.

The young people from wealthy families, who'd been challenged by the idea of visiting an old-fashioned *peña* to get drunk with poor people, were the first to slide away. What seemed like an opportunity to show off their status turned into pointless peril. *Who knew? The police, or worse still, the army, might show up any minute.*

The residents of the *población* continued to stand together in small huddles.

"Liars," someone said not too loudly. But others took over the word. It quickly sounded like a litany. "Liars!"

"Please leave," Cristóbal said into the microphone. "We can do nothing more for you. You have heard it: the government will give you better houses. Go home now."

As his words trailed off, "Liars!" rose in a crescendo. Nonetheless, people followed Cristóbal's advice. He climbed off the stage.

"I'm sorry," he said to René, who was wiping his head with a wet cloth.

"Who were they?" asked René. His left arm hung clumsily next to his body.

"Patria y Sangre," said Beatriz.

"Under the leadership of your husband," said Alejandro. "I mean your ex-husband." He seemed to be looking right through Beatriz.

"Now you've seen me hide behind the backs of others," he continued. "In the church, you weren't there, but now you've seen it. Are you satisfied now?"

———

4

Alejandro felt surrounded by the walls of his weakness. His mouth tasted vile, but he knew the decay was in his head, and he had always known that.

"I'm not like any of you," Alejandro mumbled. He let his gaze wander over the *porqueriza*, where he had sought refuge after his humiliation in the auditorium. He tried to calm himself with sips from a half-full bottle of spirits.

Beatriz was the cause of this bitter confrontation with himself. Beatriz with her nervous courage, her secret power. She had seen with her own eyes what a coward he was.

Alejandro had run away from the auditorium. Following the railway lines, he had reached the *porqueriza* without meeting a police patrol. En route, Manuel and Captain Astíz coalesced in his mind into a single tangle.

When he arrived in the pigsty, he called out curses at the people sheltering between the rubble of their houses. "Despite all the misery, the *porqueriza* is still poisoned with hope," shouted Alejandro, waving his bottle until his legs failed him. He had to sit down in the mud, screaming hope was not a gift from the gods but a torment.

The slum dwellers laughed at him. They had formed district councils and were trying to build new shelters. From morning to evening, they were working in shifts, ignoring the curfew and the police warnings. Amid all the despair and outbreaks of violence, some groups did not give up.

Alejandro lifted his head and watched the builders with bloodshot eyes. One more sip from his bottle, one last remnant of reason disappeared.

"The difference between all of you and me is I'm a cowardly rat," Alejandro mumbled after he hoisted himself up. Sloshed, he dribbled through the shantytown. In the eyes of the inhabitants, he was one of the many who had given up.

In the eyes of Beatriz, he was a coward; he did not doubt that for a second.

The aversion in her eyes was real; he had not imagined it. Alejandro blindly swung his bottle back and forth. A police jeep drove around a corner just as the bottle escaped his grip and sailed through the air before shattering against the vehicle. A young policeman with a crew-cut that made him look like a child fired in Alejandro's direction.

A fiery breath stroked along Alejandro's left shoulder. The result was not fear but drunken fury. Alejandro jumped on the jeep's bonnet. Surprised, the driver pushed the accelerator. The shock pushed Alejandro onto the driver's shoulders. With a sound like a rotten cabbage falling on concrete, the vehicle drove into a large pile of rubbish.

Alejandro, abruptly cured of his contempt for death, fell from the bonnet to the road, jumped up, and bolted away. He leapt over a pile of tires, ran past collapsed houses, and continued in the direction of the river. Close to the railway yard, brightly lit in the darkness, he couldn't go on.

Only now did he realize how exhausted he was. Gasping with shaking legs, he tried to think about what he should do. But soon, he crawled behind piles of decaying wood and fell into a restless sleep that held the poison chalice of the past to his lips.

5

Never has the Cordillera looked more like a gateway to another world. I embark on a journey within myself like my mother taught me according to ancient Indian traditions. Tonight, I am drunk enough to believe in them. I am lying in smelly mud and can hear rats scratching in the darkness. I should flee, but I have no control over my body, and I have to listen to the voices of phantom images approaching. Captain Astíz leads them. No matter what I do, I cannot refuse him access to my dreams.

Contrary to what I told Beatriz, you never laid a finger on me, Captain. That was not necessary. You sensed who I was—the wood I was cut from.

You in the darkness, and I with a bright lamp facing me, your soft voice, the contours of your body in my dark cell: that was the prologue. After days, I was taken out of my cell, handcuffed, with my heart fluttering in my throat. Now it is going to happen. Two soldiers lead me into a torture room. In the faint light, I see a naked, blindfolded man lying on a mattress.

A soldier in a uniform without insignia, with the flap of his kepi above his eyes, bends over him and places a hand on the man's crotch.

"Who are you? What are you doing?" The prisoner's voice is nothing more than a whisper.

A Bunsen burner starts hissing. In the bluish, vibrating light, I recognize the contours of Captain Astíz's body. As always, his face is invisible. He clasps the prisoner's penis. Two soldiers are bending over the burner in a corner and heating a long needle which they hand to Astíz. It glows red. Astíz holds it in front of my nose.

"We call this the toro aguja. Transforms every bull into an ox."

Quickly, he presses the tip of the hot needle against the prisoner's genitals.

I hear him screaming. My guardians hold me firmly. Not that I could pull myself loose, I can hardly stand on my legs.

"Look how that proud cock is shriveling up," says Astíz, bowing over the man on the bench. As usual, his soft voice sounds slightly ironic. "We'll leave you longing for more for a while. If your son doesn't talk, we'll insert the bull's needle."

He pulls the blindfold off the prisoner. As if that's a signal, I'm roughly pushed out of the room and led back to my cell. Piece by piece, I try to imprint the man's face in my mind and remember the timbre of his voice.

My father?

I don't know for sure. In this place, the world as I thought I knew it is far away; here, anything is possible.

I sat in my darkened cell. The captain came in and leaned against the wall. He was silent. There was an atmosphere of understanding as if we both experienced a purification ritual. I opened my mouth and was surprised by the firmness of my voice.

I betrayed the address where my friend Víctor Pérez was hiding with his family—waiting for friends from the English embassy to smuggle them from the country.

That was only the beginning. From that moment on, Astíz had a hold on me and wanted to see how far he could go. The next day, I faced a terrible choice: apply electrodes to a prisoner's body and save his child, or refuse.

I applied the electrodes.

I did other things. I never refused.

Each time I lost a part of myself.

Astíz filled that part up.

I begged Astíz to stop. He replied that it gave him satisfaction to see that the famous guitarist of Aconcagua had talents other than music.

Finally, he proposed a new choice: to carry on or to go to The Last Supper.

I wanted to carry on, but I didn't dare. I knew where I would end up: as a hangman for the regime.

But I didn't know that The Last Supper would be so hellish.

The Curse Of The Past

1

BEATRIZ NARROWED HER EYES AT THE TRAFFIC ON AVENIDA Fletcher O'Callaghan. I want to know where Alejandro is, she thought. I want to see that he's not dead. That's all I need. I couldn't bring him happiness. How could I know that it would be so difficult?

René drove recklessly down the Avenida in his old Citroën. The avenue bristled with aggressive traffic. He searched for an opening in the stream of cars. The bandage around his head already looked grubby, though it was only a day old.

"Will your father be willing to help you?"

Beatriz rubbed her hands on her tight jeans. Lately, she dressed more aggressively. "I don't know. Maybe in these circumstances. But as a fallen woman, I don't carry much grace in his eyes."

Yesterday, before the *peña*, she had driven to the EMI office in the city center and asked what it would cost to record an album. Few Terrenean bands had survived the invasion of American music over the last few years.

Those that had survived recorded their albums at EMI

and paid the production costs themselves. The amount was about the same as Beatriz's annual salary. It would have been such a nice gift for Alejandro.

"Any news about Alejandro?"

She shook her head. "João is looking for him."

"I hope he's not doing anything silly."

Did he mean what he'd said? She just nodded. At a walking pace, they approached a traffic light.

"Do you still love him?"

"Why do you ask that?"

He was quiet for a moment. "Because I was hit on my head yesterday," he replied with a crooked smile. "Sorry. It's not my business."

This time, the message of his look was unmistakable. She turned her head away. "I never imagined I would meet such a man. I met him when I didn't know what to do with my life anymore, and he felt just the same."

"Is that an answer to my question?" René cleared his throat.

"Oh, René," she said.

"Do you have a future with him?"

"I don't think about that." I am just like the girls from the *población*, she thought. I wanted to use Alejandro to boost my self-esteem, and now that he's not the romantic adventure I thought he would be, I want to pull back. Isn't that the safest attitude in this country? "Alejandro refuses to accept he can't undo the past. Yesterday, Manuel and his thugs reminded him of what he'd been through. He can't bear that."

Men refused to accept so many things. In her eyes, René Lafarge didn't want to face the fact that he was becoming a caricature of himself: the eternal father figure, always concerned about others.

"I hope João'll find him," he said. Beatriz knew how he struggled to care about Alejandro, but his voice still sounded fake.

"Why did you come to Terreno, René?"

"You might as well ask me why I became a priest."

"So why did you become a priest?"

"A year ago, you wouldn't have asked that."

"That's true."

A sidelong glance. René wore glasses when he was driving. Beatriz found that charming; it gave him a certain fragility. "I don't really remember," he said. "I think I wanted to do something useful with my life. I come from a working-class family in Charleroi, a city you'd have to see before you could understand its ugliness. An impoverished city. And Mom was a true Roman-Catholic believer. *Voilà.*"

"My father, who couldn't say ten words in his life without God being present, is now losing his faith." Beatriz laughed briefly. "I always thought that faith helped people die without fear. And what do I see? Dad's perishing from anxiety in his bed. There goes another illusion."

"You're talking tougher today," René said, smiling. She saw how many wrinkles he had on his face these days.

"Do you think so?" She laughed again; not warmly, he noticed. She seemed to have changed in recent days. How could he ever have thought of her as compliant?

Beatriz looked out of the window at the Andes Mountains: a great wall that seemed almost close enough to touch.

"When I was younger, I wanted to live high in the mountains, so high that the sky tingled in my lungs."

A nearby siren started to howl, cutting off his answer. An armored police tank swung onto the Avenida from a side street in front of them with a sharp, screeching turn. René braked hard, his car skidding sideways. The police tank skirted past and thundered in the opposite direction. The siren's screaming echoed in the avenue packed with cars. René looked at the tank in his rear-view mirror, then hit the steering wheel with his right hand.

"*Merde!*" He pulled the glasses from his nose and wiped his sleeve over his forehead. "I hate a country where the police have tanks." He started the car again. Beatriz said nothing. She looked over her shoulder and saw the armored car turn off the Avenue.

They continued in silence, Lafarge's profile grim and introspective. "I think it was because I was afraid," he said when they were near the San-Lucas Hospital. "That's why I became a priest."

What made you so afraid? She was secretly relieved when his sharp turn into the parking lot seemed to make that question inappropriate. As they silently walked through the hospital corridors, it haunted her that René and Alejandro resembled each other so much.

———

2

She felt disgusted when her father beckoned her closer with a pontifical gesture to receive his kiss. She introduced René. Don Candalti reacted blandly, a sign that he was on his guard. However, Lafarge confidently took the reins and told him in businesslike terms what had happened during the *peña*. Ernesto picked at his sheet, raised his eyes to heaven, and clicked disapprovingly with his tongue.

"I can't believe Manuel would do anything like that. With his role in the ministry!"

"He got that role because he's a member of Patria y Sangre," said Beatriz.

Her father looked at her, shocked, still wedded to his old authority. The doctors managed to reduce the cancer a bit, but his appearance had not benefited.

The medication made his eyes bulge. When Beatriz was a teenager, she thought her father was handsome with his curly grey hair, which now laid flat and thin on his skull, but his movements were still as grandiose as a theatre actor's.

Ernesto looked at Lafarge conspiratorially. "Father, I have a daughter who wanted to become a poet when she was twelve. Her imagination has continued ever since, even though she's a good child, yes, at least I can say that."

Beatriz abruptly realized that her disapproval of her father's sly ways was built on quicksand. She played the same game, an actress in gestures and facial expressions - what else was she doing right now?

"I can't judge your son-in-law's character or past," said René. "I can, however, testify that yesterday he disgraced his name. We do not want to turn to the authorities about his flagrant violation of the law for the time being. But we do ask you, Mr. Candalti, to use your influence to temper Mr. Durango in his behavior towards your daughter. Miss Beatriz is very afraid of her ex-husband. And she's not alone. What would you think if journalists were to hear about this scandal?"

There was a veiled threat in René's words. It did not escape Beatriz that her father's response was an evasive maneuver. "As a priest, you come here to defend the fact that my daughter left her husband? I find this a strange interpretation of the pastoral task."

René didn't flinch, "I'm not here as a priest, señor. I'm here as a counselor for your daughter who has reason to fear your son-in-law and because I know you're a righteous man."

Beatriz clamped her lips together. Men talked about her over her head: for years, she had been used to it. Indignation flared up while she listened to the verbal duel between the two men.

She could, at will, arouse such pity for herself that tears sprung into her eyes. She tried the talent she had used so often when she was at boarding school and found it still worked.

Both men looked surprised when Beatriz started sobbing.

René smelled the opportunity she gave him, "You can see, Señor Candalti, that your daughter is desperate. As a father, it's your Christian duty to help her."

Beatriz slowly dried her tears, silently congratulating René..

Ernesto Candalti lowered his eyes. "I will talk to my son-in-law. He will listen to an old man who doesn't have long to live anymore. I hope my daughter will finally do the same."

"Thank you, daddy." After her tears, Beatriz had no problem grabbing her father's hand and pressing a kiss to his wrinkled skin. *For what Cristóbal asked me to do, I won't shy away.* "Can I ask you one more thing, daddy?"

"Of course, child," said Ernesto Candalti, looking at René: *You see? I do everything for my daughter.*

She took a deep breath: "Can I borrow the Cessna for two days?"

He frowned. "For two days? You said a while ago that you wanted to take a small flight, nothing more."

"The university would benefit greatly," she said quickly. "We have to pick up a load of archaeological material that was excavated near Arini." She hoped that the presence of a priest as she told this lie would stop her father from getting too suspicious. René cast a surprised glance at her. She smiled at him as if she enjoyed his surprise.

"Arini?" said her father. "So close to the northern deserts? And why would *you* go and collect that cargo?"

"Our sister university in Arini has agreed to lend out the archaeological finds for an exhibition. If our paleontology department has to ask the rector for overland transport, it all will take far too long. The Cessna is precisely suited for this task. You'll be a true patron of the university if you agree, dad."

"If it's for Terreno's good, I can't refuse. As long as you are careful." Because Lafarge was with them, Ernesto Candalti added, "You're a good pilot, you'll be fine."

"Thank you, daddy," she said. "You're a darling."

Ernesto Candalti sighed. "At least you come to visit me. The others have all forgotten about me. They're too busy. But I understand that. Unlike you, Beatriz, my business associates have a hectic life." He addressed René, "Will you pray for me, Father? If the doctors can be trusted, I still have a chance of being cured."

"Every day," said René with a warm handshake. "Every single day."

———

3

The smelly river lapped noisily at his feet. Behind him, the usual mess of smashed wood, craters, corrugated iron, stones, garbage. Some ten meters further, a sewer pipe discharged a gurgling mass into the Mayu river. A street dog barked at a rat running round the end of the tube.

Alejandro Juron shuffled even closer to the water. He looked at it for a long time, his arms dangling next to his body. Eventually, his shoulders lost their tension. Juron closed his eyes. "Make me whole again," he whispered.

"Alejandro!" shouted João, running towards the river. "Don't jump! Cristóbal has found a room for you. Everything will be fine again!"

Juron slowly turned around. "João," he said with as much dignity as possible. "Can a person in this grubby country never be blissfully alone anymore?"

———

4

René Lafarge switched off the engine of his car. "I have to speak to you." The priest left his hands on the wheel and looked at the facade of Beatriz' house.

"So formal, René?" Beatriz laughed but felt uncomfortable.

"Yes, so formal."

Once inside, she suggested they sit on the patio. As soon as they sat down, Lafarge came to the point.

"What are you going to do in Arini?"

She took a deep breath: "I can't tell you that."

"Are you in trouble?"

"Not really."

"Is what you are going to do dangerous?"

She shrugged her shoulders. She was ashamed because she felt proud that René worried about her.

"Is Cristóbal behind it?"

She lowered her eyes, felt like a dumb chick, and enjoyed it.

"You don't want to talk about it?"

"No, René, preferably not."

"I'm worried about you."

"You don't have to be afraid for my sake."

"I'm not just afraid for *you*. For me too."

She looked at him, surprised.

"Someone's spread the rumor that I am one of the instigators behind a plot to murder Pelarón. Is my old friend Cristóbal behind this?"

"You surely don't think that..."

"At the *peña*, I met someone - I won't mention his name so as not to endanger you. I don't trust him. He said Cristóbal had told him that it was me who'd fished Alejandro out of the *porqueriza* to play without government permission during the party."

"Cristóbal would never say anything like that."

"No? Cornered rats, et cetera. I sense my life is in danger."

"How do you mean?" She saw how upset he was. "You have to tell me more."

"First, someone came into my confessional, a simple man judging from his choice of words. He came to ask for forgiveness because he was planning a murder. Of Pelarón. Before I could react properly, he stepped out of my confessional and left my church. I thought it was a bad joke, but shortly after that, Cristóbal asked me to meet him. He told me that the news was circulating that I was the driving force behind an assassination attempt on the general. And then, at the *peña*, that man said he knew that I had arranged Alejandro's performance. What does that mean? Is someone trying to frame me?"

"Cristóbal certainly doesn't want to cause you any harm."

René sighed: "I hope not. You do realize that these rumors are enough to make me *disappear* when they reach certain ears, don't you?"

"The death squads wouldn't dare to lay a finger on you; not now."

"Wake up, Beatriz. Nothing has changed in Terreno."

In her heart, she knew that the priest was probably right. Last night, Cristóbal had told her that her mission had to be carried out earlier than foreseen. The menacing charge of the police in Canela and the brutal actions of Patria y Sangre betrayed a new hardening of the junta's ruling style. Cristóbal told her that he was under pressure from a lot of groups demanding quick and thorough action.

"There's confusion everywhere," she said. "Things get more chaotic by the day. We're just carried along. There seems to be no way back."

Lafarge looked over her shoulder to the crisp whiteness of the mountain peaks and felt like a stone sinking underwater.

"It's my pastoral duty to try to give protection and love to others. I feel as if every day I do that less and less."

"The people of the pigsty and Canela love you."

"Love is no longer enough for me, Beatriz. I used to masturbate. I've always hidden that fact in a separate place in my mind: it was something natural that you just did. At the same time, I tried to compensate for my loneliness with spiritual ecstasy. I saw God close to me, a radiant presence that made up for everything I lacked. But over the years, God erased himself, color after color. Where once there was light, now only fear of death and darkness leer at me."

Beatriz leaned forward, took his hand, and stroked it. She felt a vibration in his muscles as if he wanted to withdraw his hand, but he only turned his head away.

"I can no longer protect the people of my parish," he whispered. "I am sidelined with my useless words and my powerless crucifix."

She moved closer, put her arm around his shoulders.

"I'm so alone, surrounded by people I don't understand," he said, hardly audible. "Is there no one I can trust?" He looked in her eyes. "You used me: you didn't just want to ask your father for protection from Manuel. You wanted something else, and you hoped that my presence would make him mild enough to say yes."

She caressed his hair.

"What are you doing, Beatriz?" She got up, stood behind him, and massaged his shoulder muscles. Manuel had forced her to do this when he was drunk: *If you stand behind me, you can hurt me. But even then, my strength is much greater than yours.*

Now, her strength was much greater than René Lafarge's. She saw it in the way he bent his neck forward. An unstoppable feeling of excitement, very different from when she was with Alejandro, took possession of her.

This priest wanted to be a father to many children, and he trembled like a child under her hands.

5

"Salud!"

João and Alejandro toasted each other on the terrace of an old-fashioned *cantina* in Calle Valdivia. Unlike the taste-lessly modernized city, the old quarter had retained its sloppy charm. Calle Valdivia had once been a picturesque artists' quarter near the Santa Lucía hill. Now, it was home to small townspeople and laborers. Most of them more than fifty years old, the Swiss-looking wooden houses were poorly maintained but had character the mansions in the expensive districts lacked.

"The sacrament of life, this wine," Alejandro said, excessively exuberant, bringing the glass to his lips. João pulled the face of someone taking off his boots after a hard day.

"But after the sacrament of life," Alejandro continued with a theatrical gesture. "*Por favor*, what comes next?"

They had just checked his room. The owner had asked for a scandalous deposit, but João paid it without quibbling. The place had previously been twice the size but was now divided into two by a wobbly partition. Next to Alejandro lived a bank clerk. Both of them were able to enjoy Rorschach patterns in the damp stains on the walls. The grubby toilet in the corridor served all the tenants. There were cracks in the frosted glass door. In Alejandro's room, there was a wardrobe, a bed with a bedside table, and a table with two more chairs. The left corner of the room smelled of damp and mice.

"What's next after the sacrament of life?" echoed João, beckoning the owner of the café. "There follows a bite to eat. *Hola, Patricio! Dos ensaladas* and white beans with bacon!"

"Is Cristóbal so well-heeled that he can buy us such a high-brow meal?"

João didn't answer Alejandro's sarcastic question. "Shall I

let Beatriz know everything is fine with you?" The painter discreetly lowered his eyes.

"Did you think I wanted to commit suicide this morning?" said Alejandro, not answering João's question.

"No, I thought you were enjoying the beauty of the surroundings," Pereira answered laconically.

"The thought of suicide has been my consolation for years. Whenever I could smell the stench of hopelessness in my cell, that possibility descended upon me like fresh dew."

Alejandro poured wine into their glasses. This morning, by the river, he thought for a while that he could see himself from a distance, and he had laughed at the folly of the thoughts that followed. Change? Shake off his falsehood? It was too late; it was as simple as that. He would never be so stupid to tell anyone that he had betrayed Víctor and his family to Captain Astíz without first enduring heroic torture.

And what he had done afterward was even worse.

"To return to your question, João. If I answer: *no, you don't have to inform Beatriz that I've found new quarters*, what would you think?"

"That it's not yet really over between the two of you," João answered with a poker face. "And that I find this rather regrettable."

"Why is Beatriz so well-loved? Are there so few women in this country worth coveting? Terreno is famous for two things: its army and its women. Where are they then, those firm breasted, seductive *señoritas*? How come we all seem to be chasing the same woman?"

Pelarón's head appeared on the portable television in the nook beneath the roof. Before answering Alejandro, João listened to what the head of government had to say. "That's because of Mister Great Buffoon over there. It seems that the general has countless concubines. For us, there's not much left."

Alejandro Juron rocked with exaggerated laughter.

6

Manuel Durango and twelve other members of Patria y Sangre gathered in the apartment in Calle Huérfanos. They sat around the large table with their eyes closed and their backs straight. Thirteen people, a personification of the sun and the twelve signs of the zodiac, tried to concentrate and regulate their breathing. Their magic circle had to make them brim with the mythical power of the solar bull, who would fertilize them with courage.

Manuel Durango tried to meditate on the ten rules of Patria y Sangre, which each member had signed with his blood, but was distracted by anger and fear. In his mind's eye, he saw his father-in-law's sickbed.

Despite his illness, Ernesto Candalti, a personal friend of General Pelarón, still possessed impressive power. Although Ernesto's time on Earth was soon to end, his influence was unbroken. "Listen carefully, Manuel, I respect you. Your efforts to force my daughter to repent are welcome. But if you ever use violence again, I will intervene. Understood?"

Manuel realized he made a mistake: at the beginning of their conversation, the old man whined, rather hesitantly, about his daughter, who suddenly seemed to be his darling again. Manuel responded brutally in the conviction he could overcome his sick father-in-law. He had seen the man change before his eyes and collided with a wall of power.

It was crystal clear to him that the smart rat Beatriz took advantage of her father's condition. Ernesto felt sure his end was not far away and wanted to tighten his bond with his daughter above all.

As a son-in-law, Manuel couldn't compete with that. He knew how strong blood ties were. They unified the members of Patria y Sangre with the homeland they defended against communism and the degradation of moral values.

Manuel glanced at his watch. The ritual stipulated that, before each meeting, the Patria y Sangre members should meditate for a few minutes on their love of the country and the traditions they defended together with the *junta*.

Ernesto Candalti's voice, however, kept on gnawing at his brain: "You're too energetic, Manuel. Leave that half-assed Alejandro alone for the time being. I know my daughter: if you stay engaged, she will, out of stubbornness, attach herself even more strongly to that gritty vagrant. Let me solve that problem. I will instruct this Belgian priest to make Beatriz understand that she needs to change her lifestyle. We will solve this like civilized people and not like street mutts, understood?"

How was it possible that Beatriz could fool the old fossil like this? Cancer had undoubtedly affected Ernesto's brain. Or he had become senile, just like Pelarón.

Manuel Durango did not understand why everything and everyone seemed to turn against him. That morning, Astíz had furiously called him: his performance during the *peña* of the Universidad Nacional had provoked extensive press comments. As a result, Pelarón was having to consider a few concessions to the inhabitants of Canela. Couldn't Manuel see further than his damned nose? "Your ridiculous private wars are destabilizing this country even further," Astíz snarled at Durango. "Another such blunder and you can expect the strictest disciplinary measures."

Manuel tried to defend himself. Had it come to the point where Patria y Sangre had to allow an agitator such as Alejandro to perform in public again? Did they have to tolerate the organization of benefit gigs for those lazy communists from Canela? If so, he no longer understood anything about his homeland. Astíz snarled at him that this remark was yet another proof of his stupidity and added that

Patria y Sangre needed reorganization. Puerile rituals and unrealistic ideals had changed the brotherhood beyond recognition in the last few years. "A bunch of boy scouts with noses bleeding from cocaine," Astíz had contemptuously concluded. The purification would be carried out *right up to the top*. Durango clearly understood what Astíz meant by the latter words.

Hate and fear made him open his eyes.

"Long live Terreno!" he declared. "The meeting is open. I have called you urgently because our brotherhood is under threat from powerful people who used to be our allies. Patria y Sangre's survival is at stake. We are the pure blood of this country. We cannot allow General Pelarón and his *junta* to deviate from the right path. Therefore, we will..."

Manuel was interrupted by the phone at the corner of the apartment. He had urged all members of the association to use this number only in emergencies. He picked up the receiver.

"Manuel Durango," Astíz said evenly. "I received a message from Bolivia: something is wrong with the supplies of our merchandise. Someone has tampered with the stock of stardust. Would you perhaps know who?"

Manuel couldn't have been more shocked if someone read him his death sentence in public.

———

7

"The glory of the old days tastes bittersweet," Alejandro mumbled to himself, half aloud. It was an old habit. That morning, he had woken up with a shock. He dreamed he and Beatriz had children, and she had risen in the middle of the night to stare at a glowing symbol in the corner of their bedroom. She told him it was a sign one of their children had to die. "Now I recall who you are," Beatriz said in his dream. "You're the reason why children die."

On waking, Alejandro immediately grabbed a piece of paper. The poetic outpouring that followed displayed a clumsiness that at first seemed funny to him.

> *My love, what does it hurt*
> *to become someone else for you.*

In his room, with the mauve of a new morning behind the dirty window, he'd come to a decision. Yesterday, João had told him about Beatriz's journey with her father's plane, but behaved rather secretively. As soon as Beatriz came back, he would go to her house and confess everything he had done in the stadium. He hadn't killed any children. He *saved* them by disciplining their parents.

A few hours later, this intention seemed insane. If Beatriz wanted him back, he still had a chance in life. If she knew what he had done, she would spit in his face.

Alejandro turned away from the window and looked in the brown speckled mirror above the washbasin. What did he see in his eyes? The glory of the old days when his name resounded all over the continent?

But not like the name of Víctor Pérez.

This afterthought made him take flight outside. He bought bread, olives, white onions, peppers, cheese and retreated to his room. With his mouth full, he struggled again with the words.

> *The glory of days bygone*
> *can be read from wall stains,*
> *armpit sweat and bubbling lips*
> *and the frosted mirror of complaints*

He started to hum the strophe, but gradually, he began to

sing with a falsetto voice. He bent over the small sink again. "I still can't write songs," he muttered to his reflection. "But my accommodation has mightily improved."

He splashed water in his face and wriggled between his bed and the table where the paper was lying. How sickeningly white it was in the gloomy room.

"I haven't been able to outsmart fame again, but if I adopt a cunning approach, I may still catch Beatriz – the graceful condor of happiness who descended on my shoulder when I was sinking in the mud." He was entertained by his theatrical performance. He threw himself on the bed. "But the question is: how long will I be able to sprinkle salt on her tail?"

Why didn't the usual trick work? The laughing fit had to come now, after all this pathetic nonsense. Instead, he felt pain filling him, the cruelty of her sudden absence.

"Beatriz has a plane, but I have to learn to get wings to flee this country," he whispered, shaking his head. "Can't leave on foot; the door of democracy is too narrow for me."

Since General Pelarón had proposed "to open the door to democracy in due course," Europe rediscovered Terreno. Journalists eagerly visited the country. Some of them painted an ironic picture of the Terrenean society in their articles because Terreneans, brainwashed by the media, believed their ally South Africa was a world power. In the display cases of shops, Pelarón's head in close-up flickered on the television screens day and night, repeating the same slogans: "Democracy without me means chaos." "Faith in my country and God is my guiding principle." "Choose between chaos and me." "Together with the US, our faithful ally, Terreno is ready to resist all vile and undermining forces!"

A possible method for leaving the country continued to haunt Alejandro, but he knew it was impossible. To reenter the public domain and become the new Víctor then? Also impossible after what happened at the university's *peña*. One more performance and then commit suicide in public? Beatriz would honor him forever. Alejandro grinned; his shoulders shook.

Could his folly be even more pathetic? A new chorus bubbled in his brain; that couldn't be a coincidence, could it?

> *A proprietor of corpses, the general said*
> *when asked about his soul.*
> *Or, if you prefer, smoking asphalt*
> *under a red sun, feeding vultures.*
> *Mirror, mirror on the wall*
> *What do you see?*
> *A white ribbon around his belly,*
> *flashing light in his eyes*
> *don't stare; he sees you on the telly.*

The words tumbled in his brain, but, *hey man, that was rock 'n roll, wasn't it?* On top of the words, he imagined a dense, smoky rock chorus. He was going to become an idol for the new generation from now on, wasn't he? "If you can't beat them, join them." When was he going to unlearn talking out loud when he was alone? He couldn't be among people while rattling away like a man with Tourette's, could he?

There was a knock on the door. Alejandro cringed. Without waiting for an answer, João came in and stepped, followed by Cristóbal, towards Alejandro. "What is going on? We heard you mumbling and humming."

Alejandro cleared his throat and lowered his eyes. "Nothing. Don't enter a room so suddenly, João, you're too ugly for that. You might scare someone to death."

Cristóbal looked around. "Not really luxurious but still nice," he said light-heartedly. João bent over the bed and stroked Alejandro's head briefly as if he wanted to say that he understood Juron's fear. Juron looked up and smiled vaguely at João who winked at him.

Cristóbal seemed uncomfortable with this scene. "I'm

sorry, Alejandro, but I don't have much time. João has an idea and wants to make a proposal."

"No, I won't share Beatriz with you, João." With a jaunty jump, Alejandro bounced off his bed and showed a cheerful façade. "We will fight for her as it behooves real men. Loosen your muscles, man; meanwhile, I'm going to get a gun."

"Speaking of fighting," said João, not in the least put out of step by Alejandro's erratic behavior, "would you fancy becoming a Superbarrio?"

8

Sweat pricked Manuel's eyes when he opened the secret storage place in his house. The stolen pouches containing small bottles of Polvo de Estrellas were untouched. Manuel stared at them for a long time, without joy or relief.

Astíz was on his trail.

Smuggling Bolivian cocaine into the United States had long been the most significant source of income for Patria y Sangre. Bolivia's large drug cartels had found strong logistic help in Terreno because the country wasn't known as a drug producer or transit country. Cargoes for America and Europe were easily shipped via Terreno's air and seaports. The Andes was a problematic but excellent smuggling route between the two countries. Astíz had hinted to Manuel high-ranking people on both sides of the border were involved in this profitable trade.

Three years earlier, after a trip to America, Astíz had an idea. A new craze had emerged in the States—cocaine was dissolved in water, mixed with patisserie flour, and then heated, turning the porridge into crystalline stones.

Addicts could heat these crystals in a simple flask and sniff the vapors. The new product was an immediate success: it was cheap and more addictive than any other substance.

The Americans called the new drug crack. The profits were so enormous that inferior crack soon appeared on the black market.

Patria y Sangre, Astíz decided, would flood the American market with a high-quality crack at a reasonable price. The bottles were decorated with the elegant banner 'Polvo de Estrellas,' star powder.

For quite some time, Manuel had been stealing star powder from the Patria y Sangre stocks to sell cheaply via the pigsty dealers. Pure profit. What was that American saying again? *The sky is the limit.*

Manuel realized that he was about to crash.

He had to act.

Fast.

———

9

"Okay, well, I understand now," said Alejandro after João detailed his Superbarrio plan. "I now declare you incurably insane, João."

The big man grinned. "In Mexico, Superbarrio was the driving force of change in government. The wrestlers performed in the streets, openly criticizing the government. It was a grand show, packed with humor. In our case, the effect will be even greater since the *junta* will be easier to caricature. We can start wearing superhero masks and only reveal our true identity after the necessary fuss in the press. When the people know you were one of the players of Superbarrio, then..."

Cristóbal interrupted him. "The opposition magazines and the foreign press would love the initiative. They've been making a lot of noise about the incident at the university - Beatriz's ex-husband attacking you. Also our own press disapproved of it. *Hermes* even—and that's normally the model of propriety, bastion of the status quo. Despite everything, you remain a resounding name, Alejandro, even internationally."

"Excuse me, but I find your plan stupid and childish," said Alejandro.

Cristóbal tightened his lips. "The government announced that it will build five hundred houses in the *porqueriza*. The right-wing press shouts the news from the roofs as if the whole pigsty is being cleaned up, but the inhabitants think it's a scandal. Five hundred houses is a joke. The tension's at breaking point in the slum area. It's now or never."

"With all the foreign journalists being interested, we can seize the moment," João added. "Performing Superbarrio, chastising and parodying the government with folk humor, we'll..."

Alejandro listened with increasing impatience. "We'll do what? Force Pelarón to resign by doing a wrestling gig in the *porqueriza*, dressed like a bunch of spidery superheroes? Madness!" He slammed his mouth shut.

"A series of street gigs with you performing music from the old days in your flashy Superbarrio costume has *power*, Juron. It can free the pent-up anger of the people," said Cristóbal, seemingly untouched by Alejandro's sarcasm. "That's a powerful weapon."

"So, I have to wriggle myself into a monkey costume and yell tired old songs for drunks and down-and-outs? Sure, that'll produce a *load* of powerful sparks."

Cristóbal sighed, and said, "What the king doesn't dare to say brings the jester onto the streets."

"Then go and stand with a placard at a crossroad," said Alejandro.

Alejandro's taunts slid like water off a duck's back to Cristóbal. "Playing Superbarrio is just a start," the man said affably. "The biggest problem of the resistance is coordination and visibility abroad. We need a central figure and international press coverage. That's why we need to be original."

"Where was the resistance in the last ten years when I was in prison? It would've been very original and got some international press coverage if you lot had got me out of there."

Cristóbal exchanged a glance with João. "João and I belong to a new group that's planning high-profile actions. Call it public relations for the resistance as a whole."

"I don't like your 'high-profile public relations for the resistance as a whole," said Alejandro. "Get me a high-profile false passport. I want to get out of this shit hole."

"Are you sure that you want this?" asked João, who had been silently following the argument while studying the papers on the table.

"No, I'm just *gagging* to jam with you in an embarrassing fluorescent wrestling suit."

João picked up the half-scripted sheets. "Why do you keep on trying to continue Víctor's work if you want to leave here so badly?"

Alejandro glared at João, clearly upset. Cristóbal made a soothing sound. "If you want to leave, we can give you a false passport. Then, abroad, as a member of Aconcagua, you could still prove important to us. But is that really what you want?"

"I think you should stay," said João, who had stepped up in front of the window and looked down. "You're an artist of the people, however much you want to deny it. With Superbarrio, we can try..."

"What can we try? How do we make the losers in the *porqueriza* aware of the mighty power of the people? Do they need *me* to show them that they live on a time bomb? Do you think they're blind as bats and deaf as posts?"

Cristóbal coughed behind his hand.

For a long time, it remained quiet in the room.

Alejandro went to stand by João near the window and bent as if he were inspecting a parade in the street downstairs. "If you think I can help, fine. I'll play your oafish Superbarrio. I don't expect anything from it, but okay, I'll loaf around in your wrestling ring if you want. I'll gird my guitar and groan myself hoarse. Why should I care anymore?"

"You underestimate the role Aconcagua's music still plays, even among young people," João said. "And you always wanted to be funny, didn't you? The people of the *porqueriza* will find Superbarrio hilarious. Humor's a powerful weapon. If things go well, you'll become more dangerous to the junta than a whole gang of armed insurgents."

Alejandro leaned with his arms on the peeling window sill, his head bent, and studied the floor under him. He sighed.

"You're right. There have been too few bursts of laughter in this fucked up country recently and too many bursts of gunfire," he said.

———

10

Gui,

I remember our trip to Binche to see the Gilles as if it were yesterday. I was twelve; you were twenty-two. You were the type that helped old ladies cross the street. Everyone said you had such a good heart, un coeur de massepain.

Jeannette Treilleur, your fiancée, believed that too.
We took the bus, you, Jeannette and I. You could afford it. As a tailor, you were earning well: everyone wanted to wear a nice suit after WWII. In

Binche, the famous carnival procession went out again, after an interruption of five years. On the way, Jeannette and I sang folk songs. I was secretly lovesick about her. She looked so sweet with her curls and her brown skirt, her white sweater, and a short jacket on top. Her face was broad, with high cheekbones and curvaceous lips. She had a high, smooth, and glossy forehead. And then that waterfall of curls that she shook when she was surprised about something. Jeannette was cheerful and compliant, and motherly. She pampered me and called me 'little brother.'

You and she were dating for three months. When we were nearing Binche, you read aloud from an old city guide. The old ramparts and city walls from the days of the knights!

In the town itself, I lacked eyes: the old buildings, the churches, the town hall. I thought everything was super; we adopted that word from American soldiers. The watery sun made Jeannette take off her jacket. Her sweater was hand-knitted and soft. You took her by the arm; she took me by the other. I looked secretly at her breasts under her clothing. I found them mysterious and attractive, and I became caught up in a state of mind that I didn't understand very well, making me shy and cocky at the same time.

The Carnival procession that crossed the cobblestones of the narrow streets was a fairy tale. I gaped at the masked Gilles dancing in clogs with their great feather headdresses as if they came from another world. The sound of the apertintailles, the bells they wore around their belly, brought me into a state of intoxication. You read from the guide that the costumes had their origin in the sixteenth century when a queen - I forgot her name - offered a party to Philip II. Inca dances had to be performed at that feast since the Spanish had just conquered Peru.

"Those Indians from Peru wore such suits?" I asked in amazement. 'My' Indians were still as good as naked then and tried to scalp cowboys in the Wild West. You were not sure either, but the brochure said so. I asked where South America was on the map. Jeannette was ahead of you. "On the other side of the rainbow," she teased me. You called her 'whacky' and

explained to me in detail how to fly to South America. I liked Jeannette's explanation more.

During the journey back home, we were in high spirits. Jeannette wore a carnival hat on her curls. You had drunk quite a lot of beer, and she teased you about your blushing cheeks. A lot of people on the bus looked at us, amused. Jeannette put her arm around your shoulders. I sat on the seat opposite you and pressed my knees together.

At the bus stop, not far from our house, we split up. You both headed for the small fair a little further through the neighborhood to get more drinks. I could go home alone, big boy that I was, couldn't I? I thought it was a pity that I wasn't part of the group anymore, but I took your city guide.

I wanted to know more about Gilles and South America and hoped that I could get more information in the guide. I thought that our father would be in his allotment, about a kilometer from our house. What I did not find in my guide, I could ask him. Father had fenced off the allotment, and the shed he had built resembled a miniature house. I knew there was a large, old feather duster lying in the shed. If I tied it around my head, I would be like an Indian from a country on the other side of the rainbow.

Father was not in his allotment, and I should've turned around and walked away. But then, when I was a few meters in front of the shed, I heard Jeannette's voice. I had Indians in my head, but the tone in her voice made me sneak to the door. I opened it silently.

You and Jeannette were lying on a blanket on the wooden floor. You had pulled her skirt down, and you were fumbling her panties. Her legs were tender and white. My knees grew cold, but at the same time, I felt a flush of warmth in my pants. You panted and mumbled something. She cried, trying to push you away. You pulled her legs open. A few months earlier, I had seen a classmate open the legs of a frog on the banks of the river Maas just like that.

After three months of fondling and petting, you wanted to go the whole way. Jeannette was different. She loved watching the farm horses rubbing proudly against each other in the nearby hamlets. She wasn't ready for the rest yet.

Excited from the beers you had, you thought she was just being childish. You struggled to keep her legs apart with one hand and pulled your trousers further down with the other. Jeannette lost her temper and scratched you. I saw how you stuck your finger in her out of pure frustration. She screamed. You instinctively slapped her around the ears. She was so surprised that she froze. That allowed you to shake your trousers to your ankles.

"Sweetheart," you muttered. "Darling, don't be angry, Jeannette. I love you."

Things went fast then.

The scene was as exciting as it was repulsive, so attractive and animalistic that a sweet pain crept from my toes to my head—a shiver that struck like a tingling shudder. I groaned when you groaned.

You looked surprised over your shoulder while your hips were still shaking. That face of yours, Gui, I'll never forget it, twisted in a grimace of pleasure, fear, and surprise combined. It's a face that I have often remembered over the past thirty-six years.

I turned around and ran away. At home, in the bathroom, I washed the sticky, weird-smelling goo out of my underpants. Afterward, trembling as if I had a fever, I put them on again.

Our parents came home a little later, and mother immediately knew something was wrong. I didn't have to lie a lot to convince her that I had a fever. In bed, with vague pain in my groin, I was overwhelmed by a feeling of guilt and fear that went so deep that I couldn't cope with it.

Clamping my teeth together to avoid making a sound, I cried until I fell asleep.

We never exchanged a word about what had happened, Gui. The following day, you avoided my eyes. We behaved formally, like two rivals who thought it wasn't the moment for openly testing their strength.

A few months later, you married Jeannette. You couldn't see anything on her wedding day, but in our neighborhood, there were whispers that she 'had to' get married. Mother burst into tears in the church; Jeannette's face had a strange shine during the reception. She tried to cuddle me, but I remained the same as I had been to her in the last few months: shy and distant.

Less than five months later, Jeannette died in childbirth, and you found nothing better than to ride your bike blind-drunk into the Meuse three weeks later, without ever coming up again.

I can confess it to you now: I wanted to be in your place when you spread Jeannette's legs. I could never forget the triangle of dark hair between them, as abundant as her curls, and the way you put your finger into her. The same frenzy that turned you from a good guy into an asshole has dwelt in me all these years. I wanted to overcome it with enforced charity. But I always knew I couldn't tame it, that it would never disappear, and was only waiting for a chance to emerge.

Yesterday, drowned brother, when I was lying in Beatriz's arms, it saw its chance.

René Lafarge opened the top drawer of his desk and placed the letter on the pile. He got up. Would he finally be able to sleep now? Suddenly, he pulled the drawer out of the desk and emptied its contents with a flourish. The unsent letters to his dead brother floated through the room while they fell to the floor.

11

In the western foothill of the *porqueriza* stood an English country house in neo-Gothic Tudor style, with a high, reddish-brown wall around it, capped with glass fragments. It seemed as if the building had slipped into the slum through a crack in time. The inhabitants of the pigsty called it *the castle*. The eccentric drug king José Luis had it built at the end of the seventies.

A year and a half previously, a gang war had started. The followers of Raoul Melisano, a fierce young rascal, were armed by Manuel Durango with the newest fully automatic hand weapons stolen from the Terrenean army barracks. They raided the house in the morning. José Luis' men couldn't compete with Melisano's better-armed gang, so they fled. José Luis simply disappeared. For a while, the slum was buzzing with all kinds of stories about his death, but his body was never found. The new master took over the house. Within a year, Raoul and his men had complete control of the drug trade in the *porqueriza*. He called himself *Rey de Los Cerdos* – the king of pigs.

Manuel stepped through the castle's metal detector. The guards at the gate treated Manuel with respect. Their boss's main drug supplier was a famous man. Raoul always had time for him. Durango supplied him with a steady stream of crack, which he had stolen from the supply line that Astíz had set up, from Colombia to the States.

Raoul received Manuel in the guest room. One of his bodyguards stood by a window, another by the door. The young man looked like he'd escaped from *Boy with the Fruit Basket*, by Michelangelo.

He kissed Manuel on both cheeks. Raoul always dressed with great taste. This time, he wore a bespoke English outfit.

"Manuel, it's always a pleasure to receive you in my house. What do you need?"

Manuel smiled. "A pair of Dracula teeth, Raoul." Raoul was a great fan of classic vampire films.

Raoul stretched his neck with a theatrical gesture. "*Soy todo tuyo*," he said.

"I only fancy maiden blood," Manuel said, chuckling. "Let's do business."

"I like to hear that," laughed Raoul. "But first, we drink as brothers."

He turned away to pour two glasses.

Manuel Durango pulled on the leather wrap around his waist under his coat.

12

"Aeródromo Olympiada, this is flight N461C. Requesting permission to land." As Beatriz prepared for landing, she felt her exhaustion.

"N461C, you have permission for runway three."

The day before, she had left early in the morning from this same small airport just outside Valtiago, owned by the Olympiada flying club. Because the Ministry of Civil Aviation in Terreno was under military control, she had to release her flight plan. The cover for her trip had worked perfectly. She had received permission without any problems.

After a bit more than four hours of flying, she'd reached Arini. Over Las Officinas, the extreme corner of the nitrate deserts that housed the ghost towns of the once flourishing salt trade, she made a turn. The blazing sun, the drained soil below her, the cumulus clouds, and the pale red wall of the Jariques volcano formed a landscape that suggested some distant, inhospitable planet. The sight had evoked a sense of resignation in her. In places like this, one saw one's own insignificance. At the critical moment, she had set course for the Carretera Panamericana, the highway that approached the mountains parallel to the Andes train track. Cristóbal Vial had explained to her that she had to pay attention to the stripes and arrows painted on the Pan-American road. They formed a perfect runway for a small plane like the Cessna. The librarian had drawn a detailed plan of the landing spot. At noon, the wide asphalt road was deserted.

The landing went smoothly. When Beatriz opened the cockpit, the 45-degree heat took her breath away. At once, her armpits were sweating. Her jeans clung to her thighs as she walked with Cristóbal's map in her hand to the nearby railway line. Less than ten meters from the rock in the shape of a horse's head that served as a landmark, she found the package. She wondered who had thrown it from the Andes train.

Using this region where the murderous heat made encounters with the army or police rare was an old smuggler method. She found the pack surprisingly small, but it was heavy, and she was soaked with sweat when she took off again.

The landing in Arini had also gone smoothly. After meeting the Jesuit who ran the San-Pedro museum of archaeology, Beatriz had spent the night in town.

The military rector of Arini's small university, who thought she'd come to interview the museum's curator, had provided accommodation in an old guesthouse. The town was hardly more than a compound for wage laborers employed by Chemical United. In Casablanca, the local cinema, The Towering Inferno was playing. In the neon advertising of the cinema name, the C. was missing. Beatriz had slept badly.

At five o'clock in the morning, a few cockerels started crowing in the back gardens, and dogs reacted with fierce barking.

In her rough sheets, she had mulled over René. Her compassion for Renè had by now repressed her anger. She realized it was difficult for her to see Renè as an ordinary man. He remained someone with a vocation, a priest with a challenging task. That's why she found it so painful he reminded her of Manuel in bed.

When she undressed, determined to free René from his deep suffering, he crawled on top of her like a frantic dog. Trembling with a powerful emotion that had frightened her, he had pushed her legs open. "Stop René," she'd said. "I don't like this." She'd seen something in his eyes that silenced her. Instinctively, she wrapped her arms around him and let him have his way. Renè's tempo was so fast and mechanical that she bit her tongue. Fortunately, it took him just a moment to come, curving his back as if ejaculation brought pain instead of pleasure.

He immediately detached himself from her, stood up, and stared at her as if she were a total stranger. "*Je suis désolé*," he'd said, apparently unaware that he was speaking French. She hadn't been able to stop her tears. She kept crying while he quickly dressed and ran out of her house. She pulled the sheets off the bed and put them in a garbage bag.

As she made herself get dressed, her emotions spilled into compassion for the priest. She sensed that, without realizing it, she had released a hidden desire in him that he probably suppressed all his life.

Beatriz concluded she didn't understand men. Nor did men comprehend her. Alejandro had run away from her because he couldn't bear that she knew he was afraid. René had left her in the lurch because he couldn't bear that she had seen his lust.

Trapped in morning sluggishness, she began to wonder what it would be like to meet Alejandro again. She would visit him in his new room, and they would end up in his bed together. The fantasy, however, seemed somehow impossible and wasn't exciting anyway.

All her fretting made her so restless that at half-past six, she stood in the rusty shower at the end of the corridor of Arini's only guesthouse. The water had a reddish color, and the trail of feet back and forth had stained the enamel to a dirty brown. Next to the shower was an old-fashioned toilet bearing a rumpled pink label on its seat. *Desinfectado,* it declared in faded letters. The smelly pot, however, did not seem to have been scrubbed in years. *What do I still want with my life?* she thought as she squatted above the toilet to pee. *If only I could escape myself and others.*

Around ten o'clock, she'd left the motel. During the flight back home, the Cessna had kept itself steady, despite the strong westerly wind that caused a lot of turbulence. The plane jolted up and down as it flew through a thick layer of cumulus clouds above Valtiago. Beatriz rebalanced the wings. A little later, she pushed the aircraft's nose down steeply. A warning light began flashing, but she knew the Cessna could take this angle of descent. The runway of the flying club seemed to jump at her. At the last moment, she pulled up the nose and made contact with the tarmac with a small bump. She saw the university van waiting for the antiquities to be loaded, together with the hidden explosive charge. Her relief was even deeper than her satisfaction with her landing. She looked at her watch: just after two. Despite the rough weather, she'd made good time.

Her radio started rustling. "Nice landing, N461C." The voice of the air traffic controller sounded laconic. "A bit brisk, but well done."

"Thank you, Olympiada," she said. She knew that the air traffic controller would tell tales to her father about her daring landing. He was one of the club's financiers. Dad would give her a roasting, but at the same time, he glowed with pride. Beatriz smiled crookedly: what wouldn't a daughter do to spice up the last moments of a father?

She turned the Cessna and taxied to the pickup. Cristóbal got out and waved. Beatriz wondered: was she now someone who had done something useful in her life, or was this all meaningless?

———

13

Manuel pulled the whip from his hips with a shake of his wrist. When Raoul turned and reached for the holster on his waistband, the strap swished fiercely over his face. The young drug king fell to the floor with a bleeding cut across his nose and cheeks. The two bodyguards didn't move and watched without emotion as Manuel hit the writhing body on the floor until a random pattern of blood smears formed on the parquet.

An outburst of rage accompanied each strike because Raoul had not been able to keep his ass-sucking mouth shut about how many drugs he could trade, all thanks to his good friend Manuel Durango. And what had his excellent friend Manuel Durango told him over and over again? Absolute secrecy, no bragging!

Raoul was no longer angelically beautiful. When he lost consciousness, Durango stopped. He sweated, and his feet seemed to be on fire in his expensive shoes. Durango wiped his mouth. He inspected his clothes for any splashes of blood. The two bodyguards were still looking on motionlessly. Durango beckoned them closer. "Now show me that I'm not paying you too much." The two men stepped forward and lifted Melisano's limp body from the floor. "Don't make any mistakes when you smuggle him out," said Manuel.

"He's joining in with the next load of stardust," said the biggest bodyguard, a mestizo with a crescent-shaped scar on his cheek. Clay-colored wound tissue filled the sickle. "Tonight you have him where you want him."

"You wanted to fly high," said Manuel to the smashed

face. "If that's what you want, you must also be able to fall low."

――――――

14

"René Lafarge," said the tinny voice. "You've been sentenced to death for threatening domestic security."

"What-" René started. The connection was cut off. René hung up and turned around. The window of his office was open. He closed it. His gaze skidded over the lower slum—a kilometer-long patchwork of pale colors, with large, frayed wounds left by the earthquake. Behind the pigsty, against the mountains, lay the Valtiago garbage dump where long queues of trucks drove past the watch-house in the morning. High poplars were planted in front of it to shield the garbage from view.

The *porqueriza* had dominated Lafarge's life for years. He worked for its occupants until he was exhausted, but its degradation had simply deepened. The rise of drugs and alcohol was unstoppable.

René closed the curtains. Who had issued his death sentence? The little Captain in his church whose masculinity he wounded? Manuel Durango, who could not cope with the loss of Beatriz? A dealer who wanted to put an end to his interference?

His thoughts strayed on until, at last, something shifted, and his spirit hardened. He grabbed his handkerchief and wrapped it around the telephone handset. He dialed a number.

"Beatriz Candalti here."

René took a deep breath.

"Who is it?" said Beatriz.

"Beatriz." The priest spoke with his lips near his handkerchief. "I know you have a small heart-shaped mole on your left thigh. By this, I will recognize you when you burn in hell, bitch."

He thrust the receiver back on the hook and walked back and forth with his hands against his temples until he put his forehead against the window.

It was not the first time he had called Beatriz like this. She told him about the nasty phone calls that undoubtedly came from Manuel. René had reacted with concern and sympathy.

The priest thought about his dead brother and how he had written letters to him for years without posting them. *Did you make me like this, Gui? Or am I fooling myself? Is it nothing to do with you? All Beatriz wanted to give me was tender warmth and perhaps a little love. And what did I make of it?*

I don't understand myself. I'm someone who wants to do good for others, right? Am I really such a person?

His forehead felt feverish against the glass. He turned around, walked to his desk, and opened the bottom drawer. In a plastic bag lay the mask he had worn ten years earlier for his visits to the Valtiago football stadium. The soldiers who guarded the stadium had called him *El Enmascarado*. There was a hint of ridicule in it but also awe. The mask helped him exercise a special kind of authority in that awful place.

No one had known who he was, except his former bishop, the old Monsignor Tibeira, and general Jiménez, who was at that time the spokesman for the new junta. Monsignor Tibeira had pleaded with the general for a priest to be allowed to remove the children from the stadium. Jiménez, a general of the old style, had given his permission but demanded that the priest remain anonymous and sworn to secrecy.

Monsignor Tibeira explained to René why he had chosen him—if anyone ever discovered his identity, his Belgian nationality could protect him from reprisals. The bishop had not mentioned what reprisals might follow. René accepted the assignment and chose this theatrical disguise. He knew well how keenly its dark symbolism would affect the Terrenean soldiers.

René unfolded the hood and let it slide over his head. He walked to the mirror in the corner of the room. Looking back at him was *El Enmascarado del Estadio Nacional*, the mysterious benefactor about whom even the official right-wing newspaper *Hermes* had written. "What is the masked man doing in the stadium, and who does he represent?" the newspaper asked in giant letters on page one.

What did the masked man in the stadium do? He collected children of convicts who were then sent to adoptive families via the sisters of the Holy Congregation of the Virgin Mary. The objective behind this bizarre mission was straightforward: take the children whose parents were sentenced to death.

"Take care of the little ones first," Monsignor Tibeira had said. His house had been a crisis center during those hectic days of tank shelling and bombings. "First, the youngest children, René." The bishop lowered his eyes, rubbed his sparse grey hair, and with a trembling voice, he added, "They don't care about them."

René followed Ribeira's order, knowing well the concession granted to the bishop by the regime could be withdrawn at any time. Every day he made life and death decisions in the stadium.

Saving all the children was impossible. René told himself he had to apply rational criteria when choosing. Parents looked forward with fear to *El Enmascarado*'s visit to the crowded, sweating stadium. If he chose their children, it was a signal that they were condemned to death.

Accompanied by two very young soldiers, René walked through the corridors of the former locker rooms. He felt the sidelong glances. He wore black trousers and had replaced his priest's shirt with a black sweater. He heard the hissing of boiling water, the blunt rhythm of blows with batons. Everywhere there were voices, hoarse or hissing, resounding with plaintive groans and sobs.

Through this pandemonium, René had walked without turning his head, his eyes focused on the double entrance door to the stadium, the *Puerta de la Maratón,* which was later called *the Puerta de la Muerta.* The door swung open, and the sunlight flooded in, immediately heating the linen mask around his head. René saw the seemingly endless rows of stands full of waiting prisoners.

The soldiers accompanied him to protect him from the desperate anger of the parents as he selected the children. Mothers clung, crying and moaning to their children. In the beginning, he tried to reason with them. The children would be well cared for, and later they would be reunited. Nobody believed him. After a few days, he'd learned to make his choice in silence.

Once, a father leapt from the highest stand after René walked away with his crying daughter. René turned when he heard the scream. It had sounded unintelligible, but he had known that it was a scourge, a curse that had fallen on his shoulders. The man's body crashed against the iron fences below, and René felt the shock deep in his bones. The whole stadium vibrated like a *fata morgana* while he pressed the sobbing little girl against his chest.

"The parents are terrified of me," he told Monsignor Tibeira that evening. The old bishop had cried, his tears running down his cheeks. But he didn't turn his eyes away from René for a single moment. "I am the executioner from their nightmares, coming to take their children as supreme torture."

Monsignor Tibeira had raised his hand as if to repel a blow and topped up René's wine glass: "Enough, René. Be silent now. Drink."

After signing the paperwork, René watched the children leave in military vehicles to a reception center set up by the

Church. He had felt no relief about his 'catch of the day,' as the sergeant in charge called the operation. Every day, he told himself he would not return to that hell on earth.

But he had returned until fate again showed its omnipotence. One day, he had recognized Víctor Pérez's wife, Lucía Altameda, among the rows of prisoners and stepped up to her. Whispering, he'd asked her where Víctor was. She had looked at the soldiers behind him with the eyes of a cornered animal and did not answer.

René pointed to Carmencita. He couldn't save the wife of the singer he admired so much, but he could rescue their child. Lucía nodded almost imperceptibly when he took the girl's hand. She knew what her sentence was. The eyes she cast at René caused a shiver to run down his back.

At the exit of the stadium, a blond man with pale eyes, oozing authority, stopped him and took Pérez's daughter as if she were stolen goods. Two days later, Monsignor Tibeira told him that the *junta* had withdrawn the concession for the children. *El Enmascarado* no longer had permission to enter the stadium.

René swore he would never forget the pale-eyed man. The years had refuted that oath. When he had placed the mask in his desk for the last time, he thought of Tibeira's advice: "Forget that it happened, René. Don't think of the lives you still could've saved, don't draw the line between what was good and evil, or it will cut through your heart like steel wire." What better way to forget than to plunge into his work for the inhabitants of the slum?

René picked up the phone and redialed Beatriz's number. It took a while before she answered. She didn't say her name.

"Beatriz?"

"Yes," she said. "Is it you, René?"

"Yes."

She took a deep breath: "Did you just do that?"

"Yes."

She was silent for a long time. "Why do you do something like that, René?" she said softly.

"Can I explain it to you, Beatriz?"

15

The shiny black Chevy hearse stopped in front of the castle gate. The bodyguard with the scar opened the window and said to the guard, "We have a load for the *enterrador*." The guard looked casually through the Chevrolet's rear window and saw the coffin. For some time now, Raoul used American hearses to transport his drugs through the city. Raouls's men called the operation 'driving to the undertaker'. There was little concern of military stopping such a car. After all, most Terrenean soldiers were deeply religious.

The guard nodded. The gate of the big house opened.

16

Beatriz knocked on Alejandro's door while he was telling himself time what a liar and coward he was for the umpteenth time. When Alejandro did not answer; she opened the door herself. Immediately, Alejandro's self-hatred disappeared as if he had only imagined it. In The Last Supper, Alejandro had to jump from his bed and stand to attention when a guard came into his cell. Now he jumped up just as fast; his body seemed weightless as a balloon. Beatriz noticed how pale Alejandro was and how hollow his eyes were. She feared he was drunk, but he had not touched a drop.

"Beatriz," he said. He didn't move to embrace her. He stood there perplexed, just as she did.

"Sit down," said Beatriz. "You don't look good." She remembered the evening when she first visited him, how unapproachable and indifferent he seemed at that time.

"I'm tired," she continued, sitting on the bed. She wanted to spend the night with him, feel him close to her body, nothing more. She didn't know if he would understand that.

He sat down on the chair. "João told me you took a flight." He didn't intend it to be sarcastic, but that's how it sounded.

"That's right. I've picked up explosives which the resistance wants for an act of sabotage." She said it carelessly. "Cristóbal was against it, but others pushed it through."

"That doesn't surprise me."

His reaction shocked her. She had expected a surprise.

"What do you mean?"

"That you'd do something like that. You're someone who thinks you're afraid but who acts courageously. I'm just the opposite."

She smiled, "Don't delude yourself. I've been terrified." She added bluntly, "I'm afraid for you, too."

An uncomfortable silence fell. "I thought Cristóbal was the one making the decisions," he finally said.

"The majority were in favor of an attack. There's been promise after promise from the *junta*—but they don't fulfill a single one. 'A symbolic gesture of resistance'—that's what Cristóbal calls the plan, but he's sarcastic. He thinks this action could pressure them into acting on their promises." She shook her head. "It took Cristóbal a long time to agree to it, even reluctantly, but now he's talking as if it was all his idea." Alejandro didn't answer. He looked at her as if he couldn't comprehend what she was saying.

Beatriz decided it was time to say why she had come. "It's normal that you reacted like you did in the auditorium," she said. "You shouldn't beat yourself up about it, especially after what you've been through."

Alejandro turned his head away. "You want to find everything I do normal," he answered, falsely cheerful. "I don't think that's normal!"

She smiled thinly.

"Beatriz," he continued. "Would you come with me if I left Terreno?"

"No, I wouldn't."

He laughed, but she saw how his shoulders slumped. "See? You are brave! Or is it because René loves you and João is mad about you? Do you enjoy all that attention?"

"Why do you think René loves me?"

He made a crooked face. "In a city that's world-famous for its beautiful women, our man of God has eyes for no one but you. Yearning eyes."

"Oh yeah?"

That same snigger appeared round Alejandro's mouth. "What do you think? Would I be able to leave Terreno without you?"

"Yes, Alejandro. You'd do anything to get out of here. But you're afraid that afterward, you'll no longer have the courage to face yourself."

He remained silent for a while. "I'll stay here," he said. "Stay here, and do what João asks. Playing Superbarrio." He grinned, shaking his head as if he couldn't believe it himself.

"What's wrong with it? In Mexico, the wrestlers who play Superbarrio have become truly famous. The police are afraid to arrest them, even though they ridicule the government and call on the poor to revolt. I think it's a smart idea, given that the opposition has almost no resources."

"Smart? You're just like João. Head in the clouds. You still have illusions."

"No, it is precisely because we've lost our illusions that we are coming up with ideas like this."

"You don't understand," he said, with a tone of resignation. "Aconcagua's most popular songs were the protest songs:

they divided everything into good and evil and black or white. It's not that simple. That's the illusion we've lost."

"I recall another illusion you've lost," she said.

"What do you mean by that, Beatriz?" He said it so softly that she barely heard him.

She got up and pulled him out of his chair. She felt compassion, not lust or tenderness, or anything she would call love. With his head turned away, he let her lead him to the bed.

"Undress and lie with me," she said. "And keep your mouth shut now, Alejandro."

<hr />

17

In the most profound secrecy, at regular intervals, at the military airbase El Bosque in Valtiago, Terrenean taxpayer money was used to 'transport sheep,' as the relevant army unit called it.

The 'sheep' were drugged, jute-bagged political enemies of the *junta* who had to disappear without a trace. Twenty-two sheep were on the program that night. Nowhere were they mentioned in cargo lists. The military command had decided that the program should be carried out without a single document to indicate its existence.

Manuel had influential friends at the base. It also helped that they knew how generous Manuel could be. Tonight, unexpectedly, a twenty-third sheep was added. The sheep's handling would be lucrative for the servicemen in charge of the mission.

Manuel was on board the Lockheed C-130 when it lifted itself, roaring and vibrating from the runway. Death-row convicts packed the floor of the cargo aircraft. Manuel looked at the sausage-like shape at his feet. The other sheep lay still, not this one. It wriggled like a giant worm across the floor.

When, sometime later, the plane flew over the sea, the soldiers leapt into action. The sheep were thrown out of the hold one by one. They offered no resistance. They tumbled witlessly through the dark, to their watery deaths, hundreds of meters below the plane. As each of them hit the water's surface, the soldiers saw a white spot appear on the midnight grey of the ocean. Manuel pulled Raoul's head out of the jute bag. The man snarled like a desperate cat. The whip had terribly damaged his beauty.

"*Cara Ancha*," said Manuel, "Your lack of discretion put me in mortal danger, so no nightcap for you to soften your last journey." He kept his head close to Raoul. He wanted to be understood above the droning engines. "Every centimeter of your fall to oblivion, you'll be wishing you'd managed to hold your tongue, frog-mouth."

Manuel looked into the eyes of the man who'd helped him earn a fortune. They were blacker than ever and seemed deeper than the sea.

Raoul spat Manuel in the face.

A little later, Raoul tumbled out of the plane.

In the plane, Manuel felt as if it was not Raoul, but himself who hit the water's dark surface with a bone-breaking blast.

18

Beatriz woke up in the middle of the night. Listening to Alejandro's breathing, she got the feeling that his eyes were open. She wanted to tell him about the miserable sex with René, about his muffled voice in the phone saying disgusting things just to hurt, and then about the second conversation in which Lafarge had talked to her as if the phone were his life-line. Beatriz wanted to tell Alejandro that, just like René, he had to face his self-delusion.

She turned around. Alejandro lay on his back. Beatriz wondered what he would do if she told him about René. The memory of being in bed with the priest disturbed her, and she wanted to get up. But Alejandro turned on his side and embraced her. He pressed his head against her shoulder. Her heart was beating fast as if she wanted to flee, but she took a deep breath and caressed his chest.

"Why don't you say anything?" she whispered after a while.

It took him a while to answer, "In The Last Supper, I learned to be thankful for the slightest thing the guards permitted me. As long as you care about me, I'll accept that with gratitude, Beatriz, and for the rest, I'll leave you free."

She felt herself becoming languid as if her muscles lost their tension. Alejandro wrapped his arms around her.

"You're a weird prison customer," she said with a small laugh. "What must I give you to get some gratitude?"

"You could make love to me."

It took her a long time, but then she gently pinched his back. "Okay," she said.

He hid his face in her neck, resting his lips on her skin. "If I were to stay in this country," he whispered, "If I could over-come all my doubts and contradictions and engage myself again, would you stay with me? If I could go back to the man I used to be?"

She did not answer, and he stayed with his head where it was, his body close to her, a warm no man's land demanding nothing more. That's how René should have been; why hadn't René been like that, a father figure who loved her?

The Two Faces Of A Man

1

"WHAT DO YOU THINK OF THE ARENA I BUILT FOR OUR sensational Superbarrio show?" said João with a wide grin. "Lightweight stuff. We can put it together in no time, and we only need a small space."

It was sultry hot in the concrete basement of the Instituto de Extensíon Musical where Terrenean dancers could practice European ballets when the *junta* remembered that culture was an excellent façade.

"Marvelous," said Alejandro absently. He showed very little interest in the painted canvas floor. He looked around the room and smiled faintly at Beatriz, who stood watching by the door.

When he had woken that morning, his genitals had been resting in her palm. He had caressed her belly, his fingers following the muscles under her skin. But he had not grown in the relaxed shell of her hand. His body felt as if it were float-ing, and a sweet laxness penetrated all his muscles. He didn't know how long he had been there, lying there with her and yet alone. Her voice, muted and strangely shy, had reminded him that they had to leave for their appointment with João, who wanted to rehearse the Superbarrio show.

João looked impressive in his blue wrestling suit that made his muscular buttocks stand out. "You're standing there in the corner with Pelarón, singing and poking the dragon," he said as he jumped over the ropes of the ring and hopped nimbly on the springy canvas. "I'm storming wildly towards you because I love Pelarón, and we start fighting. Shall we try that for a moment?"

Alejandro grabbed his guitar, crawled under the ropes, and winked at Beatriz. He started playing a rhythmic tune. He hadn't invented the words in advance; they just poured out of his mouth:

> *Jo, Jo, Superbarrio,*
> *Pelarón earns a lot of bucks,*
> *But any fool can do that, Chucks.*
> *Hey, Hey, Superbarrio,*
> *Pelarón has a belly*
> *like a horny hatch!*
> *He's so ugly,*
> *What a batch!*

From the corners of his eyes, Alejandro saw João approaching. "How dare you to insult our Generalissimo, dried-up earthworm!" João roared. Alejandro hardly had time to drop his guitar. João grabbed him by the waist; Alejandro took a breathtaking swing from João's right shoulder to his own and ended with a bump, flat out on the canvas. Squealing, Alejandro turned on his belly. His eyes stared straight into those of Beatriz. He tried to look dog faithful, but that didn't work out so well in this situation, mainly because that silly tune started to play through his head again.

> *Oh, my love, what does it hurt*

to be someone else for you.

Grinning, he blew her a kiss, but her gaze remained severe as if she were registering an important meeting.

"First lesson," said João pleasantly. "When I throw you on the canvas, you have to breathe out when you fall. Maybe you thought this was hard, but I've broken your fall quite a bit, and you're already groaning like an old drunk with a hangover. You look like a flagpole; that's how stiff you are. Remember: I'll have to throw you a lot of times. You have to look exhausted before you unexpectedly get me back. And then you still have to be able to sing your final song, the Victory song."

"Yes, yes," sighed Alejandro. "And what comes after that? Are we bowing and curtseying for the flash of the photographers and the cameras of the international television teams?"

"After that, we run away like lightning before the cops catch us," said João laconically as he sat on Alejandro's back and administered a lock to his right arm.

"A bit gentler, *por favor*, João?" groaned Alejandro.

"Come now! You're Superbarrio for a reason, aren't you?" João threw himself on Alejandro and almost squashed him under his weight. He enthusiastically started strangling Alejandro, screaming: "Dog dirt, you're not even good enough to lick the toilets clean in The Last Supper!"

His eyes stared ferociously in Alejandro's. Alejandro blinked and hit João with his knee in his balls.

I know why you show off your masculinity like that, João, but you won't have her. Not my nervous deer who loves to have her back massaged with short circles between the third and fourth vertebra at the top, the woman I just can't love enough but whom I can't hand over to anyone else either.

João groaned and let go of Alejandro to take care of his crown jewels.

"Why did you do that?" said Beatriz.

"Playing Superbarrio?" answered Alejandro innocently, making a few billy goat leaps in João's direction. "Because in this ridiculous getup, I can believe that I'm funny, Beatriz."

Of course, he knew she had asked something else, but he acted as if he'd misunderstood her. Was it possible that the look in her eyes betrayed something more than doubt?

———

2

Belgium no longer had a consulate in Terreno. The Belgian *Chargé d'Affaires* performed all consular tasks on the 17th floor of a building on Avenida General Pelarón. In the elevator to the top, René noticed the double security doors. He got out in a small area with an armored door and a counter with safety glass next to it. Behind the glass, a disinterested man watched him; his face was weathered like a sailor's.

"What is the reason for your visit?" the man asked bluntly in French. René told him that he wanted to speak to the Belgian Chargé d'Affaires.

"Your passport." René put his passport in a wall slot and saw it disappear. A little later, the slot unloaded a document on which he had to fill in the reason for his visit. After a quarter of an hour waiting, the armored door slid open, and the man beckoned him. Silently, he led René through the brightly lit office space.

The first secretary of the Chargé d'Affaires, well dressed in a suit and still young, sat behind a large desk in a solemnly decorated room, dominated by the portrait of the Belgian King Baudouin. The secretary casually loosened his tie. What a difference compared to the redheaded consul with the walrus mustache who opened the Belgian consulate for refugees ten years ago, without paying attention to political pressure, or direct threats. The Belgian government transferred the consul immediately when the *junta* was firmly in power. The Chargé d'Affaires who arrived soon after had 'excellent' contacts with the government and was convinced that democracy would return to Terreno when the time was right.

When René finished talking, the assistant said, "Of course, we will give you all the help that a compatriot deserves, Father. But in the light of developments in this country, I'm sure we can regard this threat as a joke. Nevertheless, we'll ask for an explanation through diplomatic channels. Meanwhile, I don't think that you have anything to fear. The military government is well aware that an extremist attack on a Belgian priest would be extremely ill-advised at the moment."

The man smiled, charmingly, at René. "If you like, you can, of course, leave the country. You can use the channels of the Church or get an airplane ticket from us. However, you'll have to repay it when you're back in Belgium. I am—please forgive me—not well informed of the Church's hierarchical channels. Perhaps our services work faster. The choice is yours."

"You're probably right," said René. "It's unlikely that things will change so fast. And it's hard for me to abandon my parishioners."

The secretary stood up and offered René a hand. "In any case, keep us informed if you receive any new threats. For our part, we'll take the necessary steps and will contact you in due course."

At the door, the priest turned around. A new dossier already had the first secretary's full attention. "One more thing," said René. "If something happens to me, will your services warn my family in Belgium?"

"Father," the secretary began, "We are convinced that..."

"In that case, be sure to write a letter to Gui Lafarge," said René. "The address is Rue de la Marcinelle 19, 6000

Charleroi. At least, that was it more than thirty years ago, but I'm sure that my brother hasn't moved in the meantime."

3

"*Rómpete una pierna*," said João to Alejandro, who stood in front of the mirror wall of the dance hall and peered at the bold **SUPERBARRIO** letters on his red tights. "That's how actors say it, right?"

"For a premiere, not a dress rehearsal," said Alejandro. "And you should say it in English. That's where the saying came from: *break a leg*."

"It was ingenious of Cristóbal to let us train here in the cellars of the university," João continued, putting on a testicle protector. "For three days, we've been working right under the soldiers' noses."

João looked at himself in the mirrors, waddling around like a bear. "I am ugly, but I am big, and I have countless dollars!" he roared. "Viva America!" He nodded to himself. "Tomorrow is the day. I'm going ballistic with mirth. Isn't that spoken like a true poet, singer-songwriter?"

"Are you sure, João, that your ukulele, or what's his name, that Voodoo demon you told me about, didn't whisper this crazy plan into your ears?" Alejandro asked as he came to stand next to João. Beside the giant painter, he looked like a skimpy little fellow in a fake Superman suit. João grinned at him in the mirror, and Alejandro involuntarily smiled too.

"Don't laugh at Exu Tiriri," said João. "The deity deliberately chose a foolish name which everyone laughs at so he can better conceal his power. Among other things, he's given me healing hands. When the day before yesterday you so shamelessly punched my balls..."

"An accident, João, an unfortunate accident."

"The pain was over immediately once I embraced my jewels with my healing hands, you little nitpicker."

"Your glee, João, is it incurable?"

Alejandro was surprised by the change in the painter's face. "You think my joy is real, but that's because I play it so often that it becomes real. Yesterday: the protest of the dock workers in Coquimba—how many dead, Alejandro?"

Alejandro cast João a sideways glance, full of speculations about his friend's true state of mind. "More than three hundred."

The day before, the army had brutally suppressed a demonstration of Coquimba's dockworkers. They demanded better working conditions. A government announcement on radio, television, and government-loyal newspapers had spoken of an "intolerable disruption of the Terrenean economy that was nipped in the bud."

"More than three hundred dead," João repeated. "And with what do we counter this slaughter? With a street show of two masked buffoons. In the face of our impotence, I only have my smile. And I will continue to smile until..."

The door of the dance hall swung open. Cristóbal, René, and Beatriz came in. Alejandro crossed his hands over his bright red torso.

"No audience at a dress rehearsal. That brings misfortune, and we already have more than..."

"I have to ask you something." René cut him off. The priest looked like he hadn't slept or eaten properly in days. "Would you recognize the daughter of Víctor Pérez if you saw her?"

Alejandro's left hand sank away from his chest; the other hand remained on his heart, exactly where the B was located.

———

4

When he'd stopped talking about his new plan and waited for the opinion of his table companion, Manuel persuaded himself that he looked distinguished in his blue suit, cream shirt, and blue and white striped tie. He had carefully chosen a hotel bar in one of Valtiago's most expensive streets, the Avenida Timparán. Chez Pierre, with its Italian marble, etched mirrors, and baroque murals, reminded visitors of a neoclassical French château.

Across the table, Astíz pursed his lips and looked at him expressionlessly. "An audacious plan, Manuel. I can tell that you have read *Il Principe* well."

Since he had left G2, the Terrenean secret service, with a generous allowance and the rank of colonel, Astíz did everything he could to adopt an intellectual air.

Manuel smiled and declared, "After a small injury, a person avenges himself; after a major one, he can't. That is why we must punish people so harshly that we no longer have to fear their revenge."

"Right," Astíz said. He took a sip of his ginger blossom tea and nibbled on an English biscuit. Manuel drank his cocktail. He had hoped for more enthusiasm from the colonel. The older man opposite him seemed absent-minded. Where was the sharp voice from a few days ago that questioned him over the phone about the drug leak? You never knew what to expect from Astíz. Manuel had never found out whether this unpredictability was all part of his image or simply part of his character.

"If general Pelarón implements my plan, he'll have the opportunity to wipe the opposition off the map."

Colonel Astíz still didn't seem to be focusing on the conversation. "You have come to the wrong person with your plan. I'm retired. I've done my duty for my country; I have a quiet old age to enjoy." The man looked out the window at the British-style gardens.

Manuel tried to hide his disappointment. *That's easy for you to say, with the strings of Patria y Sangre tightly in your hands, with all your high-ranking friends in the army.* He straightened his back, drank from his glass. *I may be the leader of Patria y Sangre in name, but you wield the real power, and I am your puppet.*

"Of course, you would lead the whole operation," said Manuel in honeyed tones. "You did think it was a good idea to spread the rumor that the Belgian priest was involved in a plot against Pelarón, didn't you?"

Astíz wiped his hands on the napkin adorned with Chez Pierre's excessively curly monogram. "Making the priest an object of suspicion: yes. Scattering rumors about him to stop him getting in our way: okay, fine. But with the scheme you're proposing now, you're getting above yourself. You hate that priest because he helped your wife divorce you - that's why you've got this overblown plan up your sleeve."

"My plan is watertight!" Manuel protested. "We inform several senior officers who want nothing less than hard measures, and…".

"We?" Astíz interrupted him. He no longer had the air of an absent-minded professor. The eyes that looked at Manuel had the color of the salt lakes in the Andes deserts.

"I mean… You have so many contacts and…"

"You're too ambitious, Durango; that's your problem."

As Astíz placed his napkin carefully on the table, Manuel had the feeling that the man's eyes were looking through him. "I asked you to find the leak in Patria y Sangre as soon as possible. I have a special surprise in store for the traitor who has tampered with the supplies of drugs. What did I tell you during our last conversation?"

"That you expected quick results," Manuel replied sluggishly.

He didn't dare look Astíz in the eye. He concentrated on the man's eyebrows.

They rose, slowly and meaningfully.

5

"I can't believe it," said Cristóbal after René had told them about his role in the stadium.

"Why not?" Pereira had become agitated during René's story.

"The Terrenean army is modeled on the Prussian one," said Cristóbal, somewhat condescendingly. "No Terrenean officer would raise the child of one of his victims as his own. Such a child can never be a member of the clan. It's inconceivable."

"The man who did it was not an ordinary officer," replied René. "At least, he wasn't in uniform, although the others called him captain. I think he belonged to the Special Forces."

"I can't believe such a thing could happen," Cristóbal repeated.

The priest turned to him: "You believe I'm behind some crazy assassination plot against Pelarón, but this you don't believe?"

Cristóbal coughed, marking the priest's indiscretion. "Rumors in this country are like time bombs. The rumors that surround you can endanger our resistance network."

Alejandro observed Beatriz. He saw how attentively she looked at both men. Unexpectedly, he became aware of a possibility. If Carmencita was still alive, it would be an unmistakable sign of fate.

"If what you claim is true," he said to René, "We should kidnap Carmencita and show her to the foreign press as an example of what the Terrenean army is capable of."

Cristóbal shook his head as if someone had made him a low offer.

"This is not the time to make jokes."

"I am glad you said that," said Alejandro. "Since I joined your whacky plan to play Superbarrio, I can't remember what's funny and what isn't."

"Alejandro is right," João intervened. "How long have we discussed ways of weakening the regime from the inside? If Carmencita Pérez is still alive, we can spread that story. It will strike like a bomb."

"I think it's an insane plan," Cristóbal coughed again. He turned to Beatriz. "And you?"

Her eyes were on Cristóbal, but Alejandro felt that her answer was meant for him. "I believe we should think about it."

"I'm surrounded by frenzied fanatics," said Cristóbal with a dramatic arm swing. "This is a very different order of things from giving street shows in carnival suits, encouraging people to make their voices heard."

"That's right," João said dryly.

"How do we find out if I'm right?" René Lafarge sat on one of the wooden benches against the wall. "During the *peña*, I was overwhelmed by the certainty that Fitzroy's daughter was Carmencita Pérez, but since then, I have been unsure. Pérez's daughter was still very young when I tried to save her. I didn't recognize Kurt Fitzroy. If he was that secret service officer, he's changed a lot."

"I'll know if it's her when I see her," said Alejandro. "But if that girl is Carmencita Pérez, I don't understand why Kurt Fitzroy took her to the *peña*. I could have recognized her there, couldn't I?"

"He didn't know you were going to perform," said René, wearily. "He was shocked when Cristóbal told him you were going to do an unannounced performance. After that, he talked to me. Of course, he doesn't know that I was El Enmascarado of the stadium. He'd already sent the girl home, supposedly because the atmosphere wasn't appropriate for a bourgeois child. He pretended I had stirred you up to perform again. I think that was his way of putting me under pressure."

"Kurt does that with everyone," Cristóbal said. "He likes confusion around him, a little thrill, a whiff of fear. Don't underestimate him."

"We can break into his house and take her with us if she really *is* Carmencita Pérez," said João. He turned to Cristóbal: "Afterwards, you could contact foreign journalists."

"You don't know what you're talking about," said Cristóbal, shaking his head.

"I sure do. Yesterday in Coquimba, more than three hundred people were slaughtered because they wanted a better life. That's what we're talking about. Kurt won't tell the police or the army if we kidnap Carmencita—assuming the girl *is* Carmencita. No one in the army or the *carabineros* would help him. By adopting that child, he tarnished the honor of the Terrenean army and put the reputation of the government at grave risk."

Cristóbal shook his head but refrained from commenting.

"Where does he live?" Alejandro asked René.

"Close to the park next to the Cerro Santa Lucia," replied the priest. "His caretaker lives in a janitor's house at the entrance of his grounds."

"I'm not thirty anymore, but I can still handle a caretaker," said João with an edge of bitterness.

"What's the matter with you, all of a sudden?" Cristóbal said vehemently.

The big man took one step forward, Cristóbal one step backward. "For years, I have listened to you. *Violence doesn't solve anything; diplomacy does.* And so, what have we done all these years? Falsified some passports, smuggled a few people out of the country, distributed leaflets, talked and argued, stewed and nagged. After ten years, a woman has pulled the chestnuts out of the fire for us: we now have explosives. Are we going to blow up the general as we should? No, we're going to commit a 'symbolic act of resistance.'"

João shook his head as if he couldn't believe what he was saying.

"The terrible thing is that we have come to think that our petty plans are examples of heroic resistance," João continued. "The day before yesterday, they murdered the dock workers, and this afternoon, Pelarón reports on television, without a word about the victims, that the government has reduced the prices of staple foodstuffs. We're so well trained that we welcome that communication. If we don't wake up now, we'll end up without a drop of blood in our veins."

In the silence that followed, João looked at them one by one. "We're not just dealing with the murder and manslaughter of civilians by the military. It goes beyond that: one of the murderers of the parents claimed a child for himself. What kind of resonance will that story have if we can get it out into the foreign press?"

"I can make an appointment with Kurt and smuggle you into his place," said René matter-of-factly.

"Into his home?" Alejandro asked.

René turned his gaze up from the floor. He smiled bitterly: "He'll like it when the fly comes to the web."

"Why do you say that?" said Cristóbal.

"Because I think he's one of the people behind the rumors about me. I've listened to the elderly people in the pigsty. Behind the scenes, the quarter's drug traffic is a major source of income for certain individuals in this government. I suspect Kurt is one of those people."

Alejandro grabbed the carnival mask he'd wanted to wear the following day as Superbarrio. "You're not the only one who can put on a mask," he said to René. "If you can make an appointment, João and I can hide in your car and sneak into his house."

Beatriz shook her head: "If Kurt is who you believe him to be, he can bring in private militias when you've kidnapped the girl. They're worse than the army."

"I've spoken to the staff of the Belgian Chargé d'Affaires," said René. "I can take refuge in the consulate at any time. Then they'll send me home." For a moment, Beatriz and the priest looked each other in the eye. Alejandro had the feeling that they were somehow complicit.

"Do you want to leave Terreno?" he said.

René cast an inscrutable glance at him. "It's time I left this country."

"It's settled then," said Alejandro. He put on his Superbarrio mask and looked at himself in the mirror wall.

"Viva Superbarrio," he muttered.

He turned around when he felt the eyes of the others on his back.

———

6

The driveway to Kurt's house was dozens of meters long and covered with mosaic cobblestones.

"I'll advise the caretaker that you're coming," Kurt had said on the phone that morning. And what gave him the honor of receiving René Lafarge in his house? Well, René had something to discuss with Kurt, and could his lovely daughter also be present at the conversation? *My daughter?* Yes, Kurt, in the light of the relief efforts for the needy in the *porqueriza*, I have an idea whereby young people from good families can play an important role. The press will undoubtedly pay a great deal of attention to the initiative. I want to ask Amanda's help with my plan; she seems very intelligent for her age.

"Why, especially, Amanda, René?"

"Monsignor Subercaseaux recommended you and your daughter to me when I proposed my idea to him."

After that, Kurt had sounded less suspicious. René was allowed to visit the same day just after noon. René hoped that Kurt would not contact Monsignor Subercaseaux in the meantime.

The caretaker, a small man with sparse hair shining with brilliantine, let the priest through the wrought-iron gate. He checked René's identity but didn't look into the priest's Citroën Mehari.

Another fifty meters. René looked into the rear-view mirror. The guard had disappeared into his house. Fitzroy's spacious house was surrounded by expensive weeping willows, like those planted in the nearby El Melocotón nature reserve. The house was white and in the Spanish colonial style, with Moorish accents. Next to it, on the clipped lawn, stood a large parabolic antenna.

"How's it going in the back?" asked René.

From the rear of the Citroën, a muted voice muttered, "Alejandro's shoving his big toe into my left eye." René shook his head. He turned off the engine in a parking lot marked with white stones, got out, and walked to the front door. A maid opened it. When René said his name, she nodded and took him to a room decorated in vulgar American taste.

"René, I didn't think I'd ever see you in my home," said Fitzroy, who'd come in behind him. Kurt stood in the doorway, his arm slightly bent in front of his chest, the wrist limp —an aging gentleman, tastefully dressed and a little tired.

"Why not?"

"Oh," said Kurt. "A premonition that's no longer important."

"Where's your daughter?" René asked.

Kurt pursed his lips. "I don't remember you finding her so interesting two days ago. Why are you so nervous, my friend? She'll be here in a minute."

"I've been receiving threatening calls lately," René said. "That's why I'm not quite my normal self."

"Is someone threatening you?" Kurt sat in an opulently floral armchair. "That doesn't surprise me. Thanks to your excellent work in the *porqueriza*, you have many enemies in this city, old chap. How seriously do you take the threats?"

"Very seriously," said René. "I am not cut from the right cloth to play the sacrificial lamb. And there's another thing: a rumor is spreading that I'm involved in an upcoming attack on Pelarón. Can it get any more ridiculous?"

Kurt laughed. "Who makes up such stories?"

"Yes, who?" said René, feeling a tingle down his spine.

"I thought you came to tell me about your bold plan for the *porqueriza* – something involving youngsters from the better families?"

René did not answer him.

For a moment, the conversation paused.

Kurt looked at him quizzically as if worried that he might have caused offense.

Then René took from his pocket the mask he had worn ten years ago. "Do you recognize this, Kurt?"

"That cloth?" Kurt put his right hand under his chin. "Why should I recognize it?"

"I'll refresh your memory," René replied with a dry mouth, ignoring the inner warning: *too early, you fool!* He put on the mask.

Kurt rose from his armchair. The door was thrown open, and two grotesquely dressed figures ran inside. The first, a large man in a bright red wrestling suit, on which was written in brilliant blue letters: I AM UGLY, BUT I GOT LOTS OF DOLLARS, pointed a pistol at Fitzroy. The second, in a clattering blue suit with SUPERBARRIO in glossy letters, saw René's black mask and stopped in his tracks.

"Don't move, either of you," said João.

Alejandro slipped out of his role. "What are you doing?" he spat at René.

"That's not important," replied René. "We have to find Carmencita."

"Not important?" shouted Alejandro. "You idiot! We...."

"What's the meaning of this?" Kurt intervened, more angry than afraid. The man looked at the door and assessed his chances.

"You're daft," hissed Alejandro to René. "Do you want to play some angel of doom, you idiot?"

The door swung open for the second time, and a skinny teenage girl came in, wearing her oil-black hair in a bun.

She took two steps into the room and then stood still in surprise.

"Amanda!" called Kurt. "Run!"

João pushed Kurt violently. Kurt fell against a sofa and tumbled backward. Alejandro darted towards the door, pushed it shut, turned the key around, leaned his back against it.

"Carmencita," he panted. "Carmencita, do you remember me?"

The girl stared at the masked man in a SUPERBARRIO wrestling suit in front of her, brought her hand to her mouth, and screamed.

———

7

Beatriz woke up from a dream in which a slate grey wall kept blocking her way. The wall had seemed alive. She kept staring at the ceiling, her body a lump of lead. In this country, where executioners wished to play fathers, she had remained child-less. In her daydreams, she often imagined what it would be like to have a child. Salmon-pink romantic nonsense, she'd known that perfectly well because she'd recognized the reality: if her womb had been fertile, who would have been the father?

Cristóbal? Two years ago, at the start of her divorce, he'd behaved like a gallant father, the diplomat who didn't want to risk being turned down. He had immediately retreated when João began to court her in his boyish way. A baby with João then? A large baby with surprisingly light eyes, full of health and optimism? There was something animalistic in that idea that disturbed her. From Alejandro? Alejandro was weary of life and only cared about his music, which had to justify him. Her contemplation always ended in the same way: René then? And the sweet, cherished pain she felt thinking about him.

I am crazy, she thought, but nobody notices it. In Terreno, it is the most normal thing in the world.

In her opinion, it was indeed like that: reality in Terreno was not normal. She seemed to have understood that quicker than the men. João had woken up, but Cristóbal still clung to his utopias. A little while ago, when Cristóbal was driving her home, he'd said, "At this moment, we're more in danger than we've been for the past ten years. When the *junta* ruled with an iron fist, we knew what to expect. Now, chaos can erupt at any moment." She didn't ask him why, then, he had agreed to the planned act of sabotage.

She suspected Cristóbal made concessions to the militant groups in the resistance to maintain his leadership position. Despite his intelligence, Cristóbal stubbornly believed in an ideology that tried to bury the present under plans for the future. The hundreds of thousands in the pigsty remained indifferent to this ideology: Cristóbal's message of hope drowned in a pool of desolation. Hundreds of thousands of people were getting more restless by the minute: Cristóbal did not understand their hopelessness; for him, every person was just a statistic.

Beatriz shook her head, stretched her legs, and shuddered.

The phone rang; she rolled on her side and picked up the receiver.

It was the director of the university hospital who told her that her father had unexpectedly died of a brain lesion.

Although she answered dispassionately, Beatriz saw the image of the grey wall in front of her again. She ended the conversation and stayed lying on her side. *Daddy, may I have a dog? I so much want a dog. Of course, sweetie, you can ask me the world if you always stay daddy's dearest and nicest girl.*

She hadn't stayed daddy's dearest and nicest girl, and his love had degenerated into self-serving generosity. She felt malevolence. Over the last year, she should have hated him more fervently than ever before, but she had not done so. She'd needed his money too much. She knew she wouldn't inherit his fortune now: others would manage his trading empire, and she'd get nothing but a meager allowance.

Guantanamera. He had hummed that song long ago, the day he rubbed brilliantine in his hair in front of the mirror, looking smart in his suit, young and energetic and cheerful. He had lifted her and held his face next to her in the mirror. *Guantanamera, sing with me, Beatriz, you will be the richest girl in Terreno, a fairytale princess.*

Despite everything that had happened between them, it seemed as if she'd lost a protector in a country where every shield against doom was critical.

———

8

Colonel Kurt Fitzroy scrambled up. "Amanda!" he cried.

"Run! " He plunged forward to free the girl.

"Damn!" said João. He lowered his gun and kicked Kurt against his breastbone. The man fell again.

For Alejandro, what happened in the room looked like a

puppet show delivered by a drunken puppeteer. The girl jumped at him, trying to push him aside. He grabbed her left arm and ignored the slaps she gave him with her free hand. On her left shoulder, he saw the little mole in the shape of a mouse.

"It's her," cried Alejandro. "Carmencita!" He wanted to take off his mask so the girl would recognize him, but René stopped him.

"Don't," said the priest, with a nod to Kurt, who was trying to get up. Then he called out to João, using the stage name they had come up with for him a few days earlier. "*Generalissimo*! Come with us!"

The painter struggled with Kurt, who clung to him with all his strength. Finally, for the third time, João pushed Kurt backward, pointing his gun at his head.

"I'll finish him off," he snarled.

"No," said René. "Not that. We have to get her out..."

"Daddy!" Carmencita screamed again, a cry of pure panic that surprised the three men. Crying, she struggled fiercely in Alejandro's arms.

João looked aside. Kurt was standing still, his mouth half-open, his grey blond beard smeared with stripes of blood. João lowered the gun to chest level.

"To the car," he said.

René helped Alejandro with the fighting girl. With two quick steps, João stood in front of Kurt. His fist shot forward. Kurt collapsed.

Alejandro fiddled with the door key. João pushed him aside. The giant pounded his shoulder against the door; it flew open with a bang.

"Give her to me," João said to Alejandro. In one movement, he swung the girl over his shoulder. They ran through the corridor. The maid and a dark man in an overall came out of the kitchen, but when they saw the three masked men running towards the hall, they retreated with their hands over their heads. René opened the front door. They ran to the Mehari. João pushed the wailing girl next to him in the front, and René squeezed himself beside her on the driver's side. Alejandro crawled in the back. René started the car and put his foot down too brusquely; the engine stalled. "Start this fucking wreck, you buffoon," João snarled. René glanced at him in shock and restarted the car. The Mehari came to life. As they drove down the driveway, Alejandro looked back. Even before they reached the bend, Kurt came running out through the open front door.

"Amanda!" he cried.

"Daddy!" screamed the girl. João pushed her roughly. She shut up.

Alejandro couldn't keep his eyes off the man who was staring after the Mehari, his arms lying limp along his body. *She loves him*, he thought, *and he loves her.*

"René," said João, "Why the hell did you put on your mask in front of Kurt?"

"The gate," René interrupted, snapping his gearstick down when the Mehari swayed dangerously around the corner. "What do we do at the fence?"

The girl sat gasping with her hands in front of her eyes between them.

"The caretaker is armed," said Alejandro.

"Drive on," said João. "Run him over if necessary."

"This is a Citroën," said René without turning his eyes off the road. "Not a tank."

The caretaker's cabin came in sight.

"Duck!" René said. With his left hand, he pulled off his mask. João put his hand on the back of Carmencita's head and pressed it down. The big man let himself sink as close as he could to the bottom of the car.

René honked from a distance as the caretaker had told him to do. If Kurt managed to call him, they had to prepare for the worst.

The man came out of his house and walked to the fence. The automatic gate swung open. There was still quite a distance between the Mehari and the fence: someone who was not very suspicious might not notice the extra people in the car. When he got closer, René suddenly gave full throttle, cursing the Mehari's weak engine. The caretaker stared as the car approached at full speed and he jumped aside.

"We made it," said René, sending the old car into the street with its tires screaming.

"No, we didn't make it," said João, who sat straight and pulled up the girl. "What's gotten into you, René? If this is Carmencita, Kurt was the stadium's main executioner. And in front of such a guy, you gave away that you were *El Enmascarado*? Now Kurt will have you arrested. Then all he has to do is look for us in your circle of acquaintances."

"It was an insane plan from the beginning," said Alejandro. "Did you hear how Kurt called for her, René? He lov-"

"I heard it," the priest interrupted him, his hands white-knuckled around the steering wheel. He glanced at João. "I'll make sure I don't betray you, trust me," he said. João shook his head and looked outside.

"I should've shot him," the painter said. His hand stroked his ludicrous carnival mask. "Damn it," he continued. "It's so difficult to shoot a man, even someone like him."

A Fire In The Heart

1

BEATRIZ WAITED FOR THEM AT THE FOOT OF THE FIFTEEN-meter-high statue of Mary dominating Valtiago. René braked when he saw her car but let the engine run. João got out and held the girl by her arm. She went with him with her head down. Beatriz took a few steps forward and put a hand on João's arm. João reluctantly stepped back. Silently, Beatriz embraced the girl. Alejandro saw Carmencita supported limply in her arms, her eyes full of fear and confusion.

"We did a fantastic job," said João bitterly. "Especially our padre here, who pulled a stunt."

"What happened?" said Beatriz, still holding the child.

"Nothing special," said Alejandro. "Just the normal crazy run of things. Want to hear a good one? Kurt loves her. And she *is* Carmencita, I know for sure. Carmencita had a small mole on her left shoulder, roughly in the shape of a mouse." He nodded towards the girl. Beatriz looked at the left shoulder. Alejandro wanted to scratch his head; his hand slipped over his carnival mask.

"Let's not forget we did a good job," João intervened, irritated. "The journalists will go crazy for this. No one loses any sleep these days about the *pau de arara*, electric shocks, unlawful executions… But this!" He crossed his arms in front of his chest. "An executioner who raises the child of his victim as a loving father would do." In the light of the monument and the glitter of the city below them, his patrician mask made him look like a demon from the Roman theatre.

René stepped out of the car and stood a few meters away from them like a spectator at a street fight. Alejandro frowned when he saw that the priest had put on his black mask again.

"What's wrong with you?" asked Beatriz. She looked at René as if he were a stranger. She let go of Carmencita. João grabbed the girl by the arm. "Yes, what is wrong with you, Lafarge?" he said. "Why did you put on that stupid mask? And what are you looking at now, Mr. Horrorshow?"

"What happened?" said Beatriz.

"Let me guess," Alejandro intervened. "You did it because you wanted to force yourself to leave Terreno, didn't you, René? You wanted to make sure that you have to leave."

René nodded. His smooth black mask and dark suit made him a shadow.

"Yes," he said quietly. "That's it, Alejandro. I wanted to force myself to leave Terreno."

"And how are you going to do that?" said João scornfully. "I bet that at this very moment, Kurt is drumming up a death squad for you."

Beatriz went closer to the priest. René took a step backward. "I've arranged everything," he said in that same flat tone. "Tonight I stay with a friend, and tomorrow I will be safe with the Belgian Chargé d'Affaires. Tomorrow evening, I'll be on a plane."

"Why did you do it, René?" asked Beatriz, who was now close to him.

She plucked at the fabric of René's mask as if she wanted to wipe away some dust.

"To show myself as I am," said René. "Finally."

"What do you mean?"

The priest seemed to falter for a moment, as if a strong wind from the mountains hit him, then he turned around and stepped into his car.

"René!" Beatriz shouted. The Mehari drove a few meters back, turned, and headed full speed to Valtiago.

"He's crazy," said João. "He's put us in great danger."

"João," said Beatriz. "Do you still believe that everything is so black or white?"

―――――

2

They shouldn't find my letters to you, Gui. They would love to declare me a lunatic, my prelates, the junta, the press.

When he had entered his house, René locked all the doors on his way to his study. In the room, he hadn't switched on the light. Through the window shone the glow of Valtiago at night. It was enough for what he came to do.

René stood obliquely in front of the window and watched the dark slum on the other side of the river.

What a clear night it was: the clouds were like soapy water against the dark mass of mountains. To his left lay the city, with its whimsical strings of light reflecting in the midnight blue of the Mayu River. In the distance, he saw the skyscraper of International Copper Mines, the square in front of it lit like a football stadium.

To his right was the almost endless darkness of the *porqueriza*, pierced here and there, like leaking wounds, with dots of light. The priest shook his head.

Maybe I always knew I would end up like you, Gui. Don't ask me why. I don't know. I should say it's the hand of God, according to the rules of the profession I have practiced for so long.

"Fweet," said a nasal voice behind him. René turned around. The parrot's eyes gleamed hypnotically. The bird looked sternly at René for a while before taking a few perky steps over René's desk. Head tilted, he looked at René again. René knelt in front of his desk. Slowly his hand came up. The parrot's beak opened, his eyes fixed steadily on René. René's fingers gently stroked the bird's head: so surprisingly soft, those thick feathers.

"*Cojónes*," whispered René. "Do you remember? If you want to be polite, it is *cojónes*, not *los huevos*." The bird winked at him. René got up. The parrot flapped away and landed on a chair; the priest opened the window. The parrot flew to the window sill and looked outside with his intense gaze.

"*Cojónes!*" he squawked suddenly. He opened his wings and flew out of the window. René looked at the flying shape, quickly becoming smaller when starlight met the city's lights. He took the letters he had written to his dead brother over the past years and bound them together. Lafarge unlocked the doors leading outside. He pulled the outside door ajar and looked down the street in both directions before stepping out. The priest walked toward the river. Across the Mayu lay the railway yard, a deserted and ugly place. In front of him, the dark water was splashing.

Just like you, I never learned to swim, Gui. That, too, must be the hand of God.

René weighed the letters in his hand. Through the years, they had become a thick and heavy pack. With measured movements, he tied it with a rope around his neck.

He was not lonely when he walked into the surprisingly cold water. Voices surrounded him. Images flashed brightly within him. Ghosts from his youth were all he heard and saw as if his adult life had made no impression on him. René walked without hesitation until the water was at his lips and the weight of his clothes and letters pulled him down, his hands folded in front of his chest.

Until the last moment, he waited for the glow of God: this time, it was not allowed to come from himself, but really, really from....

———

3

"I want to go home."

"I told you why that isn't possible for the time being, Carmencita."

"My name is Amanda!"

"You know well that your parents called you Carmencita. You still remember that, don't you?"

The girl turned away. In the green light of the old lock-up where they were holding her, her eyes were rimmed with dark circles. "When can I go outside?"

"That's not possible for now, Carmencita. I want to tell you some more about your parents. Your real parents."

The girl didn't answer. Alejandro stood next to her and followed her gaze; she peered at the small church outside La Paloma. The old lock-up stood right at the edge of the village, and the church was the only building she could see through the small window. It was Indians who had built the church originally. Against the background of the deep blue sky, with swampy clouds floating in it, the square tower, built in a mixture of Spanish and old Inca styles, looked grim.

The mountain top behind it, aligned against the background of the clouds, looked white and blurred at this distance. It resembled a sheep's head with flattened ears. The church tower stood on the edge of an area bordered by small prayer towers and crosses on a wide, low wall. João told Alejandro that even the most westernized inhabitants of La Paloma avoided this terrain: the Indians' ghosts wandered all around it. Alejandro had seen the sunrise that morning, and when the shadow of the tower had fallen over him, he'd felt a shiver that had made him look up with narrowed eyes.

He blamed this on the fatigue of the last night, which he'd spent watching over the sleeping girl as she moved restlessly back and forth on the improvised cot in the lock-up. Beatriz had relieved him for a few hours before she left for work to avoid suspicion from the university's military rector.

All night, and also now, Alejandro had kept his mask on. When Carmencita had fallen asleep, Beatriz had quietly asked, "Why don't you take off that silly thing? She's supposed to recognize you now, isn't she?"

"I don't dare," he'd replied. In his eyes, Beatriz had seen a shimmering of a past that she no longer wanted to discover. She didn't push the topic further.

"I want to go back to my daddy," said Carmencita resolutely, still looking outside. "My dad knows lots of important people. They'll find you and put you in prison."

"That's true, Carmencita," tried Alejandro. "Sooner or later, they'll find us. But after this, you'll never be able to forget who you really are."

"You don't know who I am at all!" she burst out.

"Well," said Alejandro. "I knew you very well when you were little."

The girl stared at him, and he interpreted this as doubt. Why didn't he take off his mask now? Because there was no laughing toddler in front of him but a frightened teenager?

"I don't believe you," she said gloomily. "It'll end like in a movie. My father comes with armed men. And then you'll try to kill me." She took a step back. "But I'm not afraid."

"Carmencita…"

"My name is Amanda!"

"Don't you remember your father? He was a great singer. Don't you remember the stadium? That's where your mom and dad were…"

"No!" she screamed. She clasped her hands over her ears.

"Those weren't my parents. They were child abductors. My dad saved me from them! Those crooks had taken me to that terrible place!"

"Those are lies, and you know that."

"That's not true!" she shouted while tears were running down her cheeks. "You're a liar! You are...."

Alejandro took her by the shoulders and shook her so hard that her mouth slammed shut. "I don't take off this mask because I don't dare," he said hoarsely. "I was your daddy's best friend, and I loved your mother and you. If I take off this mask and you refuse to recognize me, what happens then, Carmencita? How will I then be able to convince you?"

"You're all liars and murderers," the child whispered, trying to tear herself loose. "Dad told me that there are people who live by lies: they try to destroy everything in Terreno because they're jealous of our money."

Alejandro let her go. "Are you the daughter of Lucía?" he said. "Are you the girl who tried to play on Víctor's guitar on Sunday mornings when we had breakfast with all the members of Aconcagua at your home? Remember? The smell of roasted meat in the air and the mimosa in full bloom? Surely you remember that? You made us laugh, and you even sang a few verses of..."

With her arms slack along her body, Carmencita started to cry. The sound she made resembled the plaintive sound of the *quena* played by Alejandro's mother.

"That's not true," she sobbed, exhausted. "You're lying to me. In that big building, the stadium, I was terrified. Daddy found me and brought me home: I was a rich girl, and when I was very young, I was kidnapped and raised by false parents for a while until daddy found me again. I am Amanda Astíz-Fitzroy, and no one else!"

Alejandro Juron staggered backward as if she had beaten him: "Astíz?"

She drew herself up to her full height, and with fever-ishly shining eyes, she shouted, "I am Amanda Astíz-Fitzroy!"

Juron turned around and ran out of the lock-up. With trembling hands, he closed the door and walked into the street, still in his wrestling suit and mask, oblivious to the glances from two passers-by on their way to the bean fields. At the church, he slowed his stride. The sunlight speckled on the roughly plastered church tower. He paused at the first prayer turret on the wall around the old cemetery. He looked through the half circles of the openings to the niche inside—where worshippers placed their sacrifices for the Blessed Virgin, a hazelnut-shaped space under the stone cross crowning the small dome. He put his hands in the niche and placed his palms on the cold stone.

The executioner had used the name of his own mother to introduce himself to his victims; he defiled the name of his mother.

"So, here you are," said João Pereira behind him. "Still in the outfit? You're standing in the spotlight on the main podium like that, my man. I don't want my colleagues in the village to get strange thoughts. Remove that thingy in front of your ugly face, Alejandro. This village is getting to look more like a masked ball than anything else."

Alejandro turned his head around without pulling his hands out of the niche.

"Astíz," he muttered. "Kurt Fitzroy is captain Astíz. He used his mother's name in the stadium. João. The spirits of the Indians don't return, but those of the torturers do."

———

4

"Nothing in the press," said Cristóbal. "I'm beginning to think that Alejandro was right. Kurt doesn't dare to use his connections."

"I walked past his house." Beatriz stood at the window of Cristóbal's office. "There is nothing special to see on the outside. I couldn't bring myself to ring the bell."

"Who are you talking about?"

Beatriz turned around. Cristóbal noticed that her face looked puffy. The make-up she had applied couldn't quite disguise the dark circles under her eyes.

"About René."

"I'm sure he's done what he said," said Cristóbal, who pretended to busy himself with all kinds of papers. "I don't doubt he's safe and sound in Belgium by now."

"I don't know, Cristóbal. What he did at Kurt's house—do you think that was normal? What's more, he's recently..." She thought of his violent domination of her and the look in his eyes afterward.

"You liked him, didn't you?" Cristóbal anxiously avoided her gaze.

"He's a tormented man." Her tone betrayed that she wanted to say something else.

"Aren't we all?"

She smiled, but he could tell it wasn't sincere. She felt Cristóbal was losing his flair. He tried to keep up his old facade but managed it less and less.

"I made contacts," he continued nonchalantly. "Journalists from *The New York Times* and *Newsweek* are interested in the story. Big fish. McCullerson of *The New York Times* immediately came up with a title for his story: 'Only in Terreno executioners love their victims.' He could hardly believe what we told him, and he wants to interview Carmencita as soon as possible. We must make sure now that things don't go wrong.

Have you heard the rumors? The European Community is going to impose sanctions on Terreno for the death of the dockers." Cristóbal shook his head. "We are the pillory of the world."

"That is how René felt—the pillory of his world," said Beatriz.

———

5

After searching the house, Kurt Astíz-Fitzroy put his gun away when he entered René's office for the second time. He sat down at the priest's desk. The past two days, he had spent long hours in his bed, paralyzed by fatigue and pains in his joints, waiting for a ransom demand, a message from the kidnappers. He fought off the urge to send members of Patria y Sangre to René's house. There came no word. He urged himself to act, but Amanda's kidnapping seemed to have robbed him of his zest for life.

Kurt forced himself to think. Everything indicated that the priest had fled the country in great haste. Kurt had inquired of the diocese, and they were surprised to hear that René was not at his post. No one in Canela had seen the priest for the last two days. The asshole left no clue whatsoever. Kurt's lips turned into a thin line. He looked with red-fringed eyes at the room's dark window.

When had his work become more than his duty to the fatherland? It started with the imperative of forcing hard-headed prisoners to talk. Gradually, he devised inventive methods to break their resistance. The results he achieved were praised. The ideological basis of his actions had become less important than the prestige he gained. In the long run, the army command had allowed him to act at will.

What had his father, colonel of an elite unit of the Terrenean army, told him once? *A good soldier is two men in one: the one he is and the one he must be. He should dedicate his whole life to become the second man.*

Kurt now realized he had chosen a third possibility. Slowly, he had become the man he thought he should be. The allure of feeling powerful became more important than the government he served. He convinced himself that he was delving deeper into the art of breaking the human spirit. Little by little, he looked into himself and discovered, behind the clichés of 'duty and obedience' and 'the end justifies the means' a hidden *desire.*

Kurt gained even more influence when he married an American woman, which had produced numerous contacts. She was five years older than he, the daughter of an ex-senator, and her only hobby was excessive drinking. She spent three months a year in Terreno and regarded that time as a holiday in a backward exotic country where her husband passed muster as her not-so-exciting occasional lover. Eight years ago, they divorced. In the meantime, Kurt had become influential and wealthy enough. He could easily do without her. Amanda swallowed without question the story that her mother had died shortly after her birth. As was customary in Terreno, he had even given her the name of his mother.

Amanda soaked up everything he had told her. After all, he could believe his own lies perfectly well. As an interrogator, Kurt hadn't just *played* his roles like his colleagues did; he *became* them. In an impulse of curiosity, he saved Amanda from the stadium. *What will happen if I try to put the daughter of a world-famous father on the right track? She's like a puppy, a shy little bitch, a study object.*

The little bitch had grown bigger, and she learned to lick the hand that fed her. When had he realized how much he had come to love her? At first, love seemed superfluous: the lies did an excellent job. Kurt told Amanda that the 'gypsies' Víctor and Lucía kidnapped her when she was very young and that he had always searched for her. *Amanda, you have to learn to love me, just as I have always loved you.*

Love: with that formula, he achieved the results he'd wanted. Amused, he saw her fear and disbelief turn into desire to hear the story over and over again. At night, she slept in his bed, pressed close to him. He felt content when she put an arm over his chest and settled her head in his shoulder cavity. He had managed to gain her trust and to transform her into another person. It was so simple for someone with his talents. Over the years, the success of his most daring experiment had given him moments of deep satisfaction. He had re-educated the child of a left-wing agitator until she became exactly what he wanted: a loving daughter who, like him, looked down on the lower classes and who seemed to have forgotten her origins entirely.

But, on the sly, the magic spell had also changed *him*. He'd realized this on the day, five years ago now, when Amanda suddenly had difficulty breathing. He lifted her and ran to his car. Recklessly speeding, he drove through Valtiago, ignoring traffic lights, yelling at other drivers. Once they arrived in the family doctor's waiting room, he ran straight into the consulting room with his daughter in his arms. It turned out to be an attack of viral fever. During the days that Amanda had to spend in the hospital, he watched over her constantly.

His daughter: that was what she had become in his heart. He'd overwhelmed her with kisses and read to her every evening until she fell asleep. Before his eyes, he saw her change into his flesh and blood.

And because she'd become his daughter, he abandoned his usual caution. Gradually, he became an aging man who couldn't refuse her. Slowly and subtly, she'd changed too. Kurt realized now that he had missed the changes in Amanda. They'd come about all too gradually. Amanda had learned the power of seduction, the sideways glances, the kisses, the caressing of his hand, a particular inflection in her voice when she asked for favors. The way she said, "*Daddy.*"

Kurt hit the metal desk; it echoed hollowly. He had made more and more concessions. His life became swamped with carelessness and the belief anything was possible. He was retired, but he was the driving force behind Patria y Sangre, and he had excellent contacts with the highest echelons of the junta. He lived alone, but he'd built up a fortune with the drug trade. A beautiful and successful life. When he'd noticed someone was cheating him with the drug revenues from Patria y Sangre, he'd felt for the first time a vibration in his feet. They were made of clay, after all. The giant was not invincible.

Now, he concluded a pedagogic error had cost him even more. He had imprudently indulged his daughter's wishes, and as a result, he lost her. In recent months, as Pelarón came to tolerate a little opposition, so Amanda's interest in the opposition had gradually grown. She wanted to know what kind of people demanded a different form of society and how it came about that the government—in which her father so strongly believed—had to swallow so much criticism. Kurt explained his point of view to her, convinced that with the right historical facts, she would become an enlightened spirit like himself. The result he achieved was contradictory. Amanda nodded in agreement with his analyses, but still, she pleaded to go to the *peña* because she wanted to see those critics with her own eyes. She told her father that she wished to learn *what these folks were really made of*—an expression he found comical. He consented because he believed that he had overcome the past.

Overcome but not killed, as it turned out. Kurt could endure anything, except for the loss of Amanda.

A scratching sound at the window. As he pulled his pistol, Kurt let himself slide from the office chair to the ground. He looked over the edge of the desk. He heard the scratching again but saw nothing. He groped for the desk lamp and turned it towards the window. He wanted to peek over the desk when the scrabbling started anew, accompanied this time by a dull sound. Kurt pressed the button on the desk lamp. A narrow beam of light fell on the window. For a moment, he thought he saw a sparkling, staring eye—a tangle of motion.

The thing was too small for a human being, but the shimmering of its eye shocked him.

He walked to the window. Somewhere in this city of millions, they held Amanda captive. Who was it? René's cooperation in the kidnapping seemed to indicate action by the guerrillas. Or had rival groups wanted to strike the leader of Patria y Sangre? The abduction by the men in their wrestling costumes had been clumsy. If they had been members of death squads, they would've shot Amanda before his eyes.

They were members of the resistance; there was almost no other possibility. But why had they taken the risk of kidnapping Amanda? To bring her into the public domain? No Terrenean would believe that an officer from their army would raise the child of one of his victims. However, there were currently a lot of foreign journalists in the country...

A combination of circumstances that Kurt could never have dreamed of. He'd convinced himself that the *peña* was an excellent way to show Amanda the difference between winners and losers. And then, at just this ridiculous party, he'd heard that Alejandro Juron was going to perform. A surprise act! Then on top of that came an intervention of fate: the meeting with the Belgian priest René, who turned out to be El Enmascarado del Estadio Nacional. The priest had undoubtedly recognized Amanda. Kurt cursed himself for having become so careless and weak. He shivered in the night air and looked over his shoulder into the room. His deeply Catholic past played tricks on him: how the puzzle was put together had to be the work of the devil.

"The interrogator is an important judicial instrument of a

legitimate government, but he's also a human being," he declared while training new executioners. "During the interrogation, he has intimate contact with the interviewee and often gets to know him better than himself. This process creates all kinds of emotions. The interviewer must experience these if he doesn't want to lose his humanity, but at the same time, they mustn't be allowed to influence him. He must be aware of the coming and going of his emotions and take great care that they don't change his opinion. In short, he must act like a Zen master. If you don't reach that particular mindset during the torture of the interviewee, you will awaken demons in yourself that will sooner or later destroy you."

It was ironic and frightening that he had broken his code. Had his torture been a perverted form of love? Was his upbringing of Amanda a sublimated form of torture?

His anger mingled with a strange pride: he had awoken the demons about which he had spoken so pompously, and they'd struck him a heartbreaking blow. Fitzroy felt the blood rising to his cheeks. "If this is so," he whispered to the night, "I will show you that I'm ready to take you on."

However, this expansive sensation disappeared as quickly as it had come. Suddenly, Kurt felt old and powerless, a pitiful man in too weak a position to protect his own daughter. Who could he call for help? Nobody would support him. Worse still: he would be accused of subversive activities because his act of love had discredited the honor of the Terrenean army. An act of love: after all these years, it had become precisely that in his mind: he secretly smuggled the little girl out of the stadium *because he loved her.*

The anger returned with full force. A power greater than his own had intervened, and he couldn't cope with that. He turned to the window and looked at the dark shacks along the riverbank. A girl's throat could easily be cut in any of these hovels. A shiver ran along his spine thinking his daughter might already be lying at the bottom of the river. Kurt almost collapsed. A painful spasm twisted his body.

Then, he suddenly felt a flash of inspiration: he could avenge himself on many more people than just René.

He took a sharp breath. *He could take revenge for his pain.* The thought came to him as a token of the power that still resided within him, despite everything. He stood very still.

The clawing sound again. He almost fired his gun when a raw voice on the roof above him shouted, "*Cojónes!*"

A dark shape fluttered away in the darkness. For Kurt, the word was a portent.

He would prove to his torturers he had balls, big balls.

———

6

There he was, Alejandro Juron, bristling with booze, entering the lock-up, unmasked.

Beatriz had been talking to Carmencita for a long time. She immediately noticed the signs of Alejandro's inebriation: his hair tangled, the way he held his guitar, the blush on his cheeks, his self-absorbed gaze.

"Here I am, Carmencita," he said. "Do you recognize me now?" He smiled crookedly. "Now, you see me without my mask. That was what you wanted, didn't you? That was also what your fake father wanted, the father of all liars. When he tortured me in his special way, he whispered in my ear that I had to drop my mask. And I did, oh yes, I did."

"Alejandro!" said Beatriz.

"Did João tell you?" Alejandro addressed her. "Fitzroy's second surname? His mother's name, that he used in the stadium's torture chambers?"

She sighed. "João told me," she said.

He nodded but didn't look at her.

"Now you see me as I am," he said to the girl as he sat down on a chair next to the bed. "Tell me: who am I?"

Carmencita turned her head away. "I'm not saying anything anymore," she said. She cast an accusatory glance at Beatriz, who had gotten her talking about her life. Beatriz had heard the voice of a spoiled teenager who clung to the superficial and was afraid of the future. The girl praised her supposed father with an intensity that reminded Beatriz of a hidden feeling of guilt.

Alejandro jumped up from his chair, grabbed the girl, and forced her to look at him. "*Who am I?*"

Seeing how violently he shook the child back and forth, Beatriz took him by the arm. "Stop, Alejandro."

He let go of Carmencita and pushed Beatriz's arm away. "Don't touch me," he said as if he were talking to a stranger. Her fear turned to anger. She jumped up from the bed and pushed with both hands against his chest. Surprised, he took a step back.

"You don't know who you are?" Beatriz asked so softly that he could hardly catch her words. "I do now, unfortunately." She was vaguely aware of the child, huddled in the corner of the bunk, looking at them. Alejandro shook his head as if he had heard something ridiculous.

"Beatriz," he said.

She turned around and left the lock-up. Outside, in the sun, she looked around her. La Paloma seemed more idyllic than ever.

The door behind her opened. There was no sound; she looked back. Alejandro did not look at her but at the distant mountain of Aconcagua, surrounded by clouds with the color of rusty iron.

"You don't understand," he said at last. "I gave Astíz the address where Víctor, Lucía, and Carmencita were hiding. I destroyed her father and mother. And now I have to hear that my executioner has taken over the role of her father. How would you feel?"

Beatriz didn't move. He took a step toward her. "Don't you hear me?"

"I can hear you perfectly well," she said. "I've always suspected you weren't telling the whole truth. I remember the look in your eyes when you told me that you would've revealed their whereabouts to Astíz if the secret service hadn't found Víctor and his family that morning."

His arms hung limply along his body. "And it doesn't matter?"

She didn't answer.

"It certainly does," he continued. "I've just seen the look in *your* eyes."

João had told Beatriz that morning: "Alejandro has discovered that Kurt Fitzroy was his torturer." She had immediately visited Carmencita. The insistence with which Carmencita kept saying that Kurt Astíz-Fitzroy was her father seemed to indicate that the girl knew deep inside that it wasn't the truth. But the fact remained that the man had saved her from the stadium and had raised her lovingly. It wasn't Carmencita's fate that was terrible. The perversion of the situation lay elsewhere. An executioner turned out to be capable of sincerely loving the child of one of his victims. Carmencita adored Kurt. *Daddy would come and take her with him on his white steed, daddy adored her and would do everything to get her back.*

"Her adoptive father was your torturer," said Beatriz Candalti. "And what are you for her now?"

<hr/>

7

"On November the tenth," João said. "Pelarón couldn't have chosen a better date."

Cristóbal and João stood in the university library, built with an abundance of concrete and glass.

Cristóbal nodded. "On the tenth anniversary of the regime. With an evening ceremony starting at ten o'clock in the presence of the general who will inaugurate the new housing in Canela. You were right when you claimed Pelarón regards ten as his lucky number." The librarian smiled, but his eyes carefully scanned the room. It was still early, and the library was empty, except for a junior librarian behind the counter, more than ten meters away.

"Ten in the evening? The inauguration of the housing project in Canela?" said João surprised. "With Pelarón in the spotlights? Are you sure of that?"

"Without the slightest doubt. I have it from an official source."

"There must be something behind that. Does Pelarón suspect that we're planning something?"

Cristóbal coughed. "He'd have had us picked up long ago."

"Maybe he's waiting to see if more fish are caught in the trap."

The librarian sighed. "That's a risk we have to take."

"I don't trust it. Ten o'clock in the evening? With the poor lighting in Canela? Pelarón would normally never take such a risk."

"Perhaps it's precisely because of that. People always say that nobody will risk the *porqueriza* after dark," said Cristóbal. "Pelarón wants to kill two birds with one stone: prove his generosity and increase his strongman reputation. Nobody dares attack him, not even in Canela in the dark: that's the message he wants to deliver."

João nodded reluctantly. "Could be."

"Until November the tenth, Pelarón keeps the reins tight," continued Cristóbal. "The press received the program for the stone-setting a week ago, but there's a ban on publication until tomorrow." He smiled sourly. "That means that our Generalissimo is indeed on his guard. That's why the inauguration will only be announced in the press at the last minute. Moreover, Pelarón does not want an audience of poor people from the *porqueriza* when he lays the first stone of the five hundred promised houses: he has media and especially television in mind."

"First the reduction in food prices, now the houses," João nodded. "He's doing his best, our zealous leader."

"Wouldn't it be better to postpone our attack? There'll be other opportunities."

"No," replied João. "Where is the promised constitutional reform? When will the curfew be lifted? When will we have freedom of the press? With the inauguration, Pelarón symbolically celebrates the tenth anniversary of his junta. That is our chance to show that, all this time, he has plunged our country into darkness."

"Well then," said Cristóbal coughing into the cavity of his palm. "I hope you're right. What about the child?"

The painter avoided his gaze. "She keeps insisting that Kurt is her father, but Alejandro has convinced me that in three days, when your journalists arrive, she will tell the truth."

"Do you still think it was a good idea to kidnap her?"

"Yes."

"René is still missing. We don't know where he is. If he's still in Terreno, and he loses all his marbles, then..."

"René doesn't know where we're holding Carmencita. I don't think Fitzroy's got him."

"Who has, then?"

An unfathomable look slid over João's face. "My teacher in Brazil told me he could see in some people that they would soon be dead."

"Oh," Cristóbal responded politely. "In sick people, you mean?"

"In people who have decided to die soon," said João.

Cristóbal looked at the painter with narrowed eyes. He opened his mouth and closed it again.

"I have to go," he said at last. "I must receive a visitor."

"Me too. Tourists are coming to La Paloma. More than ever, everything in the village looks a hundred percent Indian."

"Who did you choose to go with you on November the tenth?"

"Jorge Espinoza. He's level-headed and reliable. He was a soldier; he knows the cracking of the whip."

"Fine." Cristóbal put his hand on João's left arm for a moment. "Be careful, okay?"

"I still have to laugh a lot in this life before I die, Cristóbal."

Cristóbal smiled, turned halfway around. "How is Alejandro doing, after hearing about Astíz?"

"Beatriz must've told you."

"Yes, but I'm asking for your opinion."

"I think those years in prison have made him even crazier than we are. We still see him as Alejandro Juron of Aconcagua. He's not that man any longer. We have to remember the man behind the symbol."

"The man behind the symbol?" said Cristóbal. "Sometimes, I think he's a marionette."

João Pereira raised his eyebrows. "Who's the puppeteer?"

The Darkness In The Soul

1

IT WAS AS IF THE GIRL HAD SAVED UP ALL HER FEAR AND ANGER until Alejandro appeared again. When he came in with his guitar, she jumped off the bed and rushed towards him. She banged her head against his chest in a blind escape attempt. Alejandro dropped the guitar.

She hit his chest with her fists and sobbed. He grabbed her by the arms and silently pulled her back to the bed. She resisted with all her might, but when he threw her on the cot, she lay there limp and crying.

Alejandro bent over her, his mouth close to her head. "When you were four, not long before soldiers took you and your parents to the stadium, your father, your real father, had a dream about you. He dreamed about who you'd be after he was gone. And your father, Víctor Pérez, the singer of Aconcagua, knew very well that there were powerful people who wanted him dead. He also knew why. Because he defended the poor and wanted them to have a better life."

"In his dream, your father saw you as a hooker in Valtiago, an orphaned girl who had to sell her body because she had nothing else. That dream shocked your father deeply because he loved you more than anything else and wanted you to have a choice in what you did in your life."

"In the months before his death, he wondered if he should leave the country with you and your mother. He was a world-famous artist, not a poor man. He could easily have emigrated. But he was also a man who saw his compassion as a duty. He felt he could not leave. It was his fate to be who he was: Víctor Pérez, the defender of the poor. He bundled his anger, his sadness, and his fear into a protest song that lashed out hard at the *junta*."

"You were the first to hear that song, Carmencita, and when he sang it for you, his voice broke at the end, and he wept. You didn't understand the words, so you danced on the refrain, and you asked me: *tío, tío, tío, am I beautiful?* You were so pretty, Carmencita, and I looked back and forth from your smiling face to the tears on your father's cheeks. Víctor clenched his teeth and kept singing. *Requiem for Carmencita*, the song he had written after his dream about you."

The girl remained dead quiet on the bed. Alejandro grabbed his guitar and sang.

> *The street, Carmencita, is your dance hall.*
> *The street that never sleeps*
> *and sells bodies as merchandise.*
> *Your feet are swollen, Carmencita,*
> *You are trapped, your arms on strings:*
> *a puppet in the street where death is yawning.*

Never had Alejandro sung with more feeling, never had his voice a more beautiful timbre. Never had he been more himself than at that moment: he was born for this, not to be afraid.

Beatriz had come in stealthily and stood there looking at him and at the child. She saw how beautiful Alejandro could be and how the girl's tears ran freely. Carmencita changed before her eyes: a new expression slid over her features—one sad and pained.

Alejandro let the last notes die away and looked up from his guitar. He put the instrument on the bed and sat next to Carmencita. "Your father's dream has come true, but the other way around—instead of a poor girl selling her body, you have become a rich girl selling her soul. *Tío, do you love me?* Yes, I loved you, Carmencita; I loved you so much that I couldn't get enough of seeing you dancing."

With a high-pitched sound, like that of a bird, Carmencita threw herself into Juron's arms. He stroked her and mumbled sweet words.

He looked up, saw Beatriz standing at the door, and trembled from head to toe.

2

"What a beautiful sky for our national holiday," mumbled João. Looking at the clear, star-strewn, violet sky, he straightened his backpack. "Don't you think so, Jorge?"

Jorge Espinoza, the tourist interpreter of La Paloma, was small and fiery. He possessed an old-fashioned dignity that seemed too big for his compact body. Jorge was one of the mildest men João knew but had eagerly volunteered for this mission. During his military service, he learned to handle explosives.

"When Pelarón organizes something, he organizes it well," the interpreter replied dryly.

"Did you know ten is Pelarón's lucky number? November the tenth, the tenth anniversary of his *junta*, ten o'clock."

Jorge shook his head as if he had been told a ridiculous joke.

João turned and looked down. Underneath them lay Valti-ago, a tangled string of abandoned stardust. To their left, a row of willows rendered the *porqueriza* invisible. Behind the city lay the mountain range, hardly darker than the purple sky. The Mayu river, bordered by ribbons of light, flowed along-side the railway.

If the trees had not obstructed the view, João would have been able to see an irregular, bright spot at the opening of the slum—the stand where artists performed in anticipation of the laying of the foundation stone.

The army placed a cordon sanitaire of tanks and half-track vehicles around the stage. Television cameras moved back and forth; flash lamps captured the 'historical moment.'

"Come," said João. "We must hurry."

They had to climb another two kilometers to the nature reserve, El Melocotón. Next to the park lay the walled private village of the national electricity company. A white plastered guardhouse flanked the wide entrance gate. A bit further on, they heard the noise of the Rio Cilata flowing from a high altitude into the valley.

"I just hope we've got the timing right," said João.

"It would be nice if Pelarón had just drunk from the bull's horn," Jorge answered phlegmatically. Every year on the national holiday, Pelarón drank a specially brewed *chicha* from a bull's horn—a symbol of his indestructible masculinity.

They climbed higher. The hydropower plant above them was built at an altitude of thirteen hundred meters. The turbines turned on the 'white coal' supplied by the Rio Cilata: enormous steel pipes led the river water with heart-breaking speed down the mountains, after which it collapsed with deaf-ening force in a narrow channel to a specially excavated catch basin.

João Pereira and Jorge Espinoza crossed the iron bridge. Below them, the river raged. The water whistled and roared.

The central machinery was higher, brightly lit at night, a massive and square building built with dark bricks.

"This is a good place!" shouted Espinoza. The noise of the river was so fierce that even close together, they had to yell.

"Fine!" João unbuckled his heavy backpack. He took out the sticks of explosives while Jorge busied himself with the detonator.

João sat next to him and assembled his rifle. "You know, Jorge," he cried, "I don't know if I could hit anyone with it now, even though I used to be a good marksman."

Jorge Espinoza was busy connecting the explosives and the detonator. Still, he replied with his head bent, "When I was in service, I was assigned to Pelarón's team of bodyguards for a while. We conscripts formed the outer ring. Professional soldiers formed the second ring, and snipers closed the ring around the general. In case of an assault, we had the highest risk positions because we were the outer ring. We always had to point our weapon with the barrel towards the ground."

"Why?"

For a moment, Jorge looked up from his work. "If we dared keep our weapon horizontal, the professional soldiers and snipers would shoot us because it meant that we were planning an attack on the generalissimo."

"You don't mean that."

"Jesus," answered Jorge, "you don't invent something like that."

João shook his head.

"Ready," said Jorge, standing up. He laid the bomb as close to the turbines as possible.

Pereira looked at the thick steel pipes that directed the water down. "A 'symbolic act of resistance' like this makes you hunger for more," he muttered.

"What did you say?"

"Nothing. Let's go."

They ran over the bridge. João kept his rifle at the ready.

In this area, soldiers regularly patrolled the narrow but well-maintained concrete roads.

"How far away should we be?"

"We have radio control," Jorge answered. "Our Cuban friends are very modern in that area. We can go a lot farther away before our party popper goes bang."

Quickly, they descended to the city. As they passed the willows, João looked to the left where, against the background of Canela's church tower, the large, irregular spot of light from the stand of honor was visible.

"A cancerous spot of light," he said. "I should have more time to paint this scene, Jorge."

Jorge Espinoza grinned. "Wait a few more minutes. Much less painting work: your whole canvas will be black."

———

3

Manuel sat in the VIP grandstand erected next to the building site in Canela. Behind the fences stood three rows of soldiers, holding their machine guns; beyond them, a dark crowd of people had gathered. On the other side of the river, some inhabitants of the *porqueriza* stood watching—surprisingly few in number. On the bridge itself, by contrast, there were packed rows of spectators from better neighborhoods, protected by two half-track vehicles, one on each side of the bridge.

At any other time, this image would have amused Manuel. Not now, with Kurt Astíz-Fitzroy sitting right next to him. The artists who had to brighten up the national holiday danced and sang on a large stage domed by a palisade of flood lights. The team from the national television station made its presence very clear. Radio people tried to work just as conspicuously, and press journalists helped themselves from a large table loaded with drinks and snacks.

Manuel peered from the corners of his eyes at Kurt Astíz-Fitzroy. His tanned skin contrasted attractively with his pepper and salt beard. His hair, though grey, was still lush. He was talking to the wife of Don Böhmer, an importer of electronics and supplier of the army. She was fluttering her lashes back at him. Her face and bosom looked youthful, but the hand she put on Kurt's arm was wrinkled and veined. Kurt murmured entertaining words that made Doña Böhmer chirp like a young girl. Kurt had charm. Manuel knew that all too well: he'd often seen him abusing it.

Kurt called Manuel a few days ago with the go-ahead for Manuel's plan to allow general Pelarón to restore order in the country. Manuel hadn't expected this sudden change of heart. He still didn't know what to make of it, especially when Fitzroy told him he had persuaded Pelarón the National Festival should occur near the *porqueriza* and coincide with the laying of the first stone. Kurt emphasized he had fully briefed Pelarón on Manuel's plan and that the general was on board with all points.

Despite a nagging unease, Manuel saw a glorious future ahead of him, with the patronage and respect of such influential people. He also knew that he couldn't back down now that the country's leader counted on him.

Martial music blared through the loudspeakers. Military motorcyclists swarmed. General Pelarón's limousine, decorated with the Terrenean national flag, came to a standstill in front of the grandstand. Kurt smiled at Doña and pointed at the general when he stepped out. There was applause. Several men in sharp suits surrounded Pelarón. He was a small man with tightly combed jet-black hair and a grey, thin mustache. On his uniform, five stars glittered like diamonds, distinguishing him from the junta's other generals, who wore four. He stepped briskly to the lectern. His sonorous voice raised the popular slogans. "The general's courage in attending this public ceremony is exemplary, don't you think

216

so, Manuel?" said Kurt without turning his gaze away from
Pelarón.

"Yes," said Manuel.

"It's time." Kurt nodded towards the stand exit.

Manuel's throat went dry. He stood and shuffled to the
exit, politely apologizing to the people in his row. Behind the
stand stood a dark figure leaning against a jeep. The man
saluted as Manuel approached. Under the helmet, his eyes
were shining in the bright lights.

"Come along, sir," said the lieutenant without introducing
himself. He was still young but wore the uniform of Pelarón's
personal bodyguard. His bodyguards were an elite group that
had sworn eternal loyalty to the dictator.

They got into the jeep, and the lieutenant quickly drove to
the start of the cordon round the festival grounds. He didn't
speak a word on the way. Manuel suspected Pelarón himself
had ordered the lieutenant to stay with him and shoot him if
he had the slightest doubt about the success of his plan.
Nevertheless, he was confident.

His plan would not fail.

He felt invincible tonight. He had set powerful mecha-
nisms in motion with his daring plan. Manuel remembered
Kurt's voice over the phone: "I reconsidered your plan and
talked about it with old friends. They approached the general.
He hesitated at first, but because of the growing tensions in
the country, he agreed."

"There is one more thing, Manuel: I need the person who
carries out your plan to be completely trustworthy. The leak in
the cocaine handling that I recently discovered has made it
impossible for me to trust Patria y Sangre. I trust only you.
You have to carry out your plan yourself."

On the phone, he had said, "Me?" He was proud and
nervous hearing his words.

"You," Fitzroy had answered dryly. "You're a sharp-
shooter, and your loyalty is beyond dispute. The other generals

of the *junta* know nothing about it. After executing your plan, Pelarón wants to strengthen his position as commander-in-chief of the army. Your scheme gives him the chance to regain complete control not only of the country but also of his generals."

His plan had triggered a complicated political move. In the speeding jeep, Manuel thought of his future and of Beatriz—on her knees begging for his forgiveness.

————

4

"Madam, I'm inviting you on a small adventure," said Alejandro when Beatriz opened the front door of her house. Alejandro had rehearsed his opening line. However, he felt he sounded distressed and foolish. He'd parked the Datsun that Cristóbal lent him on the pavement. "You're far too pretty to lock yourself up like a nun with a wart."

Beatriz smiled but stayed in the doorway without asking him to enter. "Besides, I have my guitar with me," Alejandro rattled on, constantly shifting his weight from one foot to another. "We're going to do a serenade, Beatriz, not to the moon but to darkness." He looked at his watch. "There's twenty minutes left. There's a big crowd of people in Canela. Today's a great day for Terreno. After ten years, the "General of the Poor" has finally shown up at the border of no man's land."

"And the police checks?" Beatriz asked.

"The cops are polite tonight. They'd even help old ladies across the street."

"Why do you want to go, Alejandro?"

Alejandro looked out over the wide lane lined with elm trees. "To find inspiration."

"It'll be dangerous. The police will charge when João and Jorge detonate the bomb."

"Charge? Against innocent spectators? Everyone, even the most right-wing journalist, will understand that the perpetrators of this vile terrorist attack from high in the mountains are not in Valtiago, innocently watching the ceremony. In any case, the cops will have their hands full with the evacuation of Pelarón and his entourage." He grinned. "Are you afraid?"

Beatriz shook her head. She realized that she wanted to see the consequences of the sabotage act she had made possible with her plane.

"Why do I see you so rarely lately?" Alejandro asked spitefully. With an intuition that surprised her, he added, "Do you grieve for René?"

She kept her face neutral. "You act as if René is dead."

"When João and I went to his house, the evening we were to kidnap Carmencita, he had an open book on his desk. He had underlined a sentence in red: *the hardest task in your life is to prepare for your death, and good preparation is only possible through self-knowledge.*" Alejandro shrugged his shoulders. "Lafarge has vanished without a trace for days. He was your friend. Is it normal for him not to contact you?"

"No," she said evenly.

He decided to change course and conjured up a boyish grin. "Are you coming? After all, this is a National Holiday. Missing it would be unforgivable."

"Why do you want to go?" she repeated.

"I already told you, right? The scene will make me compose a song that will strike like a bomb!"

"Why, Alejandro?"

Her calm tone sobered him. He pointed to the mountains in the direction of La Paloma. "Anything is better than sitting there with that poor child. What have I started, Beatriz? For once in my life, I wanted to be a hero. And what's the result?"

She knew that result and remained silent. Alejandro's eyes scanned her face as if he were wondering if he still had enough credit. "I thought I would free Víctor's daughter from the hands of a torturer. That idea gave me the illusion that I'd recovered my courage. But the executioner turns out to be a loving father. For once I felt myself on the right side of the dividing line, and what's the upshot? That the line doesn't exist." He nodded towards the lower parts of the city. "I think Astíz-Fitzroy once also thought he was on the right side of the dividing line…Come with me, Beatriz, take me by my shoulders. I can at least be your friend, can't I?"

––––––––

5

In the bell tower, Manuel had an excellent view of the ceremony. Using the Belgian priest's church was Astíz-Fitzroy's idea. He'd explained the details to Manuel two days ago, at their last meeting. Kurt had looked tired. In the course of the conversation, Manuel politely asked how Amanda was doing, and he was shocked by the expression in Astíz-Fitzroy's eyes. He didn't receive an answer.

"The church tower is extremely suitable," Astíz-Fitzroy said a moment later. Very briefly, a bizarre expression appeared on his face, as if he were struggling to refrain from saying something else. "Lafarge will be accused of complicity in the conspiracy." For a moment, the man's mask fell away. Manuel Durango saw Fitzroy's real face hiding underneath. He lowered his eyes and nodded.

Manuel looked through the night scope. He saw the folk dancers finish their performance and followed Pelarón with the cross threads of his rifle as the general walked to the lectern. Durango relaxed his shoulders, regulated his breathing. He admired the accuracy of the night vision's cross-threads and slightly curved his right index finger around the trigger. A beautiful weapon, this Belgian Fal assault rifle. Kurt had not overlooked a single detail. Manuel concentrated. It took him a few moments to find his mark, but then a wave of joy flooded over him and made him tingle from head to toe. *Beatriz, with this trigger, I have your destiny in my hands.*

He breathed out completely, cleared his mind, saw only the little figure in the cross-threads.

He fired.

―――――

6

"I inherited the plane from my father," said Beatriz, standing with Alejandro amid thousands of others in Canela watching the ceremony. Many people were following the show from their houses, but crowds were filling the streets as well. The atmosphere was festive. What had happened to the dock-workers in Coquimba now really did seem to be just a "regrettable mistake on the part of both demonstrators and law enforcement officials," as Pelarón stated in his speech the day before, "a provocation by communist agitators followed by a hotheaded reaction from the *carabineros.*" He'd promised the launch of an investigation and punishment for the culprits. *The government and citizens must work together to lead Terreno, this most progressive and economically developed country on the continent, to a bright future.* While uttering these words, it had seemed on the big TV screen as if the general had to hold back his tears. The cameras zoomed in eagerly.

"The Cessna? That's fantastic," Alejandro Juron answered carefully. He didn't quite know how to react. Beatriz had briefly mentioned her father's death to him. Alejandro hadn't asked any further questions. Neither of them had spoken about their relationship or its absence lately.

Alejandro had the feeling that tension was building up

under the smooth skin of Beatriz's face, the birth pains of a new Beatriz Candalti. He decided to wait and see. He had nothing more to lose. But his heart was confused and stubborn. One moment he thought he loved her; the next, his mouth felt bitter at the thought of being with her.

"That means we could fly away together," he continued. He tried to sound casual. "Would you be able to fly over the mountain tops from here?"

"I certainly could in Arini," she answered thoughtfully. "And maybe even here. There are a quite a few mountain passes." She laughed. "I love dangerous flying."

"Would you like that - to fly away together?" he asked.

"Stop dreaming, Alejandro," she said in a friendly way. Despite everything, his shy gaze endeared her. But by now she knew his tricks, and although she felt the same uncertainties as him and sometimes felt waves of desire for him, she wanted to keep this friendly distance for the time being.

"Can you see enough of the show?" he asked.

"Not much, I'm afraid," she laughed. "Our general is so small at this distance."

"Up close also, I've been told. Pelarón wears shoes with five-centimeter high heels. So a total of ten." He chuckled. "He tries to relate all major things to that number."

"How do you know all that?"

"Pelarón was a favorite subject in The Last Supper."

Was he making this up on the spot? She knew he was capable of it. Suddenly, it felt funny to her. She couldn't control herself and put an arm around his shoulders. He looked at her gratefully.

Beatriz stood on tiptoe and, closer to the river, saw a ripple in the crowd watching the inauguration ceremony. Small shapes were visible in the spotlights, waving their arms. The ripple became stronger, moved in their direction, became a wave.

"What is....?"

"Oh dear God," cried a woman about three rows in front of them. "Someone's shooting at Pelarón."

Alejandro and Beatriz saw now how the wave was formed by people fleeing towards Canela.

Echoing against the mountains behind them, a dull rumble roared like an approaching thunderstorm.

Suddenly, the city was shrouded in complete darkness.

———

7

Kurt Astíz-Fitzroy jumped up in the stands like the others when the bodyguard to the right of Pelarón collapsed. The first shot had been barely audible. The second, however, boomed as if a firecracker had been lit somewhere in the distance. A second bodyguard fell forwards. He didn't die instantly and wriggled across the stage. Soldiers jumped in front of Pelarón, pulled him off the stage, ran with him toward the row of limousines.

Astíz-Fitzroy made his way through the horrified crowd. He had foreseen the chaos. A military jeep with a driver was waiting for him behind the stage.

This is all I could do, Amanda, the only way I could avenge you. At this thought, his heart cringed. He stopped for a moment.

To his right, dense crowds of people collided in haste to get away. Cars started, engines howled. The confusion was consuming. Military motorcyclists swarmed between the fleeing vehicles, making all possible efforts to restore order. Astíz-Fitzroy quickly walked around the stand. The jeep was waiting for him with its engine running; he got in.

At that moment, a distant rumbling sounded, and all the lights in the city went out.

"*Sangre!*" the driver cursed. In front of them, two cars clashed against each other. The blast of their collision sounded louder than the explosion that had shut down the city's power station in the mountains. Astíz's abdominal muscles tightened, but the driver turned the steering wheel sharply. The jeep tilted for a moment down the verge towards the river but swung back onto the road.

"What happened?" asked the sergeant at the wheel. He'd turned on the lights of the jeep and navigated nimbly between other speeding cars. Astíz looked sideways. As agreed with Pelarón, the tanks and half-tracks had come into action. But the explosion that had paralyzed the power plant confused the soldiers. The tanks had been instructed to intervene with force at the slightest disturbance, but they hadn't expected an assault. Astíz-Fitzroy and his military supporters had convinced Pelarón that a fake assassination, orchestrated by them, was the best way of restoring order in the *porqueriza* with the support of public opinion.

"The resistance blew up the power station," said Kurt. He began to laugh. "Those idiots. Just now! Minutes after the attack on the general! They couldn't have chosen a better moment."

A little later, when the jeep drove through Canela's main street towards the church, the darkness was pierced by powerful searchlights. Oversized silhouettes appeared against the backdrop of the workers' houses. A fiery flash tore the night apart, and the rumbling sound of a 105mm cannon stunned the two occupants of the jeep. The driver braked hard. Ten years earlier, Kurt had seen how two shots from a tank cannon were enough to destroy a quarter of the presidential palace. He realized that the sudden darkness and the overall confusion made the tanks dangerous for everyone. He climbed out of the jeep. The sergeant shouted something. Kurt didn't understand him. His ears were whistling too much from the cannon blast. What target were these madmen shooting at?

A fountain of water, about a hundred meters away, provided the answer to that question.

8

Colonel Lázaro Franco, commander of the *tanquetas* assembled on the banks of the Mayu, stood with his Sherman on the bridge and forgot his good military manners, uttering a stream of vile curses into his helmet microphone. Canela was a witch's cauldron of fleeing masses to his right, and the *porqueriza* to his left was a place of chaos. Some idiot in one of his tanks had fired a warning shot in the water and panicked the crowd.

"Who fired?" he snarled at his adjutant. "That moron will face a court-martial! Retreat! Regroup at the barracks!"

The two tanks on the bridge roared in the direction of Canela, where the two armored cars stood. Colonel Franco grabbed his binoculars and tried to figure out in the darkness what exactly was going on. What should he do if the panic in the crowd got so intense that everyone was fleeing and trampling each other?

9

The jeep was surrounded by running people. They rammed into Kurt. He shouted to the sergeant but saw the man being dragged along by the uncontrolled mob. The stampeding crowd smacked his body back and forth like a rag doll. Kurt lost his balance and would've fallen if a strong arm had not grabbed him.

Manuel dragged him up. An armored car turned a hundred meters in front of them into an unpaved street. The pressure of the running crowd increased. Manuel took a pistol from his pocket and fired in the air; people fanned in all directions. The half-track at the beginning of the street tried to turn and retreat. Maneuvering was tricky in the narrow streets of the workers' quarter. Someone threw a burning bottle of home-distilled spirits at the vehicle. The primitive fire bomb burst without causing any real damage on the flank of the armored car, but the driver of the half-track panicked. The vehicle turned too sharp: there was a cloud of dust and grit as it hit the facade of a corner house.

Manuel pulled Kurt into the jeep. He started the engine and drove into a side street without regard to the running masses. A loud bang sounded; for a moment, a body was lying on the bonnet with flapping arms, then it was gone. Manuel drove in the direction of the flyover that led to the city center. The people who fled knew only one direction: from Canela deeper into the *porqueriza*. Nobody thought of escaping in the direction of Valtiago.

Even in this terrifying moment, people believed they would only be safe in the dark alleys of the slum. After the viaduct crossing the highway, Manuel turned right and drove full throttle into Avenida Santiaguillo. Kurt put a hand on his arm.

"Stop for a moment," he said, nodding to the side of the road. Manuel obeyed and drove to a parking strip. At this point, they had a good view across Canela. Kurt looked at the crowd, at this distance just an undulating patch of brown. The half-tracks cars were stuck on the river banks: flocks of running people blocked their way. Just then, the street lights on the flyover flashed back on, and here and there a lonely lantern in the workers' quarter. Astíz-Fitzroy looked at his watch: the power station's emergency generator had taken twenty minutes to start. He saw the gun of the first tank rotating in the light, followed by a thundering shot.

Water from the river splashed up as high as a house. With this second warning shot in the river, the commander of the armored vehicles wanted to force a passage through the crowd. The crowd didn't move for a moment but then spread quickly as a watercolor mass of chaos. Kurt turned his head further to the right: a stream of limousines, escorted by the military, quickly disappeared in the direction of Cerro Santa Lucia. Reinforcement was underway: military trucks advanced between the garbage dumps along the river.

Kurt signaled silently to Manuel. "Where to?" asked Durango. He was impressed. In combination with the sudden terrorist attack on the power station, his plan was having unexpected consequences. "To my house," Kurt said.

Before Manuel turned to the main highway, he saw the soldiers jumping out of the approaching trucks. The Terrenean army was going to advance against civilians. There was no going back.

———

10

"Alejandro!"

Trucks stopped with screeching tires. Soldiers jumped out of the cargo holds.

"The bridge," said Alejandro Juron. "We have to go to..."

They tried to escape against the current. It proved impossible. An armored car crashed into the corner house, startling them with its noise.

"To the church then!" Alejandro shouted, still clutching Beatriz in the swirling sea of people. "They won't do anything there!"

Shots rang out. People in the first rows were falling – a cacophony of screaming and shouting. Beatriz had never imagined that shots could sound so feeble against the noise of a crowd. "We've got to get into a house!" she cried.

Having arrived later than most spectators, they were still at the back, near the last row of houses in Canela. The street lights turned on again. From the wall of a café, some men tore down a sign promoting a beer brand that no longer existed to serve as a shield against the soldiers. Once again, a deafening cannon shot boomed out. A fountain several meters high rose from the river before collapsing. The crowd spread out in all directions. Alejandro pushed in the direction of the café and pulled Beatriz with him. The double door stood ajar; they ran inside. A little later, two more people came tumbling in. They stared at each other as if they couldn't believe that they were safe for the time being.

"We have to barricade the door," said Alejandro.

"We mustn't stay here," said one of the newcomers, an older woman wearing a dirty flowery dress with strands of grey hair in her eyes. "The tanks will drive over the houses." She laughed. "The Grim Reaper will get fat tonight."

"Tanks demolishing houses?" said Alejandro. "They would never intentionally do that. And we're in the middle of the street. It's only corner houses that are at risk. We need to close the doors."

"He's right," said the man who had arrived with the woman, a dark man in a felt hat, speaking with the accent of a half-blood. "We're safe here."

"When the soldiers come in, we're dead," said the woman. She laughed again. "But sooner or later, we all have to die, isn't that right, Giajo?"

"Before we do so, we still can close the door for a while," the half-blood answered laconically. "If more people come in, *los cerdos militares* will find us."

Alejandro and Giajo closed the doors.

"A few tables for a barricade," said Alejandro.

Together, they carried tables to the door. Behind the

windows with the dirty net curtains, there was the intensifying drone of massive engines. Shots rang out from automatic weapons. A mauve glow shone through the closed blinds. "There's liquor," Beatriz whispered to the others who were huddled together in the dark taproom. She began to put glasses on the counter and poured out *aguardiente*. For a moment, the others stayed in the middle of the small room like a gang of indecisive burglars, but then Alejandro came forward and downed the brandy in one gulp. The other two quickly followed his example.

Alejandro pushed his glass over the counter towards Beatriz: "Drink. It will be a long night."

———

11

"From this perspective, it's like a shadow play," said Manuel. He wanted to show the silent Kurt Astíz-Fitzroy next to him that he was a cultivated man with a creative vocabulary. "Don't you think there will be criticism of the army's harsh reaction?"

"Someone tries to kill the president, and two of his body-guards are dead. Simultaneously, there's an attack on the city's power station. This sabotage puts our capital in the dark for twenty minutes. So the military declares a state of siege. An over-reaction, after all that? I don't think so." Flashes of light flickered in the distant *porqueriza* as jeeps equipped with machine guns started to fire. They only aroused disquiet in Kurt. The military display of power accentuated his impotence.

"We've got the country back on the right track again, Kurt," said Manuel. "I am grateful for your support. I could never have done it without you. And you know how necessary it was. That brutal attack on the power plant: in ten years, no one has dared to try anything like that! Though as you said yourself: the resistance couldn't have picked a better moment." Enjoying the sound of his voice, Manuel took big swallows of his cognac. The fear that Kurt would discover who stole the crack had turned into a mincing feeling of camaraderie with the older man. Kurt had put his plan into operation. And he, in turn, had saved Kurt when he was in danger of being trampled. "It's like the carnival in Rio," he said, pointing at the flashes of light. "The poor idiots don't know what's happening to them."

"No," said Kurt's voice behind him. "They don't know. But I know a lame douchebag who'll know it soon enough."

Manuel turned around. Kurt was pointing a gun at him. "Colonel Astíz," said Manuel, his smile freezing on his face.

"Guess twice," Astíz said.

"I did everything you said! We're on the same side!"

"Sure, you did everything I said. And the regular army must never know that this was how it happened. That's why my contacts and I agreed that you had to die after the completion of your mission. The generalissimo also agreed to this. We're very aware of your big mouth, Manuel. So why take risks? That's one reason. The second is that I don't like to be cheated, especially not by you and a sodomite who called himself the king of the pigsty."

He knows about the crack. He knew all this time it was me, and he set me up.

"Colonel, I'll give everything back and...".

The shot spun Manuel around. He took two steps forward, and Kurt two steps back like they were hesitant tango dancers. Kurt fired again, and Manuel fell against a sofa. Kurt lost no time. He grabbed a body bag from behind the curtains. Three quick movements and Manuel's head and body disappeared behind the zipper.

You, giving everything back to me, you cocky fucker? You can never give me back what I lost. Nobody can.

12

Beatriz, who'd fallen into a restless slumber next to Alejandro, slowly woke up in the stuffy taproom. She lifted her head and looked at the window. There was a faint glow visible behind it.

Alejandro muttered something in his sleep. She looked attentively at his face.

Am I visiting you as a phantom in your sleep, Alejandro? I was born when the moon was bloodless. That's why men pour their desires and fears into me. René told me what he did in his youth to his brother's fiancé. He summed it all up into a telephone handset: his brother who had him drinking beer during Carnival at the age of twelve, his brother's girlfriend already drunk, his big brother, tanked up to the point of comatose. Just a boy, spying on them in the shed and then, like a little fox, doing what his sleeping brother couldn't manage because of the alcohol. The girl, who had covered his head with kisses, was wide open to him, like a female animal. After that, he said, he had distorted the story in his head until he had turned his brother into a half-hearted rapist.

His ambiguous repentance sounded contrived to me. A kind of certainty welled up in me after his 'confession': I knew he'd come up with this wild story to justify his failure in bed with me. I was angry at his ego, trying to make me swallow a made-up past. But at the same time, I reproached myself for assuming without proof that he'd offered me a fantasy. Maybe René was the only man I ever fell in love with. It's sad that I only discovered that after he treated me in bed like a nightmare that he had to exorcise.

Beatriz studied Alejandro's features in the sheepish light of the morning. *So, Alejandro, what nightmare did you have to exorcise?*

Her gaze wandered to the window. She felt sluggish because of too much *aguardiente*. The night before, they'd kept drinking as the rattling of automatic weapons moved toward the *porqueriza*.

Suddenly, with a powerful snapping sound, the window's

glass almost gracefully burst into dark splinters. Before she realized it, Beatriz screamed.

The others began to stir like worn-out hand puppets. Alejandro cringed when there was a banging on the door, and a loud voice shouted: "Open up!"

A salvo from a fast-fire rifle drove bullets through the door. Behind them, a few bottles splintered. They threw themselves on the floor and covered their heads with their arms.

"We're coming!" Alejandro yelled. "We comply!"

The shooting stopped. Alejandro cast Beatriz a look full of mortal fear before he jumped up, pushed the tables aside, and opened the door.

In the doorway, two soldiers stood khaki-grey in the pearly light of the morning. The first one was very young, Beatriz noticed. She stood up, together with the older woman and the half-blood.

"Drink," said the youngest soldier with his cracked voice. "Any drink here?" He moved as if there was a coil wound too tightly inside him. The other, a sergeant, was a dark, older man with a sharp nose and deep wrinkles in his forehead. He closed the door behind them. The boy walked to the Formica-covered counter and used the butt of his gun to wipe away the glasses on it. The sergeant looked at Alejandro and said softly, "My friend is a bit excited by the hard work we've done."

Alejandro noticed that the man had pale grey eyes, the color of the concrete walls in The Last Supper.

"Make some light, damn you," the boy snarled. Balancing on the balls of his feet, he looked over his shoulder, "Hey, old witch, pour me a drink. A stiff one."

The older woman went behind the counter and turned on the dirty fluorescent lamps.

"No, Pedro," said the older soldier. "If we're going to enjoy a drink, I'd rather have a charming barmaid." He gestured to Beatriz, who stood in the middle of the cantina, her hands on her hips. It seemed to Alejandro that Beatriz moved very slowly when she went behind the counter. It was silent in the room as she picked up the *aguardiente* bottle and poured two glasses. Pedro took a big sip and spat the fluid over the counter. Beatriz recoiled. The boy kicked over a chair. "Pig's piss! Vinegar instead of booze!" With a few steps, he stood behind the counter, grabbed Beatriz by the hair, and squeezed her throat with his other arm as if the action were routine. His face was thin and long in the shadows scattered by the two lamps, his grin unsettling. "You wanted to poison me," he said. "That's not nice of you, not nice at all."

"Leave her alone," said the older woman. "Have you still not had enough, even after tonight?"

"Keep silent, Imelda," said the half-blood. "They won't listen anyway."

The sergeant turned around calmly, pointed his weapon, and fired four times. In the small room, the blasts sounded almost as loud as the cannon shots hours earlier. Alejandro saw the woman and the half-blood thrown backward by the impact of the bullets. Their eyes glazed quickly. It was the first time he witnessed people dying so close by. It was somehow unreal.

"Ricardo," said the young soldier. "Where are your good manners?" He laughed, but his eyes betrayed unease.

Ricardo sighed. "I'm afraid you're right," he said, still in the same polite way. "What we experienced last night whacked me right out of balance."

Alejandro turned his eyes to Beatriz in a wordless plea for support, but in the shadows cast by the fluorescent lamps, he could barely see her face. What he did see increased his sense of unreality: Pedro's right hand moved down from her throat and was fiddling at the buttons of her blouse.

Beatriz said nothing. Alejandro did nothing. He realized he'd foreseen this from the moment the two soldiers had entered. For an instant, this awareness gave him a bizarre satisfaction, a kind of lust related to complicity, as if he could exchange intimate thoughts with the lanky young soldier.

Ricardo turned his concrete eyes to him. "You look like a gentleman, a rare breed," he said in an unbearably friendly way. "If you behave accordingly, you'll leave this place alive. Is this woman your girlfriend?"

Alejandro realized no answer could provide safety. He nodded his agreement.

"You must understand that we went through a lot last night," the sergeant continued in his sickly manner. "A lot of shocking things. So my young friend is distraught at the moment. So, please consider what he's doing as just a release of nervous tension. That'll make it easier for you."

Alejandro was sure now: the young soldier, panting heavily and kissing Beatriz's neck, wasn't mad; it was the older officer who talked like a proud thoroughbred.

13

In the corner of Cristóbal's study, the television was on. Cristóbal watched the screen and chewed on his lower lip. Despite the early hour, Pelarón's press conference was packed with journalists. Cristóbal stroked his bald skull when he noticed Pelarón was wearing sunglasses, just like at his press conference ten years before, after his coup d'état.

Later, an anonymous street artist had painted a special series portraits of Pelarón with two bloody fangs, making the general look simultaneously ridiculous and sinister. Cristóbal knew Pelarón hadn't put on his black glasses at the time of his putsch for effect. The general was fifty-eight years old then, and he had spent seventy-two hours without sleep, during which he coordinated the coup from his school for *paracaidistas* in Las Vertientes.

He wore the glasses out of vanity. He wanted to hide the bags under his eyes

But this time, Cristóbal was convinced the general wore his sunglasses to achieve a particular effect: *I know who you take me for, and you will regret that you are right.* Pelarón's black dyed hair was carefully combed back and shone unnaturally in the bright light of the press room. His face had nothing of the nice uncle he usually liked to play.

Cristóbal involuntarily wrung his hands between his knees. The statement the general read for the microphone, without looking up from his paper, was like a series of blows in his face: the proclamation of a state of emergency, the closing of the borders for fifteen days, thorough cleansing of 'murderous left-wing elements,' a clean sweep in the government itself. "Once again, it has become clear that without my full leadership, this country is sinking into chaos," concluded Pelarón. "I am ready to accept my responsibility with all the consequences that it entails."

Cristóbal got up and turned off the television. His thoughts were tumbling over each other.

"They didn't want to listen to me," he mumbled. "They didn't want to listen to me, and what's the result? Those who survive will have to listen to me from now on."

———

14

Ricardo summoned Alejandro to serve him. Drinking quietly, he had watched Pedro's escapades with Beatriz.

Hard as a stone inside, Alejandro had listened to Beatriz's appeals, her screams, then her groaning, Pedro's gasps at his disappointing fuck when he came too fast. The energy in which the boy tackled Beatriz again seemed to be squeezed out of Alejandro. His legs trembled, his heart raced in his chest. Ricardo looked at the couple on the floor, nodding to himself with absent eyes.

"I can do it five times in a row," panted Pedro. Alejandro glanced at the door, guessed the distance. Getting help was all he could do for Beatriz. With a sharp tap, Ricardo put down his empty glass. A shiver went through Alejandro when he saw Ricardo's eyes focused on him. Ricardo nodded at his glass; Alejandro filled it up. Ricardo picked up his drink and turned around. Got to run now, Alejandro told himself. He looked at the door again. When he looked back, Ricardo stood a few steps closer to Pedro, drinking and watching the soldier.

On the floor, Beatriz turned her head and looked straight at Alejandro. It took a few seconds before Alejandro realized that she was not looking at him. He followed her gaze to the counter where Ricardo had carelessly left his rifle. Alejandro only had to take two steps to get it. Her head turned with short jerks on the stone floor. Now she looked at him, with eyes telling everything: *please, grab the gun, shoot...*

Alejandro stayed behind the bar. His legs refused to move; his eyes were glued to Ricardo when he knelt at Beatriz's head, diagonally next to Pedro's half-open, panting mouth.

"It works, Ricardo," groaned Pedro happily. "I'm going to co -."

"I see," Ricardo interrupted him dryly. "Your goddess of love gets warmer with the minute, yes, even hot, I'd say." With a sharp wrist movement, he poured the liquor out of his glass over Beatriz's face. His other hand emerged, and before Beatriz's scream died away, his thumb clicked his lighter. The alcohol dripping over Beatriz's cheeks and neck burned with a blue, jerkily flickering flame.

"What are you doing, man?" Pedro exclaimed above Beatriz's screams. He pushed himself away from her body and, without thinking of the trousers still on his ankles, took off his jacket. He tried to douse the flames on her face while Beatriz sobbed, writhing in pain.

She screamed once more before she lost consciousness. It awakened Alejandro from his lethargy. Ricardo had taken a few steps backward. With a satisfied smile, shaking his head like an admonishing father, he looked at the half-naked Pedro, who shouted something unintelligible, pressing his coat against Beatriz's face to kill the last flames.

Alejandro sprinted from behind the bar. The exit seemed to jump towards him; the doors seemed to open automatically. He ran into the street, made a half turn in the middle like a runaway horse, and dashed towards a side street.

Behind him, no footsteps were heard, no shots rang.

———

15

Their footsteps thumped on the metal bridge. Beatriz could hear them panting. *I am heavier than they thought.* She could barely tolerate the rising sun on her burned face. Beatriz tried to turn it away but couldn't find the strength to do so. She clung to the pain.

It was the fulfillment of something that had always haunted her, stirred up by a remark made by her father in her youth: *you will end badly because you're a disobedient girl.*

Her father's prediction had come true. She heard boots pounding on the iron footbridge, the old bridge over the Mayu she should never have crossed to listen to René's sermons in his church. She'd wanted to hook René up. *See where this sin had brought her.*

The footsteps stopped. Tears ran down Beatriz's burning cheeks without her making any sound. She did not open her eyes.

"A journey to the end of the night," said a civilized voice in the pale unreality above her. Beatriz had expected everything: a sharp death ache, a dull blow, endlessly echoing in her brain, but not this: her stomach leaping into her throat, a woeful feeling in all her joints that made her forget the pain of her face and neck for a moment. She opened her eyes and mouth just when she hit the filthy brown water of the Mayu with a slashing blow.

Her thoughts disappeared and gave way to overpowering instinct. She didn't want to end her journey like this, to allow them a victory like this. In the same way her father had entered the bathroom and held her open wrists until the ambulance had arrived, she took a grip on her fate. Through the pain, she found willpower that set her arms and legs in motion. She lifted her head above the smelly water and coughed. She looked to the right. There, in the morning sun, the city lay like a set for a fantasy movie.

Beatriz turned her head to the left. Smoke and a sea of grey and brown. In the distance lay the new, big bridge over the river: military trucks drove off and on. The Mayu had a strong current and stinking breath. The water cooled her burns. During the previous night, quite a few things had ended up in the water. Shells had exploded in the river, causing abnormally large amounts of mud. She inhaled water and started coughing again. Her body became heavy; she sank. She felt close to abandoning herself. She splashed her arms to and fro, tried to come up again.

If she let herself drown now, Alejandro, the coward who had not helped her, would never sing another love song for her: that was the only thing the weakling was able to do. Beatriz got another gulp inside. With a final effort, her fingers grabbed something floating diagonally above her. Her head surfaced.

It was a dead body to which she clung, one of the dozens thrown into the water that night.

16

"No, sir," said Cristóbal. "You will understand that, given the state of emergency following yesterday's events, the university has canceled all exhibitions and cultural events for an indeterminate period."

"Cristóbal," said Alejandro on the other side of the line. "Can't you talk freely?"

"Give me your phone number," said Cristóbal with a neutral glance at the armed soldier who was standing at the door of his office, looking very bored. "If the situation returns to normal, I'll contact you."

"Cristóbal," said Alejandro from the phone booth, glancing in distress at the fountains of the Plaza del Centenario, deserted at this early hour. "I don't dare go back to my room. After yesterday evening, they're sure to pick me up. And Beatriz, do you know what happened to her? We were…"

"A good day to you, sir," Cristóbal said.

"Wait! I have Beatriz's car, but I don't dare to use it for long. I have the key to her house, but I don't know if I can go there. All those patrols… Something terrible has happened to Beatriz, I…."

"Maybe you should contact João Pereira," said Cristóbal. "At the moment, there are American tourists in the model village La Paloma. You get there by the road that leads past Cerro Santa Lucia. No thanks necessary, sir, have a pleasant day."

Alejandro hung up. His eyes roamed the square, with its triumphal arch and the pool full of waterlilies, to the mountains behind the city. Alejandro remained on the spot for a while, blinking against the bright blue sky. Someone tapped behind his back against the glass of the phone booth. Alejandro turned around and looked into the angry eyes of a soldier, a heavily-built young man with a thick lower lip who irascibly directed him outside.

Alejandro opened the door. So this was the end, so much more prosaic than he had imagined. He began to shudder from head to toe. Fear dominated his senses, but not his thoughts. They formulated what he had to face: *you said you loved her, but you never did. You are someone who clings to others to give a pretense of authenticity to your dreams. You could have saved her; you could have tried; now you die as uselessly as you lived.*

Tears flowed down his cheeks.

The soldier frowned and shook his head. The anger disappeared from his eyes.

"Get out, mate," he said grumpily. "I understand that you're sad your girl dumped you, but I need to make an urgent phone call. Come on, get out of my sight, and find another woman. Enough women in the world."

Alejandro felt as if he were sinking through the dirt. This silly misunderstanding could only be a sign of fate.

17

João addressed the group of Americans in front of him. "You don't have to worry, folks: the hotels in the city are functioning normally. All public life in Terreno, despite yesterday's riots, has returned to normal. I have requested a military escort only for your peace of mind. I hope that you'll revisit our friendly village, another time, in better circumstances."

Jorge Espinoza translated for the impatiently waiting tourists. The Americans applauded politely and shuffled towards the waiting buses. Once full, they turned onto the road to Valtiago. In line with the tradition, the villagers stood waving beside the road. Two military motorcyclists rode in front of the buses. Two others followed.

"We should've kept them as hostages," said Jorge. "That

would've been world news. Those gringos would've shouted fire and murder. They were already pissing their trousers."

"And us too, almost," sighed João.

Jorge raised his dark eyes at him. "Do you feel guilty, João?"

"How do you mean?"

"I believe that attack on Pelarón was bogus," Jorge continued. "Staged to heighten his aura of invincibility. And at exactly the right moment, or rather the wrong moment, we added a little extra with the city black-out. The result? Hundreds of victims and Pelarón more firmly in the saddle than ever. Fate helped Pelarón, I'll admit it, but he played it smart. And us? We had bad luck."

"Nobody could've foreseen this."

"No, but we should've listened to Cristóbal." Jorge shook his head. "Perhaps the time wasn't ripe, as he said."

"For Cristóbal, the time is never ripe," said João gruffly. "For the same reason, I could say that the whole operation failed because Exu Tiriri wasn't satisfied."

"Yeah," said Jorge. He looked at the valleys below them, which shone golden yellow in the sunlight. "Why does that Brazilian devil of yours only serve the rich and the powerful? I would sell him my soul to get Pelarón in front of my cross-hairs once, just for a few seconds."

"Damn it," blurted João when he saw a military convoy approaching in the valley beneath them.

Jorge followed his gaze. "Oh, they won't find anything," he said. "It isn't the first time they've checked us. Maybe they'll close the village for a few days to bully us, but that's all. Come, let's go to the others. We'll...."

"Listen, Jorge," interrupted Pereira. "I'll drive the pickup to the dead salt mines, and from there, I'll take the old road to Valtiago. Then, when they ask about me, tell them I went shopping in the city. Okay?"

"But they're going to..."

João didn't listen anymore. He ran to his house, went in, grabbed a hunting rifle from the wall and ammunition in a drawer. He snatched the keys of the small truck from the nail beside the door: the pickup stood on the open ground next to the old Aymara church. Pereira started the engine and raced to the lock-up at the end of the village. A few passers-by looked surprised at him. One of the men called his name. João waved and drove on.

At the lock-up, he stopped in a cloud of dust, swung out of the truck, and opened the door. Carmencita stood in front of the window and turned around when João came in.

"Come," said João in a tone that brooked no contradiction. He saw the fear on her face, and for a moment, he felt compassion. He grabbed her by the arm. Her muscles trembled.

"I won't do anything to you if you do as I tell you," he said. "We have to leave."

18

With his hands on his knees, Alejandro stared at the Indian-designed tapestry in Beatriz's living room. The incident in the telephone booth had given him the courage to drive to Candalti's house anyway. To his surprise, no soldiers patrolled this district. The army had concentrated the troops around the *barrios* of the poor. Alejandro struggled with a pang of guilt as sharp and cold as an ice pick. He tried to keep it at bay. *Follow the soldier's advice at the telephone booth*, he thought. *Find another one, forget her.*

He told himself to look at the situation pragmatically. Pelarón had declared a state of emergency and replaced one of the junta generals. The borders had been closed. Pelarón's grip on the country was tight again. Alejandro was sure that the police or the army would arrest him if they checked his identity. But it was impossible to hole up in this house very long. Sooner or later, Manuel Durango would come here. It was almost inconceivable that Beatriz was still alive. She was Ernesto Candalti's daughter, a man respected by the junta. She had a seat on the board of directors of one of the largest firms in the country. The soldiers in the cantina had probably not known this.

Nevertheless, they would realize that the army would start an investigation if their crime were discovered. More than likely, they had killed her and made the body disappear. In the pandemonium of the *porqueriza*, that wouldn't have been any trouble at all.

Alejandro concentrated again on the question of how long he was safe in this house. The front doorbell rang. He jumped up and slipped via the patio into the garden. He was already at the back gate when the bell sounded again. Manuel wouldn't ring the bell; he'd already made that clear. Soldiers didn't do that either in the current atmosphere. Maybe Beatriz was standing at the door and couldn't enter her house because her house keys were in his pocket, attached to her Land Rover keys.

João and Carmencita came onto the patio. Alejandro took a few steps as if he still wanted to flee.

"João," he said like an aggrieved father to a stupid son. "You might as well hang a huge sign around her neck with 'I am the daughter of Captain Astíz' on it. The city is bursting with soldiers."

"They're too busy in the slums just now." The painter was agitated. "We had to get her out of the village. A convoy arrived. Where's Beatriz?"

Alejandro took a deep breath. "She's not here."

"What? Her car is on the driveway."

"Don't be so upset, João," said Alejandro wearily. "You'll

blow yourself up soon. And in hindsight, that would've been a better idea than blasting that idiotic power station."

Carmencita ignored the angry glances the two men exchanged and flung her arms around Alejandro's neck. "Alejandro," she whispered. "I want to believe what you told me, but I can't. Not till I can talk to my daddy and look him in the eyes. Why can't I talk to my daddy?"

————

19

"I'm starting to wonder if you're the kind of person who brings bad luck, Alejandro," said João.

During Alejandro's report of what happened the night before, in which he had wrapped his cowardice in fog, Carmencita huddled next to him on the sofa, pale and anxious. The painter watched her like a cat concentrating on a mouse.

Alejandro massaged his eyes. "I don't immediately have a funny answer to that. Would you have done anything differently?"

"Should she hear all this?" asked João, pointing at the girl.

"This is the regime that her foster father served so faithfully. Now at least she knows what it can do to people. Carmencita, do you still think we're lying to you? Do you think I would invent what happened to Beatriz?"

The girl's eyes were pitch black with fear and disbelief. She didn't answer, pulled her head deeper into her shoulders, hunched entirely over. Alejandro looked at her, frustrated. It was so difficult to gauge her feelings. She was continuously urged to choose, and every time the choice became more opaque.

"She doesn't believe a thing of what you've said," said João. "She loves that asshole."

"You can't blame her for being loyal."

"Stop," blurted João viciously. "You sound just like Cristóbal."

"What's wrong with you? Please keep calm; she's afraid of you."

"Calm?" said João. "Do you know how many people died yesterday? On top of that, you're sitting here telling me in that death-cult tone of yours what they did to Beatriz. And then you say: *please, keep calm.*"

"Why should I believe you?" Carmencita suddenly said. "Both of you are crazy." She looked at Alejandro. "Perhaps daddy put me out to foster parents for a while when I was four, and I was too young to remember him from before that." Triumph lit up her face. "But no, I remember him from when I was even smaller: how he bent over my crib, and I grabbed his beard."

"Víctor Pérez, your real father, had a beard for a while," said Alejandro. He regretted that he'd left his guitar in the Land Rover. He had lost the small breakthrough he had forced in the lock-up in La Paloma with *Requiem for Carmencita.* Maybe, he had to try again. He thought he understood what made Pereira so sour: it was Carmencita's love, locked tight like an oyster, for an assassin.

Carmencita stared stubbornly at the floor. Alejandro shook his head. Was he feeling a touch of admiration for her unshakeable fidelity, a quality he had so flagrantly lacked in his life?

Pereira jumped from his sofa, took a few steps, and bent over to her. "You silly goose, after what happened yesterday, you still dare..."

The girl curled up and began to cry.

"Stop that," said Alejandro. "You're only making it worse."

João straightened his back and turned around. "If I hadn't

blown up that plant yesterday, maybe the whole tragedy wouldn't have been..." His voice trailed away.

"You're lying to me because you want me to go mad!" whispered Carmencita. She put her hands in front of her face and screamed from the top of her lungs, "Daddy!" She jumped up from the sofa and ran to the door. Pereira cursed and went after her. He yanked her hands away from the door-knob and pulled her back to the couch while she kicked and screamed. He threw her on the sofa. The girl curled up like a fetus and hid her head in her arms.

"Congratulations, João," said Alejandro. "We can be proud of ourselves. We're delivering a child of fourteen to the mercy of a kaleidoscope of despair, fear, doubt, and distrust. And all this without result, that's the best part of it."

The front doorbell rang.

––––––

20

The bed was like a floating abyss, in the air and underground at the same time. Its flight pushed the pain to the background like the glow of a dying campfire. Resonating voices full of authority spoke to her from a great void. Beatriz tried to flee from what she was forced to listen to, but width and length no longer existed, only up and down, and blaring voices echoing in between. What did they say? They jabbered mercilessly about delicate secrets drowned out by noise and murmur, about the most lucid insights cursed with a tail of darkness, and finally about death as a way of existence without all these contradictions.

The nurse who entered the room heard the sedated patient murmur and bent over the burnt face. She thought the woman had been lucky: the skin tissue was not profoundly affected.

A wave of gossip followed her admission to the hospital: she was said to be one of Pelarón's sweethearts who had crossed the bridge yesterday, attracted by the violent scenes in the *porqueriza*. There, the "brutalized cretins" of the slum had caught and tortured her.

The nurse bent her knees and looked closer. The skin would probably heal reasonably well, and the burns wouldn't leave the woman with awful scars after surgery. But she wouldn't be beautiful anymore.

The patient opened her eyes. The nurse looked into those eyes and felt that the fire that burned inside the woman was far worse than the flaming alcohol someone had poured over her cheeks and neck.

From the burning inside her, she would never heal.

21

"Her doctor called me," said Cristóbal. "Beatriz is in the same hospital her father was." He coughed. "Her burns seem not too bad." He cast an enigmatic glance at Alejandro.

Alejandro was sitting next to Carmencita. The girl pretended to flip through a fashion magazine, but her eyes kept going from one speaker to another. The mood in Beatriz's spacious living room reminded Alejandro of the distress in his cell, leering despair that spread its membrane over everything.

"What does this tone of yours mean, Cristóbal? That I should've stayed with her and defended her? You mean, like a gallant knight with a bar stool against two madmen with automatic rifles, mmm?"

"I just wanted to say that her wounds are not as bad as you thought," Cristóbal replied smoothly. "In your mind, she was dead or at least mutilated." Alejandro felt the weight of the glances of both men in the room. What dealings did he actually have with these people? They had dragged him along in their foolish revolt, and what was the result? That they were eyeballing each other full of suspicion. It would be better for him to leave and make sure he never had anything to do with these losers again.

Alejandro stood up. "I've got to go. I have to speak to her."

João, standing in front of the window overlooking the garden, turned around. "It's far too dangerous for you to go outside. You'll get yourself arrested in no time."

"He's right," said Cristóbal. "Besides, she'll be sedated."

"I won't meet any patrols," retorted Alejandro. He looked João in the eyes. "Your Brazilian voodoo devil Exu Tiriri has just whispered it in my ear. He's a comrade of mine."

The Cruel Need To Love

1

THE BUS STOPPED A FEW DOZEN METERS BEFORE THE CATHOLIC hospital. Along the way, through the city, Alejandro had seen an overwhelming military presence, but few checks were being carried out. The city and the army seemed to be recovering from the shock.

He was fifteen minutes too early. The city was much less crowded than usual, and the bus had found its way through the traffic unusually fast. The main building of the large hospital had been refurbished, and new signs surrounded the building site next to it. They boasted that South America's most modern scanner would be installed in the new wing. Nowhere was it written that this clinic was unaffordable for three-quarters of the city's inhabitants.

Beatriz had been found by an employee of the Banco del Estado, which had offices on the banks of the Mayu, upstream where the river was no longer the dividing line between the slums and the prosperous city districts. He had seen her unconscious on the river bank during his lunch break. After scanning her passport, his superiors had immediately called the chairman of the board of directors of the Candalti company. Humberto arranged for her to be admitted directly to the clinic.

Alejandro walked into the garden to the left of the main building. Neatly shaved lawns, gazebos, American oaks, and silver birches. "If it had been me who'd been perishing on the bank, they would've kicked me back into the ditch," he muttered. He neatly pulled a fold in his trousers and sat down on a brightly painted bench. The resentment he felt was so elusive, so devoid of a clear origin, that he couldn't fight it. He'd cherished the same kind of resentment against Víctor.

Possibly, love was its engine.

He'd failed with anyone he loved because love held up a mirror to him.

His eyes roamed the attractively pruned trees. His thoughts jumped from one memory to another like a squirrel, ready to change direction with the slightest breeze.

When he told his dad that he wanted to give up his studies to play the guitar with Aconcagua, his father had stared at him with sad eyes. "Why do you always want to hurt everyone who loves you, boy?" More than fifteen years later, his father's monk-like patience suddenly made his throat ache.

"Yes, old man," said Alejandro. "You were more than right, okay? Happy now?"

Cruel is my desire to love. It was a line from one of Aconcagua's songs that once brought a lump into his throat. It felt like pompous poetry now, rattling as hard as Cristóbal's political plans and João's revolutionary fantasies. In him, Alejandro knew, the desire to love was deceptive.

Alejandro shook his head, tossed by a tempest of self-pity. Instead of the summits of fame that he had imagined in his youth, he had a ruined life behind him. Who was Alejandro Juron? Not a troubadour, basking in the warmth of the audience, nor a conscientious citizen, nor a cold-blooded scoundrel. He realized that he had something of all these men. Resignation rose in him. He wanted to throw off his past like a dog shaking its wet fur.

"You know who I'd like to be?" Alejandro murmured at the candy wrap blowing between his feet. "Exu Kukeleku in person. That would produce some sparks, wouldn't it?"

He looked up. Visitors walked along the paths to the automatic doors of the hospital.

It was time, high time for everything.

———

2

Cristóbal was watching television in Beatriz's living room, but his attention was elsewhere. He wondered why his fellow activists didn't seem to understand the dialectics of his political goals. They made too many foolish mistakes, errors resulting from chaotic thought processes.

He wondered whether ten years of dictatorship conditioned the Terreneans' brains. There had to be an explanation for why everything was flashing in red. At noon, he'd returned to Beatriz's house to ensure João had done nothing stupid after Alejandro's departure. The TV screen replayed the attack on the general for the umpteenth time.

The image froze dramatically when the second bodyguard was lifted from the ground by the impact of the bullets. Then Pelarón appeared on the screen during his press conference, explaining with somber dignity how communist forces tried to kill him. Pelarón told the journalists in the press room that they subsequently caused a massacre of the least well-off in Canela, hoping to undermine the nation's morale.

His tone became even more strained when he told them he had ordered his army to intervene. He showed remorse and anger when he talked about the 'horrible consequences for the poor neighborhood.' He brought his hand to his forehead; his voice faltered. For a moment, the general's head floated in close-up as if it had been separated from his body and had acquired eternal validity. When Pelarón raised his head again, the camera retreated so the general could look at his people with piercing eyes. He announced far-reaching changes that would benefit all Terreneans, rich and poor.

Cristóbal looked at João, who watched the general's performance with him. "The circus will be over sooner than we thought," he said. He got up and turned off the TV. "In a few days, the borders will probably be open again. They're broadcasting the same story for the sixth time today; a sign that Pelarón thinks the situation is under control."

"I wonder who committed the attack on Pelarón," said João. "Have you seen how, ehm, *photogenically* the cameras recorded those bodyguards dying?"

Cristóbal coughed. "And how they swung to Canela's church just after the murders."

"René can't be behind all this," said João. "Pelarón must have ordered a fictitious attack on himself; there's no other explanation. That piece of shit is capable of it."

"The newspapers say that the bullets were fired from the church tower."

"Oh, Cristóbal. Don't start again."

"Why else did René show his face to Kurt? Explain that to me." Cristóbal looked tired. In the sunlight that shone through the open sliding doors of the patio, his naked skull shone as if he had smeared it with grease. "Have we overlooked something?"

"We've overlooked so many things," said João. "Especially that we're not as good at scheming as we thought." He sighed. "I have to go back to La Paloma."

"Isn't that too dangerous?"

João shrugged. "The people in the village depend on me. Nobody will suspect me; I've been cautious. I've always listened to your advice until now. And see where we're standing."

"You think that I'm too careful?"

The two men had emerged from a bitter discussion. João had wanted to smuggle Carmencita and Alejandro out of the country. According to him, the story about Carmencita would be picked up much better abroad. Moreover, in a foreign country, the child could be separated from the influence she suffered so intensely here. Cristóbal thought it was too dangerous to attempt smuggling them out.

João looked through the window. "Enough bungling, that's what I think. An armed mountain-based guerrilla organization is our last hope. Pelarón doesn't understand any other language."

Cristóbal didn't answer. João turned around. Suddenly, they were facing each other. They saw it in each other's eyes: their paths were irrevocably separating.

3

Beatriz slept. Of course, she slept. Was that perhaps why Alejandro had come? To say goodbye without her looking at him accusingly?

He had passed through the hospital corridors without any problems. Cristóbal had given him the room number. In a suit borrowed from Manuel, he looked classy, very much a representative of the Compañía de Importación Candalti.

It was warm in the room. Beatriz was sweating in her pale hospital gown; she lay on her side facing the window, with its blinds half lowered. Large plasters stuck to her face. He saw patches of discolored skin on her neck. Did he feel nothing now, even though, in the hospital garden, he'd been overwhelmed by waves of intense emotion? He sat down next to the bed in a faux-leather armchair, stared at her, turned his head away. His gaze wandered through the window. The garden suddenly appeared to be an incomprehensible place, separated from the world. In it, Juron had concluded that he would never be able to make anything of his life. His actions were controlled by unpredictable cowardice.

"Do you know why I'm such a coward, Beatriz?" Alejandro mumbled. "Dissociation is the culprit, not me. Astíz boasted to me that he studied the influence of fear and stress on the human mind. It would've been better if I'd stayed in my cell. There, in daydreams, I could flee to any place I chose and be whoever I wanted. In prison, I created a new Alejandro Juron. But it was only a scarecrow who was pecked bare in the outside world." Beatriz kicked off the blankets in her sleep and turned around; her hospital shirt crept up. He could see her buttocks. Alejandro looked at them and shook his head. Her nakedness didn't stir lust, but sadness; no desire, but loss. He kneeled in front of the bed and let his head rest against her buttocks. She groaned. *Could you have helped me to cure myself, Beatriz? What a question from someone who let you down so badly.*

A nurse entered the room. Alejandro lifted his head. "Oh," said the middle-aged, sturdy woman. Her eyes turned dark with anger. She turned around and ran outside. Alejandro followed her closely and when she ran to the right, shouting "Miguel!" he turned left. Juron ran through the passage, didn't wait for the elevators, but rushed with rumbling feet down the stairs. He walked quickly through the main hall.

When the automatic doors opened for him, he ran to the bus stop without looking back. Running, he realized more clearly than ever that he wasn't born to write love ballads or revolutionary songs as Víctor had done. Although he could imitate them, he had a blind spot for beauty, love, and emotion. Alejandro knew he only had the talent to depict the brutal, the grotesque, and the ugly. In reality, he couldn't sing cogently about a first kiss, sweet dreams, pastel tenderness.

"Me, a scarecrow plucked bare?" he mumbled. "Not even that."

———

4

Beatriz woke up. Somebody had shut the curtains. She felt as if she'd been washed ashore after an exhausting battle against a raging sea. When she realized that she was lying in a hospital room, she immediately felt that it was the room where her father had died. It was inevitable that at any moment now, she would hear her father's spirit say, "Didn't I always tell you how badly you would end, disobedient daughter?" She saw his eyes floating mockingly through the room. Her face, neck, and chest were glowing. In her fever, she saw René's face wreathed with flames, his eyes closed. She heard his voice whispering in her ear: *I'm burning in hell, Beatriz, not because I've lost my faith, but because I didn't dare to love.* She tried to deny René's presence and couldn't. *Only the dead come to visit me,* she thought vaguely. She turned around; the pain in her body shot in all directions but remained bearable because of the painkillers and sleeping pills. The memory of Alejandro's eerie numb eyes in the *cantina* was much more painful. His eyes had betrayed that he had understood her wordless supplication to grab the rifle on the counter but didn't dare to do it. "Oh, Alejandro," she moaned, swept to and fro by anger and pity.

She lingered on the bed, reflected for a long time. Then she tried to get up. Apart from the numb feeling in her body and the glow over her face and neck, she felt very little. She turned on the bedside lamp, slipped gently from the bed, and went to the wall cupboard. Humberto had brought brand new clothes. Beatriz chose an elegant black suit. When she was dressed, she looked in the mirror above the sink. Her swollen face looked the color of an old potato in the harsh light. Her eyes, her forehead, and her left cheek were free of bandages.

There were several painkillers on the bedside cabinet; she swallowed them all with a glass of water and opened the door of her room. The hospital corridor was deserted. A clock on the wall showed it was thirty minutes to midnight. Beatriz slipped outside and ran with her shoes in her hands through the hallway.

She turned around the corner to the elevators. Two doors further on, she heard talking: the night nurses. She walked with a self-confident air past the open door. Nobody reacted. The first elevator was available. She stepped inside, pressed the button for the ground floor. A little later, she alighted in a hospital lobby dominated by a large glass dome. There was no one there either. The hall was as dimly lit as the rest of the place. Beatriz turned left at the end of the row of elevators to the emergency night entrance. This corridor was narrow and brightly lit. At the end of it, there was a glass booth in which three nurses sat and talked. Next to it was a door for bringing in emergency cases. Beatriz bent down and put on her shoes. She ran past the glass cage. She heard nothing, but from the corner of her right eye, she saw movement. She pulled the door open and ran across the ambulance bays to the driveway. As soon as she'd reached the first row of trees, she looked back. Three figures were standing on the parking lot; one of them called out to her. Beatriz ran under the trees towards the street. She clambered over the white-painted enclosure—only knee-high—and ran on. The heat in her body propelled her forward; she'd never been so fast.

———

5

"Enough," said João. "I've had enough of it."

"Oh?" said Alejandro, who was playing drafts with Carmencita in Beatriz's living room. "And to what do we owe that?" After Alejandro's return to the house, he liberated Carmencita from Beatriz's bedroom. The girl seemed more willing and less preoccupied with the future.

"Owe what?" said João.

"Your turn, Carmencita," said Alejandro when he noticed that the girl was casting anxious glances in João's direction. "From your words, I gather that you think we're not doing enough and that you're going to do something."

"No one can understand your gibberish anymore," rumbled João opening the curtains of the front window. "No one can understand anything anymore in this country," he added.

In the full bus, on the way back to Beatriz's house, Alejandro felt confused and guilty. But as so often with him, a counter-reaction quickly emerged. Was he supposed to let himself be bullied *by himself*? The counter-reaction triggered a great zest for life. Up till now, he'd survived the most arduous hardships, hadn't he? He should be proud of that! And sooner or later, the highs and lows of his mind would result in a full-length album—a monument of enduring beauty that would make him immortal.

Back in Beatriz's house, João's dark face put Alejandro's feet back on the ground. Cristóbal left after yelling that "he washed his hands of them." Alejandro had tried to placate João. The effect was counterproductive.

Alejandro noticed that Carmencita was becoming increasingly wary and tried to distract her, "Will you come with me and watch television?"

"Watch television," repeated João, shaking his head. "Do

that: there'll be lots to see, I'm sure. I'm not staying here. I'm going back to the mountains."

"What can you do there?"

"It all started there," said Pereira. "In the mountains, the Terreneans once fought Spanish domination. From there, we must now tackle Pelarón."

"What would you think of traveling with me to Europe?" Alejandro said to Carmencita. "I could teach you to sing. I'm sure you'll sing very well after a bit of practice. Your mother could do it, but she didn't want to perform on stage because your father was so famous."

Carmencita looked at him bewildered. Again, Alejandro noticed how thin her face was. She tried to create an aura of indifference around herself, but he noticed that she'd started to squint. In no way did she resemble her mother or the toddler he had known. *We did not kidnap her; that happened a long time ago.*

"My father doesn't sing," she said softly. Tears welled up in her eyes. She clung to the life she had known. At that moment, Alejandro felt clear that Carmencita would never play the role they had assigned for her. But neither could she remain the devoted daughter of Kurt Astíz-Fitzroy, now that doubt had crept into her heart. The girl in front of him was the combined product of her genetic makeup and ten years of Pelarónism, a wretched hybrid who could only elicit cruelty or pity.

"Are you spewing stupidities again, Juron?" asked João. "Do you have a magic wand that will take you hotfoot to Europe?" Alejandro kept silent, but he thought in his heart: *you're nothing like the painter who told us in La Paloma about the rainbows he loved to paint. We were all kidnapped a long time ago and started playing someone other than ourselves.*

"Listen," said Alejandro. "It is too late to leave now. Let's wait another night, and tomorrow you can decide what to do." He shrugged. "I no longer have any illusions."

"Nor do I," answered João, who in all his life had never cherished them more than now.

———

6

The roar of a revved-up motorbike echoed in the street. Beatriz looked over her shoulder, ran down a few stairs to a basement, and made herself as small as possible. Her fear of being discovered on the street after the curfew wasn't mere self-preservation. It sprang from her determination to reach the goal she had in mind. The staccato of an automatic rifle tensed up her muscles. The streets were deserted; the curfew was strict, but she'd got this far already and had to continue.

A new salvo. Beatriz hid her face in her hands. She sensed someone was near and looked up. A man came running down the street. It made her recall the day she'd seen Juron again after their first meeting. It was that memory, not the shocking image of a man running for his life, that made her weep with violent spasms of her diaphragm. Behind her, a jeep turned into the street and accelerated noisily. A new volley of shots, then a noise as if linen were being torn, and a scream that faded fast in the dark, deserted street. With her body pressed firmly against the ground, Beatriz knew where she wanted to be.

High in the air.

———

7

Alejandro wasn't dreaming when he heard Beatriz calling his name in the no man's land of his early morning dozing. He lay on the sofa in her living room and blinked his eyes.

João turned around on the other sofa. "Alejandro," he whispered. "Can you hear that?"

"Yes."

Sharper than usual but unmistakable, her voice sounded in the garden. "Alejandro, open up. I know you're inside."

Alejandro started giggling. João got up and stared at him in amazement. "What are you doing, man?" he whispered.

Alejandro squawked, "She has come to look for me. She'll never leave me alone, never."

João shook his head.

"She saw her car standing on the driveway," Alejandro continued, more calmly. "She can't get into her own house because I have her keys." He swung his legs off the sofa.

"Alejandro!" Beatriz fiddled at the back door.

"You have to open the door. She'll scream the whole neighborhood awake otherwise," continued Alejandro.

"Why don't you do it?"

"Go on, open up, João. I'm not wearing any trousers."

João cursed under his breath and walked to the sliding glass doors of the patio. He pulled them open, walked across the courtyard, and switched on the garden lamps, although the sky already had the color of old ice. Alejandro looked at João's muscular back and thought of the crazy sergeant in the café who'd stood with his back to him while his rifle lay on the nearby counter.

The difference in light between inside and outside made Beatriz and João look like two elongated shadows when they entered the room. Beatriz came in first. Her face was a mass of grayish-white bandages and red, swollen skin. It made her hair seem blacker and more beautiful than ever: never had it looked more glossy and delicate.

"Sweetheart," said Alejandro. "It's not a dream!"

Beatriz looked at him as if he had just told a wild lie. Standing in front of her, dangling his arms loosely next to his body, he remembered how, in The Last Supper, he'd refashioned his past to become an artistic hero who turned against the junta and suffered for it. Was there, in reality, any distinction between Kurt Astíz-Fitzroy and Alejandro Juron?

Beatriz turned away from him and addressed João . "As soon as it gets light, I'll call Humberto," she said. "I need him to send a driver with an official limousine from dad's company. He must pick us up as soon as possible."

Carmencita pounded on the bedroom door and screamed, "Open up! Who's there, Alejandro?"

Beatriz looked at the door for a moment but didn't otherwise react. That fascinated Alejandro even more than her face.

"Calm down," he called. "Go back to sleep, Carmencita. It is still too early, not yet seven o'clock."

"I want to go back to daddy! When can I go back to daddy, Alejandro?" The girl behind the door started to moan.

"Limousine?" João said. "Where do you want to go, Beatriz? We can't go anywhere!" He shook his head; his gaze slid shyly along her face. "When is all this going to end?" he said helplessly.

———

8

Her plan, said Beatriz, was as follows: she would tell Laínez she was out of the hospital and that the limousine had to pick her up. However, she would order the chauffeur to drive her to the flying club. She would offer the pretext that there were essential documents in her plane. They would have no problems on the way to the airport: the large, American limousines, flagged with *Casa de Importación Candalti*, were untouchable, even at this tense time. With the Cessna, they could cross the Cordillera and fly to freedom. Crossing the mountain ridges close to Valtiago was risky but not impossible.

During Pelarón's coup, members of the People's Government had fled in the same way.

João listened to her quiet speech with his arms on his knees and shook his head increasingly vigorously.

"Why the sudden rush?" he said. "Leaving everyone behind? And what about Cristóbal?"

"Cristóbal is safe because of his position," she answered calmly. "Nobody suspects him. Besides, he'll never want to come along."

João hesitated.

"You helped to kidnap Carmencita and attack the power station," Beatriz continued in the same rational tone. "Sooner or later, they'll search for you, and, no doubt, they'll arrest Alejandro too. And as far as the child is concerned..." She turned her gaze towards the window and the pale sky behind it. "She has to leave this place."

"But La Paloma..." started Pereira.

"The village will manage without you. If you get caught, your reputation will reflect on La Paloma."

João nodded slowly as he stared at the ground.

"Once you're in Brazil, you'll be able to revisit your voodoo god," Alejandro said. "That'll do you good."

He felt Beatriz's eyes on him. Did they shine with irony and aversion? Alejandro lowered his eyes.

"Agreed?" Beatriz said.

9

The Stone Sentinel
and the sky wind
are night brothers.
When the mountains moan

> *deep in their lap,*
> *the wind becomes an arrow*
> *and the Guardian turns red.*

Alejandro wondered if his voice was clear enough. Several times he felt his voice catching. Beatriz had asked him to sing something. Carmencita sat close to him on the sofa as if she were looking for protection. Juron believed he could feel her confusion. *The Stone Sentinel* had been one of her favorite songs; her father had often sung it for her.

Beatriz called Humberto Laínez, who was surprised she was already home but promised that the limousine would arrive as soon as possible. Beatriz had insisted on haste because she knew that sooner or later, the hospital staff would call him and tell him that she left without a physician's consent. She could only hope that the hospital would wait as long as possible before acknowledging that a patient had simply walked away.

When Beatriz had asked Alejandro to sing a song to kill time, he sensed a double meaning behind everything she said. He was convinced that she hadn't forgotten their wordless communication in the café, although she hadn't said a word about it. "Sing a song to us, Alejandro. That would do me good," she had said when an uncomfortable silence had fallen in the living room. He obeyed and sang with body and soul. This old song full of symbolism, which Víctor had adapted from an Indian legend, suddenly seemed ambiguous to him.

> *The Stone Sentinel,*
> *guardian of the white*
> *that does not accept a footstep,*
> *only begs for innocence.*

The words resonated with profound meaning in Alejandro. He couldn't protect himself from the sadness they triggered. They aroused mesmerizing, weeping sounds in his guitar. He didn't look up when Carmencita started crying next to him, silently this time. The last strophe was coming on. Alejandro didn't know it, but he never looked more like Víctor Pérez than at this moment.

The bell rang. Carmencita jumped up, ran to the door, and swung it open so brusquely that it banged against the wall. Alejandro dropped his guitar on the floor; Beatriz stayed where she was, João jumped up, cursing.

Carmencita was already in the hall and opening the front door. Beatriz's driver was standing on the pavement. The girl tried to cling to the startled man.

"I want to go to my daddy! Help me! They're holding me captive!"

When the girl tried to squeeze past the driver, João dove through the open door and grabbed her rougher than he'd intended. A new hysteria screwed up her face.

"Miss Candalti," the driver said, astonished. "Where is she? I'm supposed to pick her up here. Who are you? What are you doing?" He was dressed in a nice suit, a man with impeccable manners, proud of his function, used to transporting busy and hasty men. He took a step in João's direction but changed his mind when the painter's size became apparent to him.

Beatriz appeared in the hall, closely followed by Alejandro. João pulled Carmencita into the corridor and took her up to the bedroom.

Beatriz stood squarely in front of the driver. "Manolo," she said. "That was fast."

The driver lowered his eyes. Alejandro couldn't tell if that was because of her face or what he had just seen.

"Alejandro," Beatriz continued without looking at him. "We have to go to the bank. I need money. Will you join me? We'll come back immediately to pick up the others. This will give Carmencita a chance to calm down." She nodded at the driver: "The girl is the daughter of an artist from La Paloma. Her father has been missing in Canela since yesterday. The poor child is distraught." The driver nodded sympathetically. Beatriz turned to Alejandro. "Are you ready?"

Alejandro looked her in the eyes and didn't know what to answer. When a muted scream came out of the bedroom, he nodded, although he didn't like the prospect of being alone in the car with Beatriz. She stepped down the garden path and walked past the driver to the black Buick on the street. Alejandro closed the front door behind him and followed her. He looked at her back, and suddenly he remembered the last lines of the song he had sung.

> *The Stone Sentinel,*
> *hollow as an ancient tree*
> *Guardian of the dream.*

10

The trip in the heavy traffic on Valtiago's central avenue passed in jolts and bumps. The limousine dipped up and down with constant acceleration and braking. Alejandro thought he could feel angry heat next to him, where Beatriz was sitting, but he gazed forward and occasionally met the driver's eyes in the rear-view mirror.

"You sang nicely," said Beatriz.

"Thank you."

"Only now do I know how beautifully you can sing." She laughed.

"Beatriz..."

She cut him off. "Do you think we'll manage, Alejandro? Flying over the mountains?"

"I don't know."

"You sound as if it no longer interests you."

He wanted to answer: *No, Beatriz, you sound as if it no longer interests you.* Instead, he said, "We've piled blunder on top of blunder."

"That's how it goes if you want to stand hollow like an old tree in front of the Stone Sentinel."

He could find no trace of irony in her voice. "What will you do if we get away from here?"

"Become beautiful again," said Beatriz. She laughed.

"How will Cristóbal react?"

"He'll form a new revolutionary committee and tell himself that he was the only one in our group who had common sense. Maybe that's even true."

Alejandro realized he wanted to ask her for forgiveness. But, he couldn't do it or didn't dare to. The reason escaped him.

"Here we are, Miss Beatriz," said the driver.

"Very well," she said calmly.

They stopped in the parking lot of the Banco del Estado, a little pool in the hustle and bustle of Valtiago. The mountain ridges shone like marble in the sun. Beatriz took out a key; Alejandro finally turned his head to her. Her gaze was open, without any accusation in it. She gave him the key and said, "It's better that you go inside: I would be walking too much in the spotlight. This is the key to my locker in the public room. Number 242. My name is on it. Don't go to the safes. They're asking for proof of identity there. You'll find a brown envelope in the locker. That's all you have to bring along."

He nodded and grabbed the key but couldn't suppress a shiver when their fingertips touched.

"Beatriz..."

How radiant and forgiving her eyes were, how soft and melodious was her voice when she replied, "Just go, Alejandro."

He got out. He turned around two steps away from the

car; she looked at him and lowered her window. Alejandro felt a tingling sensation in his body. "It's all about letting go, Alejandro," she said evenly. The electric window of the Buick slid up. Alejandro turned around, confused, at the point of discovery it seemed, but then he nodded. She was his redeeming angel who, despite all his selfishness, everything he had done wrong, was still devoted to him. That angel would take him away from this land, his birth nest he had polluted, and wanted to leave behind, so he could be cleansed. Even when he was much younger, he had dreamed of salvation, of a love that persisted despite evil.

Alejandro walked confidently into the bank. With a steady stride, he went to the locker and opened it.

It was empty.

Alejandro turned around and ran out of the building. Older ladies, dressed in the latest Paris fashion, stared at him and raised their chins in the air. A uniformed security officer stood to attention and realized then that the suspect was leaving the bank instead of trying to rob it.

"Beatriz!" called Alejandro, running through the revolving glass door.

He rushed outside.

The black limousine was no longer in the parking lot.

The Unbearable Lightness Of A Sense
Of Honor

1

WHEN SHE SAW THE STEEL WIRE FENCE ALONG THE RUNWAY OF the *Aerodromo Olympiada,* Beatriz Candalti thought of Carmencita. She regretted not having the chance to know the child better. "I could've taught you a lot, girl," she murmured.

"You said something, Miss?" the driver asked. Only then did Beatriz notice his inquisitive eyes in the rear-view mirror. She bit on her lower lip. She'd told him that she first had to retrieve important papers from her plane before driving to the headquarters of Casa de Importación Candalti, where Humberto was waiting for her. The driver accepted her explanation, but she had to be careful. He had already witnessed some quite unusual events.

"That my face is still hurting," she said, looking into his mirrored eyes. He turned his gaze away and stopped at the gate of the tiny airport. "It won't take long," she said, stepping out. "Take some time to read your newspaper."

He smiled. "There is only bad news in it, señorita," he said. He glanced at Beatriz's face and realized she may have misinterpreted his joke. "Shall I come along to help you?"

"No," she said. "That won't be necessary."

Beatriz opened the gate with her key and closed it again behind her, as required by the regulations of the private airport. She walked to the hangar where her plane was parked. At this early hour, there were already some people in the small control tower. She had to submit a flight plan. She knew how to avoid that. Ironically, Manuel had given her inspiration when he told her about how terrorists could plan aerial attacks on the city. She blinked at the sun and felt its heat spreading painfully over her face. Her face, the defense-less face she'd shown all the men in her life, had earned the right to hurt. The pain kept her sharp. Beatriz opened the hangar where the Cessna was parked and walked around it. Images came to her of films in which airplanes performed daring maneuvers. At the back of the hangar, there were cans of oil and a jerry can with petrol.

Pouring gasoline and mixing it with the oil was not a chore: she felt skillful, secure, and determined. Holding the flame of a lighter to this mixture was a joy; seeing it flare was a self-confirmation. The smoke, black and bulging like some apparition from a nightmare, would soon be visible outside the hangar. Beatriz climbed into the Cessna's cockpit. Usually, airport personnel pushed the plane out of the hangar, but she didn't doubt that she could taxi it out. The sun reflected in the cockpit; it blinded her for a moment. The wings vibrated as she crossed the grass strip separating her from the runway. She went too fast, slipped a little, corrected immediately.

"N641C, you have not provided your flight path," the radio said. Beatriz didn't answer, braked at the beginning of the runway, and got out of the plane. One of the oil drums she had put near the fire burst apart. Heavy smoke rippled outside. She waved her arms at the tower and made gestures of surprise and panic towards the hangar. It was not long before a man threw open the glass door of the control tower and came running out. Beatriz stepped back into her plane.

The concrete rolled away beneath her when she took off. The radio remained silent. Below her, she saw several men sprinting toward the hangar.

As she had expected, the burning hangar absorbed the attention of the three staff members. Manuel once spent days telling her scenarios whereby terrorists could attack the capital. During his airport story, she hadn't been bored because she liked flying. The airport operated under the Terrenean Ministry of Civil Aviation, which was accountable to the military air force. Any aircraft that took off without a flight plan would be reported by the control tower to the military base north of Valtiago. If a plane took off without permission, it would be less than ten minutes—a timeframe that Manuel had emphasized with much patriotism—before army jets surrounded it. Last night in the hospital, in a haze of pain and bitterness, she thought about how to avoid this—by providing so much distraction at the airport that no one would report her departure for several minutes.

That was all the time she needed.

She rose up from the valley in which Valtiago lay. She could imagine her driver, who undoubtedly had looked upwards in amazement when she took off.

It would have been a lot better if Alejandro had been standing there.

———

2

"How do you mean, *taken off?*" Humberto was not only irritated but also bewildered.

"Yes, sir," replied the driver in his car phone. "Miss Candalti told me to drive to the airport and to wait for her. I didn't suspect anything, sir."

"Taken off?" repeated Humberto Laínez. "When?"

"Just now, sir. And there's a fire at the airport. The hangar that housed Miss Candalti's plane is on fire. They're busy putting it out."

The driver had often had to deal with Laínez's domineering behavior. The silence on the other side of the line was more beautiful than any music in his ears. He peered at the sky through the limousine's reflective windows. The plane was no longer visible.

"There is something else, sir," he said, hiding his gloating delight at his boss's confusion.

"What then?"

"When I arrived at Miss Candalti's house, I noticed some odd things, sir."

———

3

"Faster, Pedro," said sergeant Ricardo Córdone Cerdá. "Are your tires made of soapsuds?" In the back of the jeep, the three soldiers smiled. They had become accustomed to their sergeant's unusual turn of phrase. Cerdá could have climbed higher in the military hierarchy if it weren't for his haughty irony towards his superiors. The soldiers had heard stories of sergeant Cerdá's past. Ten years ago, he served in a *grupo especial* that had carried out torture and group executions in the football stadium.

"What can we expect, sergeant?" asked one of the soldiers, a young peasant boy with a clean-shaven skull. "Incidentally, aren't we heading in the wrong direction? There's only blue blood living round here." The boy got what he'd hoped for: everyone laughed.

"This is the house of a Miss Candalti," Cerdá said. "Her father was the owner of a large company—he died recently. One of his colleagues just contacted the captain about some strange goings-on in her house. It's probably a false alarm, but it still woke the captain from his siesta." The soldiers laughed somewhat uneasily. You had to watch it with Cerdá. If he went into one of his moods, you could quickly be in the soup.

The driver swung into the Calle Ordoñez. "Number 44, there it is," he said. He stopped a short distance from the modern American-style house.

"Listen up, now," said Cerdá. "This is a fancy area. People are sensitive. If you get the wind up them, they'll kick up a stink and start waving their money around. So we ring the doorbell like well-brought-up soldiers. There is probably nothing wrong. And wipe your feet when they let you in, you 'orrible peasants."

The men sniggered behind his back.

———

4

René, would you believe me if I told you I loved you? Because I did. The odd thing was: I knew exactly why. You were my father figure; with you, I thought I didn't have to be on guard. However 'modern' I tried to be, I still felt safe around you because, in my eyes, you were a man who had a higher purpose in his life in which everything, including sexual desire, was subordinate. Because I felt safe, I could afford to tease you. To reap your admiration, I gave you glimpses of my body, pretending not to realize. I wanted to turn you into a father I could squeeze against my breasts without resentment, guilt, or fear.

I wanted too much, didn't I, René? I wanted Alejandro to play my tragic hero, though he wasn't that, and I had to make you play the man who had given himself to transcendence. My parents used to scold me in my youth because I always wanted too much, so all my life, I saw myself as a foolish woman full of romantic dreams.

Now I understand that I wasn't that, René. I know it now while I am sitting in my plane, and for the first time in my life, I feel entirely free.

There's a fear in this freedom I feel through my body, but there's also an irrevocable certainty.

I had the right to desire so much from life. That is why I will die differently from you, René: I am convinced you have put an end to your life because you felt you were forced to by yourself.

I have made a choice; finally, I have made a choice.

———

5

"For God's sake, turn on the television, Carmencita," João said. "Don't just sit there staring at the floor; it makes me nervous. And eat something. You haven't eaten all day."

The girl didn't lift her head. She sat bent over on the sofa with her arms wrapped around her knees. João took a step in her direction; the girl didn't move a millimeter. He turned away with a sigh and went to the window.

"Where are they?" In the past hour, he had constantly repeated the same question.

He looked out of the window and suddenly raised his shoulders like a bull ready for the attack. He turned and snatched the hunting rifle from the couch table. At that moment, the doorbell rang.

João pulled Carmencita out of the sofa and put his left hand over her mouth.

"Silence!"

The girl bit João's hand with desperate strength. He couldn't suppress a scream. Instinctively, he released the girl. Carmencita ran to the door of the living room, threw it open, and screamed. João jumped over the coffee table and grabbed her by one of her braids. Carmencita yelled again, just as the pounding on the door began. João knew he was trapped. Roaring, he emptied his rifle in the door.

6

Alejandro arrived on foot at Beatriz's house, heard the shots, saw a soldier fall to the ground, and another dive away. The wounded soldier tried to crawl backward, leaving a trail of blood in the grass. Alejandro felt a tight spot around his heart: he had known that this would end badly. *Victor, your daughter was in the wrong hands with me, no matter how well I meant it.*

Alejandro stopped at the neighbors' place. He intended not to run away this time and looked on while the soldiers searched for cover behind mimosa bushes and Beatriz's mailbox. He heard them yelling at each other. One of them gestured commandingly. Two soldiers bent down and ran to the back of the house. The sergeant who directed them fired a salvo that shattered the window of the living room. Large pieces of glass fell into the house.

Time and again, it was stronger than he was. Despite his intention, when the sergeant threw a grenade through the broken window, Alejandro ran away.

7

Wouldn't it have been most intimate, Alejandro, if you sat next to me in this plane and we held each other's hands until the last moment? For seven minutes, we would've been happy. Where are you, Alejandro, now that I could use your support and trust, even more so than in the cantina when you saw me naked and helpless? Alejandro, poor Alejandro, before my eyes, I see you walking in the city. You don't know where to go; you have the look of a beaten dog, your feet trot aimlessly on. I hear the song in your heart, Alejandro, and the sound it makes is a lament of the faraway night. Are there people born for misfortune? If so, there are also people dying to ward off evil, Alejandro, poor Alejandro, Alejandro of my dreams.

8

The tear gas grenade spread thick yellow clouds. João Pereira didn't waste a second; he pushed Carmencita up the stairs. The girl stumbled. João swung her in one powerful motion over his shoulder and ran further up. He clenched his teeth when he remembered that the tear gas grenades used by the Terrenean army contained toxic substances that did not conform to international regulations.

João was panting hard as he entered the bathroom. He wanted to open the sliding door that gave access to the sun terrace, but at that moment, a salvo splintered the glass. He crouched on the floor. Carmencita's body tightened briefly and then became limp. João slid the unconscious girl from his shoulder to the floor. He stroked his face with both hands and felt glass splinters pierce his skin. He noticed how quiet it had become. Downstairs, the whistling of the tear gas had stopped.

All the muscles of his neck tightened as he shouted through the broken window, "I have the daughter of Kurt Astíz-Fitzroy, colonel of the secret service of the goddamned Terrenean army. She's here with me! I swear I'll kill her if you don't withdraw!"

9

Alejandro walked past the old football stadium, the shortest way to leave the city. Someone had sprayed in black, shaky

letters almost a meter high on the concrete exterior wall: THE
RULES OF DEATH ARE WELL-WRITTEN.

Alejandro stopped right in front of the U of MUERTE,
and he couldn't resist; after all that had happened, he still
couldn't resist.

The rules of death are well-written,
the children learn how to write them
without understanding why.
Death keeps them in the dark.

He leaned against the wall, his fist on the U. His eyes fixed
on the distant mountains. Ten years ago, three weeks before
this stadium was to be his final destination, his father said to
him, "If I had to flee from this country unexpectedly and
without any means, I would try to cross the mountains."

The situation in Terreno had been taut then, and
Alejandro had understood what his father was referring to.
But because of his artistic reputation, which was so important
to him at that age, Alejandro looked at him impassively. They
stood on the old university campus and had an unobstructed
view of the mountains.

"If ever necessary, you can escape via the mountains,
using only determination and willpower," his father had
added without looking at his son. "Do you see that funny
tear between the two peaks over there? That's a mule track.
One can reach it after about twelve hundred meters of
climbing to the top. Behind it lies a valley. You can see the
beginning of it, that big tree over there, that *maitenes*. It stood
there long before my father was born. It'll take you days, but
if you keep following the old mule track, you'll end up in
Argentina. The first valley you'll come across is an old smuggler's spot that they call the shepherds' valley. It was a bloody
battlefield when the Spaniards advanced in the sixteenth
century. The popular belief is that on certain days, you can

still hear the fiery tongues of fallen warriors singing their songs."

Alejandro remembered the way his father had looked at him, the index finger with which he had pushed his glasses on his nose. Suddenly, he had seemed old and confused. "Things will be fine, father. They will be fine," Alejandro said.

10

"Did you hear that, sergeant? The young soldier laughed. "Have you heard what that madman is yelling there? The daughter of a colonel of..."

He shut up when he saw Ricardo's gaze. He'd seen the sergeant pensive like this before: one night when he had set fire to a journalist's house after tying the man to his bed.

"Kurt Astíz-Fitzroy. That *canalla* used the colonel's full name," said Cerdá to himself, assuming a pose of coquettish thoughtfulness reminiscent of Mussolini. "How does the fucker know that?"

The enigma seemed to entertain the sergeant. "You're staying here," he said. "Keep an eye on him, that's all, understood? Don't shoot."

Cerdá ran past the house to the patio.

11

João sat with his rifle in both hands in front of the broken window and looked out over the garden. He saw no movement. The grass had never looked greener. The trees were like a chalice, donated by the earth to the blue sky. His painter's eye saw how beautiful the world was. He looked at the mountains. Higher and higher, his gaze rose until he became dizzy from all that blue brightness, and his eyes began to well up.

"I meant what I said. I'll shoot you if the soldiers attack," he said slowly and clearly. "First you, then myself." He looked sideways. Carmencita was sitting in a corner by the door he had locked. Her eyes didn't leave João's face.

João didn't turn his gaze away, he who so often in his life had painted the most endearing children's faces.

12

Pelarón secured his house well when it was built almost nine years ago. The young dictator chose a real eagle's nest high up in the mountains behind Valtiago. The only way to reach the pompous villa with its irrigated gardens was via a concrete road crossing the terrains of a military compound. No one without wings could reach the "General of the Poor," as Pelarón liked to call himself, without first passing the barracks. And even from the air, an attack seemed impossible: every aircraft that took off without a flight plan was intercepted by Pelarón's jets. Heavy anti-aircraft artillery would shoot down any aircraft that for any reason was not caught. But, as Manuel had told Beatriz, enjoying the display of his "strategic genius," a plane that flew in the direction of Argentina and turned mid-way could approach Pelarón's villa from the rear, unthreatened by anti-aircraft artillery. Of course, Manuel had added, this hypothetical plane would be destroyed by jet fighters shortly after take-off, so such a scenario was impossible.

It took Beatriz a few minutes to reach the turning point. She was confident her plan wouldn't fail.

How blue it was, the expanse of heaven all around her, utterly different from the grey wall she had seen so often in her dreams. For years, Beatriz had thought that the wall in her dreams symbolized her death.

Now she understood that the grey wall had been her life.

―――――

13

Sergeant Ricardo Córdone Cerdá stood in Beatriz's living room and browsed the telephone directory. His former superior was listed as Kurt Fitzroy without any reference to profession or rank. Ten years ago, this ex-officer of the Servicio de Inteligencia, better known as G2, had been Cerdá's superior in the secret service. Fitzroy had done an excellent job in the stadium. Just before his retirement, he was appointed a colonel. How did the terrorist entrenched on the first floor of the house know that? In G2, Fitzroy had adopted the habit of working under the name of his mother, as many torturers did. But the man upstairs had yelled Fitzroy's full name. Ricardo Cerdá imagined the position of the subversive: the fear, the grimness, the panic of a cat in dire straits. Cats in dire straits perform strange jumps; Ricardo Córdone Cerdá knew that.

While dialing Colonel Astíz's number, he suddenly felt goosebumps on his arms. He shivered with pleasure.

Oh, how he loved those strange jumps.

―――――

14

"What?" barked Kurt Astíz-Fitzroy into the receiver.

He listened attentively.

"A moment," he said, restrained. "I'm letting a visitor out. Stay on the line."

Kurt pressed the telephone receiver against his hip, his

thoughts a spinning spiral. Sergeant Cerdá: how could he forget that psychopath? Brilliant soldier; a pity he was insane. Cerdá could have gone far, but he was overconfident and thought he was unstoppable. They tamed him, and now he was a sergeant who knew his place. So he warned a former superior that a terrorist was running amuck in Beatriz Candalti's house, had fired on his soldiers, and had gravely injured one. That was not all: the terrorist claimed the daughter of colonel Kurt Astíz-Fitzroy was his hostage.

"He mentioned your full name and your rank, colonel... Mr. Astíz, I thought it strange that he knew this. Excuse me, sir, but...you don't have any children, do you? He threatens to kill his hostage if we attack."

Astíz remembered the words of his first instructor in the "executioner school" of G2. "Cruelty is an instinct that helps you uncover the truth. The heart betrays itself through the eyes. Therefore, you need to practice: look the interviewee straight in the eyes. It's not easy in the beginning, but you can learn it by looking into your own eyes in the mirror and holding your gaze for as long as possible."

Kurt Astíz-Fitzroy stood on his terrace in his dressing gown, in front of the doors to his house—he hadn't worn another piece of clothing all day long. The sun made the glass reflective. He saw himself standing with the receiver pressed against his hip. He couldn't see his eyes clearly; the glass didn't reflect them sufficiently.

Dishonor, shame, a grave violation of the code of honor of the Terrenean army if I say "yes." Cerdá will no doubt capitalize on it. My instinct, what does my instinct say?

Slowly, Kurt Astíz-Fitzroy brought the telephone receiver back to his mouth. As he did this, his hair in the mirroring glass turned white, so white that it seemed to disappear. Kurt saw himself shriveling up. How was it possible that all of a sudden, one could become so old and weak, with a heart beating feebly, its life-energy draining away with every contraction?

"I don't have any daughter, sergeant. What's that mad man thinking?" said Kurt Astíz-Fitzroy in a firm voice. "Remember what they all made up in the stadium to stay alive? I have an urgent appointment, so please excuse me. All the best with your activist, Cerdá. I assume you'll take the necessary measures."

Kurt Astíz-Fitzroy no longer felt that he was shrinking when he heard his dry voice save the honor of a colonel but deprive a father of his greatest love. Stiffly in a military stance, he stood, tight and upright, staring at his image on the terrace doors, while the telephone receiver slipped out of his fingers.

Kurt felt this was just the beginning of his self-torture, but still, he couldn't look the interviewee in the eyes.

————

15

Beatriz saw war lights: lamp posts a meter high whose light formed yellow cones on the ground. Then followed a beautiful garden with a swimming pool that surrounded Pelarón's villa like an oyster snuggling its pearl.

Beatriz pushed the joystick forward and shook her head, so her shiny, black hair fanned out. It had not suffered under Cerdán's lighter fire and gleamed more than ever with a deep glow.

She plunged her plane down like a condor. The questions of whether general Pelarón was even home or if he would see her coming were no longer critical.

There was only one question.

Is this an honorable death?

————

16

When sergeant Cerdá joined his men again, he looked smug, as if he had just heard a good joke.

The sergeant peered at the sun terrace on the first floor, where nothing moved, where everything seemed to be waiting.

"We take him down," said the sergeant. He chuckled. "That clown up there is a dead man."

————

17

For many seconds, the mountains reflected the explosion of Beatriz's plane crashing into Pelarón's house, but in Valtiago, only the antennae of the crickets caught the faraway rumble. They fled into cracks and fissures, convinced that the vibration they had felt was the harbinger of an earthquake. The insects would remain vigilant for hours.

————

18

"What did you say, sir?" said Cristóbal.

Ten minutes ago, the military rector of the university convened his staff for an emergency meeting. When Cristóbal received the summons, he coughed hard. With buckling knees, he had passed the nervous guards at the door of the large auditorium. After the rector's announcement, Cristóbal trembled even harder, but not as hard as the rector. The man was so nervous his cigarette shook in his mouth. He evaded the eyes of university staff as he, in response to Cristóbal's question, repeated the official bulletin he had just read aloud.

A stunned silence hung in the auditorium. The rector

cleared his throat. "The government wants to sit down with civil society representatives as soon as possible to facilitate a transition to democracy." Someone asked what 'as soon as possible' implied. The rector looked up from his papers. "There is the talk of a term of fewer than three months." Again, it grew quiet in the auditorium. Cristóbal was afraid everyone could see the image looming up in him: a meeting of delegates from various groups of the resistance under his leadership after he had forged them in three months into a broad political party ready to take the reins of government.

He had to inform the press of his intentions and prepare a speech for the members of his group about this abrupt turn of events, the first of many to come. He would make sure that his words carried the luster of statesmanship.

Cristóbal hurried through the corridors to his office. He urgently needed to call several people. A story came to his mind, told to him once by Alejandro, about an earthquake that, according to legend, took place every time there was a brutal change of power in Terreno. When the People's Government fell, Cristóbal had felt nothing, but now a peculiar inspiration came to him: the wave of renewal he imagined would shake Terreno to its foundations. And that is why Cristóbal felt the kind of certainty one feels only once a lifetime: before long, he would sit at the head of the conference tables in the former parliament under the dazzling lights.

———

19

The Tormenta Seca broke loose in the Andes that night, the dreaded dry thunderstorm with the kilometer-long lightning bolts. Alejandro Juron didn't see the spectacle above his head nor the reddish-brown of the mountains glowing in the lightning.

He left a beaten track behind him and looked at his tired feet. The Valley of the Shepherds ahead was dozens of kilometers across, a light gray expanse in the approaching night, here and there dotted with the brown of cacti and Quillay trees.

Alejandro shuffled. Alejandro shook his head. Alejandro moistened his cork dry lips.

The night is angry at the mountains, father. I have walked all day, and my feet are tired, but I have not risen as high as I wanted. I don't hear the beat of even a single condor's wings nor a whimsical tune on your quena, mother. Everyone is quiet; everyone is silent. I don't even hear the fiery tongues of the warriors who died here long ago. I only hear my voice, and I cannot silence it. Is it not a bottomless misery, a voice that cannot keep quiet? Do you want to hear what it says to me, father? Do you want to know what it sings, mother?

Alejandro trudged on at twelve hundred meters high in a direction that might take him to Argentina. The thunderstorm doubled in strength. Alejandro looked up timidly, knowing how dangerous a storm in the Andes could be. But the source of his fears, which once seemed inexhaustible to him, was drying up. Tired to his bones, he sought shelter behind a house-high boulder. He stretched on the hard ground, his face turned to heaven. He felt inspiration bubbling up, and this time it was expressed in a sound he thought he could hear behind the thunder, a distant chant.

Do I hear the shepherds who, a long time ago, blocked commander San Martín in these mountains in his rush to conquer Terreno, father? Do they sing 'oh and woe' because they failed to stop the blinded hothead who had suffered a severe sunstroke in the Andes but who eventually managed to become the founder of this cursed country? But no, they don't sing lamentations: the thunder is their favorite bombo—the big drum designed to accompany their lust for war. The songs, the traditions, and legends defy the centuries: they are the real heroes of the people. They enchant reality. That's why I've been smart for the first time in my life, father: I've fled Terreno without leaving a trace, and if I stay smart, I'll never come back again. *I couldn't be the hero others thought they saw in me, but with a bit of luck, I can still become a tragic legend.*

Once I'm in Argentina, I will not remember my name, father. Andes fever and the hardships and tortures of G2 headsmen created a void in my head. "You look like Alejandro Juron; you are Alejandro Juron," they might say in Argentina. I will stubbornly deny it. Anonymously, I'll send songs to artists who resemble Víctor Pérez, and that's how I'll serve penance. These songs, father, will become the real folk heroes because I will present them: Beatriz, João, Cristóbal, Carmencita, everyone who thought they were dealing with the real Alejandro Juron and met their Fate.

You, Beatriz, I'll turn you into one of the brave women of this continent. You are the heroine who kills the scorpion Pelarón. He screams and coils, he shows the inferior material he's made of, and you laugh your most dazzling smile while you send him to the nether world.

You, João, I'll turn you into a mythical warrior of the mountains—a fierce and determined commander, an idealist forced to paint scenes of blood but still dreams of chasing the rainbow on the horizon.

You, Cristóbal, I'll turn you into Terreno's new president, a leader who dares drive through the streets in an open car, bursting out in fits of laughter, proclaiming national holidays by the dozen; a president who provides good news on the radio and ventures a dance step in front of the cameras.

You, Carmencita, I'll turn you into a girl who never grows up and prefers to experiment with all sorts of dance styles when her father plays his guitar. Your hair has the color of freshly polished copper, and you will stay four years old forever. Your body is golden brown, and when you laugh, it tickles in your belly.

And for myself, I create a troubadour, an indestructible lover, someone who always tells the truth and never speaks a word without a musical inflection in his throat.

All of you will hear from me.

The earth vibrated beneath Alejandro Juron. He didn't have the time to think about the myth that in Terreno the Earth trembles after an unexpected change of power. Terrified, he jumped up, threw his head backward, and opened his eyes to the sky that seemed ripped in half by a giant sword of light.

Querida!

For an eternity, the lightning clarified everything.

Dear reader,

We hope you enjoyed reading *Alejandro's Lie*. Please take a moment to leave a review, even if it's a short one. Your opinion is important to us.

Discover more books by Bob Van Laerhoven at https://www.nextchapter.pub/authors/bobvanlaerhoven

Want to know when one of our books is free or discounted? Join the newsletter at http://eepurl.com/bqqB3H

Best regards,

Bob Van Laerhoven and the Next Chapter Team

About the Author

Bob Van Laerhoven is a 67-year-old Belgian/Flemish author who has published (traditionally) more than 45 books in Holland and Belgium. His cross-over between literature and noir/suspense is published in French, English, German, Spanish, Swedish, Slovenian, Italian, Polish, (Brazilian) Portuguese, and Russian. In Belgium, Laerhoven was a four-time finalist of the 'Hercule Poirot Prize for Best Mystery Novel of the Year' with the novels' Djinn,' 'The Finger of God,' 'Return to Hiroshima,' and 'The Firehand Files.' In 2007, he became the winner of the Hercule Poirot Prize with 'Baudelaire's Revenge.' The novel was published in 2014 in the USA and won the USA Best Book Award 2014 in the category 'mystery/suspense. In 2015 followed Месть Бодлера, the Russian edition of 'Baudelaire's Revenge.' His collection of short stories, ' Dangerous Obsessions,' first published in the USA in 2015, was chosen as the 'best short story collection of 2015' by the San Diego Book Review. The collection is translated into Italian, Portuguese, Spanish, and Swedish. 'Return to Hiroshima,' his second crime novel in English, was first published in May 2018. The British quality review blog Murder, Mayhem & More chose 'Return to Hiroshima' as one of the ten best international crime novels of 2018. Also, in 2018, Laerhoven's second collection of short stories, "Heart Fever," came out in the USA. 'Heart Fever' was one of the five finalists of the American Silver Falchion Award. Laerhoven was the only non-American finalist. The collection has been translated into Italian, Spanish, and German.

The context and themes of Laerhoven's stories aren't invented behind his desk; instead, they are rooted in personal experience. As a freelance travel writer, he explored conflicts and trouble-spots across the globe from 1990 to 2003: Somalia, Serbia, Bosnia, Liberia, Sudan, Gaza, Iran, Iraq, Lebanon, Mozambique, Myanmar... to name but a few. Echoes of his experiences on the road trickle through in his novels.

Printed in Great Britain
by Amazon

25226157R00169